MURDER TIMES TWO

Haughton Murphy

FAWCETT CREST · NEW YORK

A Fawcett Crest Book
Published by Ballantine Books
Copyright © 1990 by Haughton Murphy

Library of Congress Catalog Card Number: 89-26151

ISBN 0-449-21947-X

This edition published by arrangement with Simon and Schuster, Inc.

Manufactured in the United States of America

First Ballantine Books Edition: March 1991

For Martha,
with, if possible, even more love than before.

Let us, my brethen who have not our names in the Red Book, console ourselves by thinking comfortably how miserable our betters may be, and that Damocles, who sits on satin cushions, and is served on gold plate, has an awful sword hanging over his head in the shape of a bailiff, or an hereditary disease, or a family secret, which peeps out every now and then from the embroidered arras in a ghastly manner, and will be sure to drop one day or the other in the right place.

In comparing, too, the poor man's situation with that of the great, there is . . . another source of comfort for the former. You who have little or no patrimony to bequeath or inherit, may be on good terms with your father or your son, whereas the heir of a great prince . . . must naturally be angry at being kept out of his kingdom, and eye the occupant of it with no very agreeable glances. . . . If you were heir to a dukedom and a thousand pounds a day, do you say you would not wish for possession? Pooh!

WILLIAM MAKEPEACE THACKERAY,
VANITY FAIR

JUNE

RECOLLECTIONS

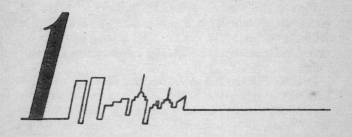

REUBEN FROST SAT DOWN AT HIS PERSONAL COMPUTER AND got it up and working. A mechanical illiterate all his life, he had been astonished at his ability to cope with his hard-disk, 40-megabyte machine, complete with a 16-MHz microprocessor (whatever that might be). The pleasant young saleswoman at the computer store had assured him that the model he bought was state of the art, though she could scarcely conceal her surprise at the prospect of a dignified seventy-year-old buying his first PC.

"What are you going to do with it?" she had asked.

"Prepare my will," Frost had been tempted to answer, but instead had mumbled something about, "writing letters." "That is, if I can make it do anything."

"You won't have any problem, Mr. Frost. It's very user friendly."

The truth was that Reuben had bought his PC on a dare. For months his ancient friend Douglas Gilmore, retired chairman of Hastings Industries, had talked of little else but home computers whenever they met at the Gotham Club.

"Douglas, you're an old fool," Frost had impatiently told Gilmore on at least one occasion. "Those damnable things are for *young* people, not the likes of us. I've always used a

3

live secretary and I expect to continue to do so for the few years I've got left.''

"Easier said than done, Reuben," Gilmore had replied. "I don't know how it is at your old law firm, but at Hastings it's damned hard for someone who's been retired as long as I have to get a decent secretary.''

Frost had been forced to concede Gilmore's point. His old colleagues at Chase & Ward were unfailingly polite when he visited the office, but he had the nagging impression that his occasional requests for stenographic help were thought a nuisance.

One day Gilmore had finally said that Frost was undoubtedly right, that he probably couldn't cope with a PC, that he was indeed a very old dog to whom new tricks would not come easily. Thus challenged, and also encouraged by his wife, Cynthia, who was eager for her husband to fill up his days, Reuben had taken the plunge.

To his amazement, he and the computer got on well. He shared his triumphs with Gilmore and his younger clubmates, many of them writers who used PCs in their work. At the Gotham bar, the conversation often concerned laptops, printers, modems and other electronic esoterica that intrigued the aging hackers gathered for their preluncheon drinks. Frost imagined that this talk must resemble an earlier day's conversations, right at the same bar, about the wonders of the newfangled automobile.

Right now, on a sunny afternoon in mid-June, Frost wanted to be anywhere but before his computer in the library of his townhouse on the East Side of New York. The City had looked temptingly fresh and green when he had returned from lunch. But he had promised his wife that he would reply to an urgent request from their mutual friend, the writer Eleanor Daggett, to provide her with background on the Vandermeer family.

The City's news media had been fascinated with the tale of the Vandermeers and their fortune ever since the poisoning of the family scion, Tobias, the previous March, at a meeting of his wife's reading club at which the Frosts had been present. Daggett, a well-known free-lance journalist, had become a specialist in so-called "true crime" sagas. The denouement of *l'affaire* Vandermeer had been astonishing and, now that the drama was over, or at least ready to be transferred to the courts, she wanted to find out all she could about Tobias, his wife, Robyn, and the whole unsavory cast of players.

Frost stayed at his computer all afternoon, composing a long letter to the reporter:

DEAR ELEANOR,

As you requested, I will try to set forth what I know about the background of the Vandermeers. I will also include a certain amount of hearsay, but, knowing what a good reporter you are, I am certain you will not use anything in your book that you do not check for accuracy.

My own exposure to the family goes back to my early days as an associate lawyer at Chase & Ward in the late 1930s. The firm, then as now, handled the Vandermeers' trust and estates work and occasional corporate problems. One way or another, I became the corporate "expert" on their affairs, and then, in 1964, I did a special piece of research for Tobias that I will describe later.

I should say at the outset that both Cynthia and I always had mixed feelings about Tobias. I don't like drunks, particularly loutish ones, which Tobias became in the years before his death, though I can't deny there were many times when he was utterly charming. Despite his often terrible behavior, he had a rather romantic streak that could be appealing.

It was fascinating, and singular in my experience, to observe a man not only so rich that he didn't have to do anything—there are plenty of those—but one who actually *didn't* do anything, except of course play jazz piano, stitch needlepoint and, late in life, build a collection of Dutch genre paintings. It is certainly unique when one's only workaday concern is to keep off the *Forbes 400* list of the country's wealthiest individuals—an obsession with Tobias.

As for Robyn, her social climbing and cultural pretensions never appealed to us. But you couldn't help feeling sorry for her as Tobias grew more sodden and meaner toward the end. And one also had to admire her deep commitment to the cause of literacy.

The Vandermeers were one of the old Dutch families in New York, arriving at the end of the seventeenth century. They didn't come over with Henry Hudson or Peter Minuit, but they were here not much after them. (A competitor of theirs in the real estate business once remarked to me that it was too bad they didn't come with Minuit; with the help of a Vandermeer, he probably would have gotten the Manhattoe Indians to cut their price for Manhattan below $24.)

By the early 1800s the Vandermeers had money to invest, and they put it into land and shipping. Manhattan had begun to burst out from its boundaries at the lower end of the island, and the Vandermeers shrewdly invested in well-located properties, many along Bloomingdale Road (no relation to the store; it is now Broadway). The ships they commissioned and chartered out sailed the world, not necessarily in the most respectable commerce. There is pretty good evidence, for example, that they were willing to engage in the slave and rum trades in the Caribbean and Africa and the opium trade in the Far East.

The family liquidated its shipping interests in the 1840s, producing massive new funds for investment, virtually all of which went into New York City real estate.

After the Civil War the first Tobias Vandermeer looked after the family fortune. He stuck to real estate, buying, selling and exchanging properties all over the city.

I never knew Tobias I, who died in his nineties about 1930. But I remember tough old partners at the firm, unfazed by almost anybody, who still shuddered at the mention of Tobias I's name a decade later. And he was supposed to be as close as the next second. From all I've ever been able to gather, he died unloved and unmourned—and very rich.

The modern era of the family begins with Hendrik, who took Great Kill over when his father died. (The name of the family company has always been Great Kill Holdings Corporation—an ironic title given all that's recently happened. But it is old Dutch, referring to a stream that ran through several Vandermeer parcels and emptied into the Hudson River around Forty-second Street.)

Consolidation and expansion of Great Kill's assets became Hendrik's whole life. His wife had died in 1925, in the course of giving birth to Hendrik's sole heir, the second Tobias.

Hendrik's technique for making money was simplicity itself. He leased the land that Great Kill owned to eager developers, providing a steady and reliable stream of ground rents to Great Kill.

Hendrik's skill in preserving the Vandermeer patrimony was the pride of his life. He never remarried after the death of his wife, and he had a very small circle of friends. One of them was Dr. Cates, the rector of the Collegiate Church of St. Nicholas, which used to be at Forty-eighth and Fifth. He accomplished a feat that no one else had theretofore been able to manage—to arouse a Vandermeer's social conscience. Under intense pressure from the good doctor, Hendrik established the now notorious Bloemendael Foundation in the early 1960s, with an original gift of, as I recall, two million.

Hendrik's only source of discontent was his son, Tobias. I've always understood—he even said so himself, in unguarded moments—that the boy had had a wretched childhood. He was raised by a series of governesses until shipped off to Hotchkiss at an indecently young age. One gathers that Hendrik tried to befriend his son, but I don't think he ever could break through his Dutch reserve to show him anything approaching real affection.

Tobias joined the Navy in 1943, when he was eighteen, and sat out the rest of the war at a supply depot in New Orleans. He collected no medals for heroism—but he did learn three skills during his tour of duty: how to play jazz piano, how to do needlepoint and how to drink. None of which he ever forgot.

After the War, Tobias enrolled at Brown, but that lasted barely two years, after which he went to work for his father. That continued for another two and was a disaster, since the boy had no business judgment whatsoever. And his lifestyle, centered on the City's jazz clubs and late-night drinking, conflicted with the austere work ethic his father imposed on himself and wanted his son to emulate.

Finally, they reached an understanding: Tobias would leave Great Kill and do as he pleased, supported by a healthy allowance from his father. (I believe it was $100,000 a year—big money in 1951.) All his father asked was that the boy avoid public scandal and publicity. Tobias more or less obliged; the jazz bars on Fifty-second Street and in the Village where he hung out did not attract Walter Winchell and the other gossip columnists. And Tobias at this stage did not carouse and get disruptive in public; his drinking was quiet and steady, mostly vodka and orange juice, from the time he got up at noon until the jazz clubs closed in the early morning.

When Tobias announced in 1954 that he wanted to move to Paris, Hendrik was relieved. Jazz was apparently booming in France then, and Tobias wanted to be a part of the scene. His father encouraged him, glad to have the Atlantic separating them.

It was in Paris that Tobias met Ines Amarante de Sousa, a glamorous Brazilian of twenty-two and the daughter of a well-to-do Rio industrialist, Nascimento Amarante de Sousa, who owned a string of paper mills scattered throughout Brazil.

As Tobias told me the story years later, he met Ines at the Club Saint-Germain, where he spent most evenings. Ines was astoundingly beautiful, sitting in the club's dim light. The product of a strict Sacred Heart education, she was still very much under her parents' control and hungered to escape.

Tobias, always happiest around music bars, his amiability fueled by his regular drinking, seemed to offer a way out, and she pursued him around Paris. After a brief time they were married in Paris and then set off to meet her parents in Rio de Janeiro and his father in New York.

Ines captivated Hendrik. She was polite and cultivated, and these qualities appealed to the old man, as did her unquestioned beauty. She was not perhaps the upright Protestant bride he would have chosen for his son, but he thought she might actually reform Tobias, and, as he told me at the time, "she certainly beats the low-class types the boy used to bring home."

Tobias did not reform, and it was not long before Ines began creating a private world for herself. She took courses in drawing and painting and, as her English improved, art history, first at the New School and then at the Institute of Fine Arts.

Amply subsidized by her own father, Ines began to patronize the galleries and soon was a part of the art scene, leading an independent life amid an ever larger circle of artists, gallery owners and hangers-on. Tobias did not seem to mind so long as his daily (or more precisely, nocturnal) routine was not disturbed.

As their lives diverged, Ines and Tobias became, in effect, independent boarders, sleeping apart in the duplex maisonette at Park Avenue and Seventy-fourth Street. While no longer interested in each other, neither one was attracted to anyone else, so there was no reason to alter the status quo.

All that changed when Tobias and the Principessa Montefiore del'Udine (née Robyn Mayes) started their affair in, I would say, 1963. At the time I did not know all the intriguing circumstances of how Tobias had first met the Principessa, only that he was seen more and more frequently with an American divorcee with an Italian title.

Then, in the summer of 1964, the explosion occurred. Tobias announced to Ines that he wanted a divorce so that he could marry the Principessa. Indifferent as she had become to her husband, Ines summoned up a full dose of wronged-woman indignation and vowed that she would never give him a divorce.

Tobias told her he would take up residence in Nevada and get what we lawyers call an *ex parte* divorce without her consent. (You will recall that the only ground for divorce in New York in those days was adultery.) Ines, in her fury, told him to go ahead, with the dire warning that if he got such a divorce and married the Principessa, she would have him jailed for bigamy.

This threat sent a very scared Tobias right into the arms of Chase & Ward. Up until then, I had the impression that he was slightly distrustful of our firm, which represented his father and had represented his grandfather before him.

My trust and estates partner who would normally have dealt with Tobias' problem was away on an extended vacation so, at Tobias' insistence, I had to tend to the matter. I knew next to nothing about out-of-state divorces and, God knows, even less about bigamy; I'd heard others mention the bad repute of "mail-order Mexicans" and "one-day Albamas," but it was a subject I'd never encountered in my rather staid corporate practice.

With the help of a bright young associate, I educated myself and concluded that if Tobias established residence in Nevada for six weeks, he could indeed get an *ex parte* divorce without Ines' consent that probably would be valid. And if he married Robyn in Reno or Las Vegas, where the divorce would clearly be recognized, there would be no question of bigamy. To my ignorant surprise, having never considered the matter in my life, the crime of bigamy is the *act* of marrying a second spouse while still married to the first; it has nothing to do with ongoing living arrangements.

I have seldom had a client more grateful for advice given than Tobias. For better or worse, it made him—and Robyn—our friends for life. We maintained the relationship through the years—helped a good deal by the Vandermeers' generous contributions to Cynthia's work at the National Ballet—and because of it we ended up as members of that damnable reading club of Robyn's where Tobias was murdered.

Tobias and Robyn were married just before Christmas in 1964, and she immediately set out to achieve two goals: to beguile Hendrik and to establish herself in New York society.

Accomplishing her first objective was necessary to realize the second for, at the time she married Tobias, she had practically no money. Il Principe Montefiore del'Udine had given her a title, but little else. Indeed, it turned out that he had managed to squander what money she had brought to their marriage. And Tobias' allowance from his father, while ample, really could not sustain the level of charitable giving Robyn felt necessary to buy her way into society.

Disarming Hendrik was a formidable task. He had been horrified when Tobias dumped Ines, whom Hendrik had grown to like. And Robyn struck him as something of an adventuress.

In that he was probably correct, though to give her proper credit, she did work hard at her charities, most notably READ. Ensconced in the Vandermeer living quarters—Ines had fled to Brazil as soon as it was clear that Tobias really was going to leave her—she surveyed the charity scene and saw that literacy was a cause without a wealthy and visible sponsor. There were some small groups dedicated to childhood literacy—teaching little wide-eyed minority children to read had its drawing power—but no one was much attracted to the plight of poor, and generally not very appealing, adult illiterates. To her credit, she set out to form a committee that would promote literacy programs for adults as well as for children, and the impossibly named READ (Reading Education for American Democracy) was created.

The first time I ever met Robyn was when she came to One Metropolitan Plaza to talk with a group of us about setting up READ. Having expected a *femme fatale*, I was impressed. She wore what even I could recognize as a Chanel suit, a glamorous red one that showed off her lustrous brunette hair, dark eyes and trim figure to perfection. Her slight overbite, a legacy from her less-than-grand childhood, was her only imperfect feature. She was very businesslike and seemed, despite the years she had spent abroad, very knowledgeable in the ways of the not-for-profit world.

READ was a spectacular success. The annual READ ball almost immediately became a must-be-seen-at social event. By inviting well-known authors eager for social pampering, she made the ball more interesting than the usual charity benefit; soon both socialites and authors were clamoring for invitations, the former at ever escalating prices and the latter, of course, for free. For years it has been the only benefit I know of that has a waiting list.

Robyn's success with READ eventually won Hendrik over. He became an enthusiastic contributor and, even in his nineties, made rare public appearances at the READ ball.

The upshot of Hendrik's approval was the now famous codicil that allowed Tobias to appoint a life estate to Robyn, if she survived him, in the income from the so-called Vandermeer Trust that Hendrik set up in his will.

With the usual Vandermeer financial good luck, when Hendrik died in 1974, at the age of ninety-four, the New York real estate market was badly depressed. Thus his estate was valued at a mere (!) $90 million for estate-tax purposes (this at a time when the Federal estate-tax rate was a crippling 61 percent and the New York rate was an additional 21 percent). The canny old fellow had enough liquid assets squirreled away to pay these taxes, leaving the Bloemendael Foundation and the Vandermeer Trust each with half the Great Kill stock, each half being worth roughly $30 million. The Great Kill stock is now being reappraised and, given the huge increases in New York City land values since Hendrik's death, each half is probably now worth on the order of $150 million.

The years between Hendrik's death and the tragedies of this spring you know about, though I'll be happy to talk with you concerning them.

I realize that this letter is terribly disjointed, and I apologize for my stilted old lawyer's prose. I do hope, however, that it helps to fill in the background. Cynthia and I both wish you luck with your project.

Fondly,
REUBEN

MARCH

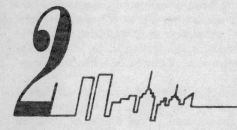

KATHLEEN BOYLE WAS IN A FOUL MOOD. HER IRISH CAPAC-
ity for resentment, honed and refined over forty years as a
domestic servant, was on display as she angrily plumped up
the pillows on the sofa in the Vandermeer living room.

Minutes before, Robyn Vandermeer had swept through,
calling out instructions for things to be done. Her litany had
included an icy order to remove a silver sugar bowl from the
coffee table, her tone implying that she questioned why it
was there in the first place.

The maid bristled at the innuendo, but said nothing. She
was perfectly aware that the sugar bowl should be removed,
and she would take it away in her own good time. The only
reason it was out on view at all was because of the overbearing Bill Kearney, the man who ran Mr. Vandermeer's business and came to see him every Sunday. In his imperious
way, Kearney had demanded a cup of coffee even before he
had his coat off. Then, after he had been summoned by Tobias Vandermeer to the study on the next floor, the offending
dish had been left behind.

Kathleen Boyle's grievances reframed themselves in her
mind as questions. Why was Kearney around on Sunday anyway? Why didn't he and Mr. Tobias do their business during
the week like normal people? Getting a weekly report on

how the books stood was probably not servile work, forbidden on the Sabbath, but it did seem inappropriate to her.

And how could Mr. Tobias stand Kearney in the first place? Haughty to her, and even to Miss Robyn, always speaking to them in the condescending tones of an old-school monsignor, he changed completely when speaking to Mr. Tobias. No turnip-snagging peasant was more obsequious to his landlord than William Kearney was to Tobias Vandermeer. Sure, Mr. Tobias' senses were usually clouded with drink, but even he must see what a toady his manager was. He must be good at what he does, Kathleen had reluctantly concluded.

Normally she was able to avoid Kearney. All day Sunday and Tuesday afternoons were her time off. Except, for the last year or two, those Sundays every four months when it was Mrs. Vandermeer's turn to entertain her reading club for supper and, what seemed to Kathleen the one time she stayed around for the whole event, interminable gabble about the book they all had copies of. She resented the reading club and its interference with her Sunday free time. Not that her Sundays were particularly exciting—generally a movie in the afternoon and the evening spent before the TV in her tiny quarters behind the kitchen. It was the smallest room in the eighteen-room Vandermeer complex, but it was comfortable and private.

Spending her Sunday getting ready for the reading club did interfere with her routine. She couldn't attend the eleven-thirty mass at St. Vincent's, her favorite church, with the amiable Dominican friars and the choir, but instead had to trudge uptown to St. Jean Baptiste for the evening mass. And endless, endless sermons and ''folk'' music by a guitar-piano duo that struck her untutored ears as being not much short of sacrilegious. Vatican II and the sainted Pope John may have accomplished a great deal of good, but St. Jean's folk mass did not prove it to Kathleen Boyle.

Mulling over her immediate resentments as she worked about the living room inevitably fueled thoughts of older gripes and her growing apprehensions about working for the Vandermeers.

There was, of course, the matter of the television. She had been insisting for months that her small set no longer worked properly. The picture was fuzzy, but Mrs. Vandermeer, after a personal inspection, pronounced it an irreparable fault of the cable hookup, not of the tiny set itself. This seemed wrong to Kathleen, since the large set in Mr. Tobias' study always had a clear and distinct picture. To her, the struggle over the TV was simply one more example of the Missus' increasing closeness with money. Never in Kathleen's experience exactly openhanded, Robyn had some time ago become obsessed with saving money on the smallest items. Couldn't the maid empty out the disposable bag in the vacuum cleaner and use it again? the Missus had asked her not long before. And she knew that Robyn Vandermeer reviewed the accounts of the new Japanese-American cook, Mr. Obuchi, all the time.

Kathleen shrewdly guessed that Mr. Tobias must be keeping his wife on a short string, though she had no inkling why. Maybe it was just part of the overall change she had noticed in Mr. Tobias' own habits.

When she had come to work for the Vandermeers six years earlier, her predecessor, before packing up and retiring to County Clare, had warned her that Mr. Tobias "liked his whiskey." This had not fazed Kathleen; after all, she had put up with a brother who not only liked whiskey but appeared to nourish himself on it.

There was no denying, though, that Mr. Tobias' drinking had become more intense. She recalled listening to him play the Steinway in the living room whenever it took his fancy, day or night. She had never cared much for the jazz music he pounded out, but she had recognized that his playing had deteriorated and become more discordant and painful to listen to as time went on. Jesus, Mary and Joseph, what a noise he could make!

Mr. Tobias had become a mean blackguard, Kathleen thought. Fits of temper were now frequent, or, what Kathleen found worse, he lapsed into a morose state that sometimes lasted throughout the day, almost as if he were haunted by some unspoken reality. Maybe he was keeping a closer watch on his checkbook as part of this withdrawal.

The matter of money had come up specifically in connection with Kathleen's extra duties on the reading club Sundays. When approached about the matter, Kathleen, trying to be obliging, had worked the first one and then protested. Serving supper to eleven people, and then acting as their waitress while they went on about their book over drinks, was too much. Besides, Mr. Obuchi had made clear when he was hired that he would *never* work on Sunday, reading club or no reading club. Robyn's efforts to persuade him otherwise had been without avail; his command of English, such as it was, disappeared completely whenever the subject was raised. He had eventually agreed to prepare a supper in advance, the result being that Kathleen became an unwilling kitchen helper as well as a server in the dining room.

After listening to Kathleen's complaints, Robyn Vandermeer offered to pay her more money for the extra work. But Kathleen was more interested in her Sunday freedom and insisted that additional help was needed. Robyn was petulant and only agreed most reluctantly to hire a waiter to assist and to relieve Kathleen in the late afternoon (a much more expensive proposition than paying her overtime). He came from Bright Lights, the catering agency that Robyn, and half the hostesses in New York, used for their larger parties. The creation of Byron Hayden, a former child actor who outgrew his talent, Bright Lights possessed a Rolodex full of the names of hungry, out-of-work actors eager to staff everything from a small at-home dinner to a charity banquet in the Sixty-sixth Street Armory.

This March Sunday, Bright Lights had served up Pace Padgett, an unemployed actor who had worked at the Vandermeers' on several recent occasions, including the reading club supper the previous November and, that same month, a three-day "house party" when the Vandermeers entertained a dozen of Robyn's friends who had flown in from Europe to attend the READ ball.

Kathleen was of two minds about her helper. He was pleasant enough and, she thought, would even be good-looking if he shaved off his mustache and had his medium-length black hair properly cut. And, having worked the Vandermeers' residence before, he did not ask a lot of dumb questions about such matters as where the wine-glasses were or how to run the dishwasher.

Pace had not won Kathleen's complete approval, however. She did not at all like the arty manner in which he set the table, with flared napkins at each place. Nor the way he took charge and treated Kathleen as his assistant, rather than as the senior servant of the household, even to the point of answering the telephone, clearly Kathleen's prerogative. And worse, going off to make calls of his own without asking her permission. He certainly makes himself at home, Kathleen thought, but did not challenge her only route to partial Sunday deliverance.

By five-thirty, all was in readiness for the reading club, which would begin with drinks at six. Kathleen Boyle looked around with satisfaction. Everything was spotless, the bar stocked and the ice bucket filled. The silver and crystal on the dining-room table gleamed. The dishes were laid out in the kitchen for the supper Mr. Obuchi had left behind. The Missus would have nothing to complain about.

Kathleen said good-bye to Pace Padgett and hurried away, eager to make her exit before the Missus or Mr. Tobias could interrupt her day off any further.

GETTING READY: II

"WELL, DEAR, I'M AS READY AS I'LL EVER BE," CYNTHIA Frost said as she walked into the library, where Reuben was puttering at his desk, working his way through a pile of accumulated paper. He looked up at his wife, pleased as always to take in the slim dancer's figure she had managed to preserve years after her retirement as a ballerina. She was carrying a paperback edition of Thackeray's *Vanity Fair*, which she waved at her husband.

"Well, so am I," he replied. "Having nothing better to do while you were off gallivanting in Chicago, I reread parts thirteen through sixteen last night."

Cynthia, who was in charge of performing-arts grants at the prestigious Brigham Foundation, had been away for two days in Chicago, trying to assist in the latest effort to establish a viable ballet company in that city. She had attended a dinner of potential backers the night before and had offered up a Brigham grant, conditioned on obtaining a matching amount from local sources.

Cynthia had been annoyed at the inconvenience of attending an out-of-town dinner on a Saturday night, even though, as she and her husband got older, the working world's distinction between weeknights and the weekend no longer was as pronounced for them as it once had been. But her annoyance had been tempered by the enthusiasm she had encountered, though she realized that it was not the first time that there were bright predictions that ballet was, at last, going to be put on a sound footing in the Windy City.

She had eaten the execrable lunch served on the plane and, after a brief report of her travels to Reuben when she arrived home, had gone immediately to her room to prepare for the evening's session of Robyn Vandermeer's reading club. It was not exactly her idea of ending a day that had begun at the Chicago Ritz at seven that morning, though she was reasonably sure she could not persuade Reuben to skip the monthly event. But it was worth a try.

"I'm afraid my gallivanting, as you call it, has taken more out of me than I thought," she said. "Do we really have to go tonight?"

"We'll talk about it in a minute," her husband answered, instinctively employing the lawyer's trick of meeting confrontation with delay. "What do you think of this? Do we need it?"

Reuben handed his wife a flier from the telephone company extolling the virtues of call-forwarding.

"This thing says you can program your phone so your calls will go to another number," Frost explained. "Like everything the phone company does, it's only pennies a day."

"What on earth would we use it for?" Cynthia asked, as she looked over the advertisement.

"Well . . ."

"Reuben, sometimes I don't understand you, even after forty what? forty-four years of marriage. I can remember when you could barely plug in a toaster—and refused to learn anything mechanical. Now, ever since Doug Gilmore persuaded you to buy that computer, you've suddenly become Dr. Steinmetz."

"Now, wait a minute. You wanted me to get my computer," he said, gesturing toward the sleek machine sitting on the side of his desk.

"Yes, I did. I thought it would—"

"—Occupy me."

"Yes, occupy you. And maybe tempt you to start writing

down some of the interesting things that have happened in your life.''

"Oh, God.''

"But it's turned out to *pre*occupy you. It, and now all these other toys you want. Call-forwarding. Or that machine you mentioned the other day, the fax.''

"Everyone has a fax,'' Frost protested.

"What would you do with it?'' Cynthia asked, then suddenly realizing that this was perhaps not the most politic question for her retired husband. "But that doesn't matter. If you want one, for heaven's sake get one. We'll end up with more electronic equipment than the Russian Mission on Sixty-seventh Street, but that's all right.''

"I'm going to buy one. All the people at the office say they're wonderful. Imagine, sending copies of things over the telephone.

"And I'm going to have a modem, too,'' he added. "Gilmore tells me that with a modem you can do all kinds of things. Like access back articles from *The New York Times*. Or get airplane schedules and stock reports. Or even play blackjack.''

"Reuben, you're impossible.''

"So be it. But you haven't answered my question about call-forwarding.''

"I really don't see what use it would be. Unless of course you want all your calls transferred while you're down with the boys at the Gotham. And, if we may go back to where we started, do we have to go to Robyn's?''

Reuben's filibuster was over. "Of course we do, dear, unless you really feel terrible. I know, we both were hoodwinked into the damn thing—Robyn called you ten minutes after writing a big check to NatBallet, and Tobias followed up right after a meeting on high-fee legal business at Chase & Ward. But as I said then, and have been saying ever since, if we do it, we have to take it seriously. That means reading the books and going to every meeting. Look at the Jeromes. They come only half the time and are completely lost when they do.''

"I don't think their being lost has anything to do with their attendance."

"Okay, Ted Jerome is dense, and his wife almost as dense. But I still say we have to go regularly to make the thing work."

"You're right, of course," Cynthia said with a sigh.

"It will improve your mind—Robyn's lofty goal for the group."

"Hah!" Cynthia snorted. "That's what she told *W* when they did that piece on reading clubs. But you know as well as I do the motive was that earlier interview with her in *Vogue*."

"Oh, yes." Reuben chuckled, recalling the story, which was sufficiently delicious that his wife now repeated it.

"I'm surprised she ever admitted it to me. But I can just see it—there she was, holding forth about READ and all its good works, helping the little illiterates and the big illiterates learn to read. Then the bitch reporter asked Robyn what *she* had read recently."

"He-hee."

"And recorded poor Robyn's hesitation in print. Well, the reading club was born instantly after that article appeared. First *Light in August* and now *Vanity Fair*. And here we are, stuck on another Sunday. Thank God the episodes we're reading this month should make for a lively discussion. Or as lively as it ever gets."

"I agree. I can't wait to hear what the group's got to say about Becky Sharp *this* time."

"Besides, I would hate to deprive you of a chance to be taken by the hand through Thackeray by Helena Newcomb."

"That's a low blow. Just because Helena doesn't look like your typical frumpy professor of English. She may be a trifle, ah, overblown, like a fading movie star, but she's very smart."

"Oh, I grant you that. She's no affirmative action case, and I'm sure got tenure at Princeton on her merits. But that long blond hair and buxom figure can't have done her any harm."

"I'm not so sure. She may have gotten ahead *in spite* of

her looks. Academics are capable of envying *anything*—from mammillae to monographs, from derrieres to—''

"Reuben, please. I'm sorry I brought it up. Helena leads the discussions very well. I wonder how Robyn found her.''

"Wrote her a letter, is what she told me. It's not too surprising. Helena reviews in the *Times* a lot and her book on Thackeray is pretty well known, I think.''

"I should go get ready,'' Cynthia said. "I must pretty up so I don't look like Barbara Givens.''

"Oh, God,'' Reuben groaned, as he thought about the wife of Dr. Wayne Givens, both the Chairman and the President of the Bloemendael Foundation and another member of the reading group. "How can anybody be so plain?''

"She must work at it,'' Cynthia said. "Those prim Laura Ashley dresses, no makeup and that straight hair that looks like it was cut in a barbershop. And she sounds as if she's going to strangle when she finally gets to say anything.''

"Well, her popinjay husband talks for both of them.''

" 'Dr. Wayne,' as he now calls himself on television.''

"America's leading expert on drug addiction, or so everybody says—including himself,'' Reuben observed. "I guess he's good, but he certainly can be insufferable.''

"I still remember his psychoanalysis of Joseph Sedley as a repressed homosexual last month.''

"One of the reading club's high points, no doubt about it.''

"Enough. Maybe it will be fun, after all. Becky's money troubles are pretty interesting. But we still have the unanswered question, as we always do at these things.''

"Do you mean what I think?''

"The unanswered question—how drunk will Tobias get?''

"He'll have to go some to beat the last time.''

"Yes, but he'll be on his home turf. It won't take two people to carry him home,'' Cynthia said, recalling with distaste the untidy conclusion of the February gathering at their house. "We've talked it over a hundred times, but after all those years spent getting plastered so quietly, why is he now drinking so violently?''

"I haven't a clue. Something must be bothering him terribly, but I have no idea what."

"His finances are all right, aren't they?"

"As far as I know. Maybe Dr. Givens—Dr. Wayne—should psychoanalyze Tobias."

"I'll be ready in ten minutes. Let's hope it's an uneventful literary evening."

Cynthia left to go upstairs, and Reuben, his joints creaking slightly, stood up.

"I hope so. I hope so," he said quietly to himself, as he followed his wife.

DRINKS AND DINNER

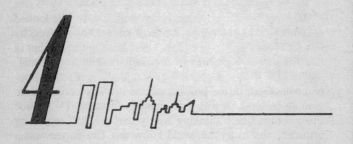

ROBYN VANDERMEER AND HELENA NEWCOMB HAD DEVISED
the rules for the reading club at its inception. They were
simplicity itself:

1. Members should not attend meetings if they had not
read the assigned selection.

2. Biographies and criticism relating to the selection could
not be consulted beforehand. Helena, as the discussion
leader, was the only one permitted to introduce secondary
material.

3. Meetings would be held on the first Sunday of each
month, alternating among the houses of the members. Drinks
were at six, supper at six-thirty and the reading discussion at
seven-thirty, or as soon as the meal was over. The members
were urged not to discuss the day's selection until after supper.

There was general agreement on the ground rules, with
some exceptions. Sherman Deybold, the art-gallery owner,
invariably cheated, although usually not too obviously, by
citing outside sources. Tobias Vandermeer thought the cocktail hour too short, though it really didn't matter since he
drank constantly through the evening. And both of the Frosts
would have preferred to start discussing the reading at hand

over supper, which would have achieved the double result of limiting the small talk and shortening the evening.

This March Sunday, the Frosts walked from their own townhouse on Seventieth Street to the Vandermeers' apartment building four blocks north, each with a Penguin copy of *Vanity Fair* in hand.

Robyn Vandermeer greeted both with kisses. She looked elegant, wearing what Cynthia Frost knew to be a Givenchy silk dress that matched her dark eyes. Standing beside her in the living room were Wayne and Barbara Givens. As usual, Wayne, Dr. Wayne, looked deeply tanned. A real tan, Reuben wondered, or the product of one of those carcinogenic tanning parlors? Or was it all makeup from the TV studio? Frost couldn't help thinking sourly that the tan, natural or artificial, was to let the world know that Dr. Wayne was a television personality. Or perhaps it was simply a beauty aid to advance his activities as a notorious skirt-chaser around Manhattan.

Mrs. Givens, predictably, was wearing one of her schoolmarm print dresses, projecting a severity accented by her lack of makeup and straight brown hair.

"Hello, Reuben, ready for Lord Steyne?" Dr. Wayne asked jauntily. His wife dug in her purse for a cigarette and lit it with a Bic lighter.

"Oh, let me get you an ashtray," Robyn Vandermeer said.

Since Barbara Givens chain-smoked—her husband's clinical expertise in treating addiction not seeming to extend to her smoking habit—Reuben was sure that the absence of ashtrays was an oblique and hostile comment by the hostess. Pace Padgett, Bright Lights' contribution to the party, appeared, and Robyn asked him to bring an ashtray.

"I'm sorry, Robyn," Barbara said. "I should give up smoking. It's become so difficult, everywhere you go." The woman's global observation did not exclude the Vandermeer living room.

"Think nothing of it," Robyn said sweetly.

"You know, it must be awful running a restaurant these days," Reuben said. "Smoking areas, nonsmoking areas, and everybody getting angry when the lines are crossed."

"Yes," Dr. Givens replied, "restaurant owners must be ready to kill Norman, our dear Mayor. But I guess if you can't solve the big addiction problems you go for the little ones, and regulate smoking in restaurants."

"Now, now," Robyn said. "Let's not be too harsh on Norman. He's giving me an award for READ a couple of weeks from now."

"Yes, we got an invitation to the ceremony," Cynthia said. "What are they going to give you, Robyn?"

"It's all very muddled. They said they wanted to honor me, but I don't know whether it's a scroll, the keys to Gracie Mansion, or something else."

"Maybe a free Chinese dinner with the Mayor," Dr. Givens said.

"Oh, Wayne, it wouldn't be that," his wife contradicted, as usual missing the point that her husband had been making a joke.

"I suspect, my dear, you'll get a crystal apple," Reuben observed.

"I hope so, Reuben. I have so many plaques and scrolls now I don't know what to do with them. A crystal apple would be fine."

"Who is this?" Cynthia interrupted, having spotted in a corner a dog that she had not seen before.

"Oh! My goodness, you haven't met Neil. My new baby darling!" She picked up the dog and stroked his back. He responded with pleasure. Yet he did not make a sound.

"He's very well-behaved," Reuben marveled, always expecting the worst from pets.

"He's a basenji," Robyn explained. "He doesn't bark."

"He what?" Reuben said.

"He doesn't bark. Basenjis don't, you know."

"I've never heard of such a thing," Reuben said.

"Well, you have now. Just the strong, silent type, aren't you, Neil?"

"What happened to your retriever? Dolly, wasn't it?" Cynthia asked.

Robyn looked stricken. "It's a long story that I won't bore you with. We had to get rid of her."

"She was a beautiful dog," Cynthia said, trying not to make an invidious comparison with the much less prepossessing Neil.

"Yes, she was. But she's gone and I must forget her."

"Robyn, have you been away?" Cynthia asked, tactfully changing the subject.

"Yes, I have," Robyn answered. "A *tremendously* interesting trip to Duke University. A conference on rural illiteracy and what could be done about it—three days and *very* stimulating. And they gave me an honorary degree!"

"That's wonderful," Cynthia said.

"So you are now Dr. Vandermeer," Reuben said.

"My dear, I've been that for eons. This was my *sixth* honorary degree. The Duke hood, white with blue piping, made me feel like a bride again."

As they talked, Reuben took in the familiar room, covered with Dutch genre paintings of all sizes, collected by Tobias Vandermeer under the tutelage of Sherman Deybold. He knew that Tobias' collection was distinguished, though it was in sharp contrast to the tough and solid contemporary works that had graced the same walls when Ines Vandermeer had been the collector-in-residence. That collection she had taken with her when she decamped for Brazil in 1964.

Deybold, a specialist in seventeenth-century Dutch painting, had regarded the blank walls Ines had left behind as an opportunity to be seized. He had persuaded Tobias that it would be appropriate for one of his Netherlandish heritage to collect works of the sort that Deybold, just by coincidence, specialized in. And he didn't have to point out that the paintings he had in mind were about as different from the abstracts Ines had assembled as one could imagine.

A clattering noise on the stairs to the floor above, followed by heaving, unsteady footsteps, diverted Reuben from his visual tour of the room. Robyn, who had been laughing over her new doctor's degree, turned away to talk to Pace Padgett, asking him to heat up the meal Mr. Obuchi had left and get ready to serve supper. She was not panicked, but she was nervous.

Her guests, certain that Tobias Vandermeer was coming

down the stairs, also became tense. Then their host appeared, a glass of whiskey in one hand, the prerequisite copy of *Vanity Fair* in the other.

Tobias Vandermeer immediately dominated the room. At six feet four, he was an enormous man, and his bold hound's tooth jacket made him look even larger. He wore a relatively neat shirt and tie, but there were two cuts on his florid face from a botched job of shaving.

Given his heavy tread on the stairway, Cynthia was surprised to see that he was wearing velvet slippers, complete with fox heads in silver thread on the tongue over his initials, "TV." Except for their large size—his feet were huge—the slippers, with their bright colors and tiny animals, might have delighted a child.

Tobias did not shake hands with his guests nor, as Cynthia noted with relief, did he kiss any of them. Instead he grunted affably and settled into a large overstuffed chair, especially built to accommodate his formidable bulk. The others, who had been standing until now, dutifully sat down around him.

Soon the doorbell rang once, and then, after a pause, a second time.

"Where is that young man?" Robyn said, with impatience. "Probably talking to his agent," she grumbled crossly, before realizing that she had dispatched Padgett to make the last-minute preparations for supper. She herself went to the door to let in Helena Newcomb.

Reuben noted with approval the woman's bright-red silk shirt, which nicely showed off her ample bosom, though he had to concede that her silk trousers were less suited to her equally ample posterior.

"Here comes teacher," Tobias said, in a heavy, gravelly voice. "Let me get you a drink. I was headed that way myself," he said, finishing in a single gulp the one in his hand as he went across to the bar.

Looking around the room, as if taking attendance, Ms. Newcomb asked where the Jeromes were.

"They're not coming," Robyn said.

"Unprepared?" Reuben asked, using the dreaded word he remembered from long-ago law school classes.

"I'm afraid so," Robyn said. "Charlotte said life had been so hectic in Hobe Sound that they simply hadn't had time to do the reading for tonight."

"And how about S & M?" Tobias called over his shoulder from the bar, referring to Sherman Deybold and his young companion, Michael Costas.

"Tobias! That isn't nice at all," Robyn scolded.

"It may not be nice, but that's what everybody calls them," he replied matter-of-factly. His guests did not comment.

"They're always late," Robyn said.

The unkindly named S & M arrived shortly afterward. All the guests wondered at Sherman Deybold's appearance. Until very recently, his skin had been as dark as Wayne Given's, or even darker, the product of diligent sunbathing on Fire Island in the summer and Saint Thomas in the winter.

Now Deybold's face was completely white, a condition that had given rise to the inevitable rumor that he had AIDS. The reality was quite different. The art dealer was simply reflecting the new health chic that viewed suntans as dangerous to the skin. He had been unenthusiastic when his dermatologist had lectured him about staying out of the sun (this after removal of a small melanoma from Deybold's forehead) but then, as many of the brown beautiful people changed their sunning habits, he changed his.

Michael Costas, by contrast, was as dark and handsome as ever. He was the older man's assistant in running the traditional Deybold Gallery and its downtown modern offshoot, called Deybold/Costas. Everyone assumed, from the way they behaved together, that he was Deybold's lover. This was a source of envy among Deybold's friends of both sexes, since Costas was uncommonly good-looking.

Today Deybold and Costas looked like versions of Mr. Bibendum, the Michelin man, with their billowing Armani pants and jackets. Except for the difference in their complexions and their similar dress, they could have been father and son, Deybold in his early fifties and Costas not yet thirty.

Robyn Vandermeer urged S & M to have a quick drink, since supper was ready to be served.

"Has Mr. Obuchi outdone himself tonight?" Deybold asked.

"He may have," Robyn said. She was justifiably proud of her new chef. "Come, we'll find out."

"I've got to make a quick stop at the little boys' room," Deybold said. "We've been at a brunch that lasted all afternoon and I'm *floating*."

"Me, too," Michael said.

"Well, hurry up," Robyn said. "We've got to keep on schedule. Michael, you know where the john is down here, right off the hallway. Sherman, you go and use Tobias' bathroom upstairs. Right at the top to the right."

The two Michelin men went as directed while everyone else headed into the dining room. Robyn arranged the seating and Reuben found himself between his hostess and Helena Newcomb. Sherman Deybold soon returned and sat down on the other side of Helena.

"Oh, Robyn, you're trying to torture me again," he said, turning to his hostess. "Putting me across from that Jasper Johns." Deybold had been attempting for years to persuade the Vandermeers to sell the painting, a dynamic and colorful oil, mostly bright red, green and yellow, that showed the numerals 0 through 9 superimposed over each other.

"How much do you think it's worth this week?" Tobias asked, picking up on the dealer's remark.

"After those recent auctions it's hard to say. Ten million anyway."

"Good! It's going up!" Tobias said. "I can't stand it myself, but I can't afford to let it go. At least not till Bush reduces the capital-gains tax."

The Johns had a curious history. It had been purchased by Ines Vandermeer in 1961 for ten thousand dollars and had been on loan to an exhibition at the Modern Museum at the time she left Tobias. Later, when she discovered her forgetfulness, she had fought bitterly to have Tobias return it. Although he disliked the work, he had stubbornly refused, and Ines had eventually given up trying to get it back—so that Tobias, with typical Vandermeer good fortune, now possessed a painting of immense value.

"Let's have a drink to Jasper Johns!" Tobias thundered. "Kid, are we going to have any wine with this meal or not?" he demanded of Pace Padgett, who was placing a large soup tureen next to Robyn.

"Yes, sir. Just a moment, sir," he replied, quickly grabbing a bottle of the Montrachet from the ice bucket on the sideboard and hurrying to Tobias' place.

"Kid, you've got to hop fast around here. This is a thirsty crowd."

"I know, sir. I've worked here before."

Tobias gulped his wine and was demanding a refill before the hapless Padgett had made the rounds of the table.

Robyn dished up what she explained was turtle soup, with "calipash and calipee," as it had been served to Joseph Sedley in Cavendish Square in an earlier episode of *Vanity Fair*. Her guests' compliments were effusive.

"I think Mr. Obuchi's done very well," Deybold said.

"Where did you get him?" Cynthia asked.

"Straight from the Culinary Institute of America," Robyn answered.

"Where does the American part come from?" her husband demanded, from his end of the table. "Pretty damned Oriental, I'd say. But then, everything is. I went to hear this gal stride piano player the other night. Name's Judy Carmichael and she's terrific. Really got it. You know where she was playing? A joint called the Fortune Garden, that's where! A Chinese restaurant. Jazz in a Chinese restaurant! We've come to that."

The rest of the table listened in silence to their host.

"You say this woman pianist was good?" Helena Newcomb finally asked.

"Capital! First-rate! Best woman stride player I've ever heard."

"Are there that many?"

"No, not at all. Mary Lou Williams years ago. A few others. But this gal was doing 'Carolina Shout' as good as Eubie Blake."

"I don't know it," Helena said.

"You don't? James P. Johnson. Nineteen twenty. I'll play

it for you.'' Vandermeer edged himself out of his chair and lurched toward the piano in the living room. Robyn was horror-struck and showed it, yet she did not protest.

Tobias, to no one's surprise, was too drunk to play. He got hopelessly confused in Johnson's demanding crosshand figures—a challenge to a skillful pianist when sober—and finally stopped in mid-phrase. Silence, this time a heavy, embarrassed silence, pervaded the dining room as Tobias made his way back to the table.

''Out of practice,'' he muttered dejectedly as he sat down, reaching for the wine bottle Pace Padgett had left on the table. ''I'll play it for you some other time.''

''I get the idea,'' Helena said generously. ''It sounds fiendishly difficult.''

''It is.''

Tobias' disgrace was forgotten as Padgett served the delicious beef stew the versatile Mr. Obuchi had prepared as the main course.

The red Château Talbot '78, which Padgett now served, went well with the stew. Reuben turned to Helena Newcomb, basking in the double pleasure of the wine's bouquet and her good looks.

''Just a nice, simple Sunday supper,'' he said.

Helena laughed and agreed with him.

''How are things at my alma mater?'' Frost asked.

''No change, Mr. Frost. The students are smarter than ever and keep you jumping.''

''Glad to hear it. It must be fun teaching bright ones. Looking back on it, I often wonder how the teachers in my day stood it, teaching all the 'gentlemen third groupers.' ''

''There're still some of them. But mostly they've been replaced by, what would you call them, 'lady A' students.''

''Except you're not supposed to call them ladies, I thought.''

''I trust your discretion, Mr. Frost. I assume you won't turn me in to the Sexist Language League.''

''Is there such a thing?'' Reuben asked in surprise.

''No, no. There might as well be, though.''

''Hmn.'' Reuben drank deeply from his wine and then

turned to the mango sorbet that had been served to him for dessert.

When dessert was finished, Robyn declared the meal at an end.

"We must get started," she said. "The Crawleys are waiting. We'll have coffee in the living room."

"I look forward to this, Ms. Newcomb," Frost said. "There are dramatic events in this evening's text."

The guests moved into the living room, and as they did so, Robyn took Reuben's arm and asked if she could see him privately for a moment. Reuben, puzzled, followed her across the hall to the library.

Robyn closed the door and turned to Frost, her face now more drawn than it had seemed at dinner.

"Reuben, this is dreadfully embarrassing, but I thought you would understand."

"What's the matter?"

"Do you have any money with you? I haven't a cent and Tobias says he doesn't either. I need to borrow enough to pay the waiter."

"How much do you need?"

"Let's see. He got here at four and I can let him go at eight-thirty. I'm sure that's seventy-five, carfare included. Plus a ten-dollar tip. Do you have eighty-five dollars?"

Frost checked his wallet and had enough to make the requested loan.

"Oh, Reuben, I can't thank you enough. It's so awkward, never having cash. Tobias . . . never mind. Let's just say I'm immensely grateful and I'll pay you back tomorrow if I can."

"Think nothing of it, Robyn."

"And you won't say anything to the others?"

"Of course not."

"You're a lifesaver."

Thus praised, he walked across to the living room while Robyn went off to settle up with Pace Padgett. The wife of a multimillionaire with no cash. Odd, Reuben thought.

THE READING CLUB

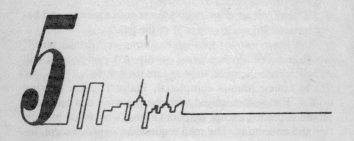

WHEN REUBEN ENTERED THE LIVING ROOM, THE EVENING'S students had already begun to assemble in a semicircle around Helena Newcomb.

Professor Newcomb sat on an upholstered bench in front of the immense marble fireplace along one wall of the room. She had declined a more comfortable seat, both so she could dominate the group from a slightly higher perch and (she had to admit to herself) so that she would remain fully alert. Tobias Vandermeer was at her left, sitting in his custom-built chair, his omnipresent needlepoint on a side table at his right.

Sherman Deybold was at Tobias' left in another armchair, separated by another side table. Michael Costas was next to him, sitting on one of three Breuer chairs—the comfortable kind, with arms—facing Ms. Newcomb. The middle chair was empty, and Wayne Givens occupied the third.

The semicircle was completed by a large sofa that faced Tobias, Cynthia Frost sitting on the end nearest Givens and Barbara Givens on the other.

Reuben was about to put himself between Costas and Wayne Givens when Robyn came in and directed him to sit on the sofa between Cynthia and Barbara.

"It means you'll have to sit beside your wife, Reuben," she said, "but that's less bourgeois than having all the men huddled together." As she spoke she no longer seemed as distraught as she had only moments before in the library.

"You sure? Wouldn't you be more comfortable on the sofa?"

"Heavens, no, this is fine," she insisted, and the seating was completed.

Pace Padgett appeared with a silver coffee service and began passing out demitasse cups to the guests.

"I suggest you have the waiter bring you drinks now," Robyn said. "He'll be leaving shortly. After he goes, it will be self-service. You all know where the bar is."

The coffee rounds completed, Padgett began serving drinks. The women stayed with the red wine that had been served at dinner, except Barbara Givens, who asked for Perrier and an ashtray. The men requested Cognac, except Tobias, who demanded separate glasses of Scotch and Drambuie, and a third glass with only ice in it. Once served, he mixed the Scotch and Drambuie together in the glass with ice and contentedly began stirring the mixture with his long but pudgy index finger.

Sherman Deybold watched the concocting going on next to him with fascination. "What's that called, Tobias?"

"Rusty nail. Good for the digestion," Tobias replied, taking a large and contented sip of his creation. "Want one?"

"No, no, brandy's all I can handle."

Helena Newcomb was going to speak when Tobias again drew the group's attention by picking up his needlepoint.

"What are you working on?" Barbara Givens asked.

"Oh, ha, ha, just one of the Seven Deadly Sins. Hieronymus Bosch. This one's Pride," he said, holding up the frame for all to see. The panel, showing a vain woman looking in a mirror, was nearly completed, including, in the title at the bottom, the first three letters of "Pride" and part of the "d."

"It's very beautiful," Mrs. Givens said, then fell silent as Helena Newcomb cleared her throat and began.

"As you know, tonight we are having a look at parts thirteen through sixteen of Thackeray's *Vanity Fair*. These parts, which comprise a fifth of the total, came out in monthly numbers from January through April 1848. Shall we start at the beginning, with the O'Dowds and Major Dobbin in Madras?''

"Oh, that's too boring," Robyn said. "Mrs. O'Dowd with her pretensions and her sister, Glorvina, a husband-hunter who isn't very exciting."

"Okay. Then let me ask what you thought was the most interesting thing you read?"

"When Rawdon caught Becky with Lord Steyne and threw the diamond pin at him," Tobias said.

"Very good," Professor Newcomb commented. "A major Thackeray scholar, George Saintsbury, called that one of the greatest scenes in English prose."

"Poor old Rawdon," Tobias observed. "Beaten into the ground by his wife, being called 'Mrs. Crawley's husband' everywhere he went. I'd almost given up on him. It seemed like he was going to fade away. Then he gets mad and gives that old cat just what he deserved."

"Are we sure of that, Mr. Vandermeer?" Ms. Newcomb asked. "Becky says in that scene, after she's found out, 'I am innocent.' Was she? Or was she the 'odious little adventuress' the country ladies called her? 'Unworthy to sit down with Christian people,' as her sister-in-law said?"

"The country ladies were right," Tobias said.

"I disagree," Deybold countered. "Look at her situation. She was desperately poor, worried about her future and always short of 'ready-money,' as Thackeray calls it. Her in-laws were terrible, her husband ineffectual. When foolish—and rich—old Lord Steyne came along, who can blame her for flirting with him?"

"If Becky was innocent, she's the most worldly innocent I've ever come across," Cynthia said. "In the old days in the ballet there were dancers like Becky—or her mother. They took old fools like Lord Steyne for plenty. But, believe me, they weren't innocent flirtations."

"I guess I'd go along with Sherman, but from a different perspective," Dr. Givens added. "If Becky were on the couch today, I think almost any psychiatrist would say she was suffering from deep-seated neurotic anxiety—anxiety over money, anxiety over being respected in society. Her response was not untypical—pretty consistent lying, aggressiveness, hostility—remember that confrontation with Lady Bareacres?—more love for her dog than her son, and, yes, probably sleeping with Lord Steyne.''

As Dr. Givens was talking, Reuben had been sipping at his Cognac. What was he doing, drinking such stuff? he thought to himself. He knew it disagreed with him; much better to have a Scotch. He looked around for the waiter, who had disappeared. Perhaps his time was up, Reuben concluded, and the ''self-help'' period had begun. He stood up, as unobtrusively as possible so as not to disturb Givens' monologue, and headed toward the bar. As he did so, Tobias beckoned to him from across the way, wigwagging his half-empty rusty nail. ''Scotch,'' he mouthed silently.

Reuben obediently prepared two Scotches, one for himself and the other for his host. Returning, he handed a glass across the coffee table to Tobias, who put it down carefully beside his needlepoint at his right, which he had temporarily abandoned, seemingly intrigued with Wayne's discourse. ''My reserve supply,'' he whispered audibly to Helena Newcomb. She was trying hard to concentrate on what Dr. Givens was saying so that she could draw the others into evaluating his analysis, if and when he finished it.

''In my view Becky was clearly psychopathic,'' Givens concluded. ''And Thackeray seems to have thought so, too. That scene with the charades at the party, where she frightened everyone when she acted out Clytemnestra, waving a knife. Or when she said back at the beginning that she wanted to see the headmistress floating dead in the water. This is psychotic stuff!''

''Any comments?'' Helena asked, as Givens finished.

To the surprise of everyone, Barbara Givens spoke up. Helena had seen the telltale sign that Barbara was getting ready to speak—she had got red in the face and fidgeted with her cigarette—and gently asked her what she thought.

''Wayne, on your analysis you could justify anybody's conduct. Anxiety, indeed. We all have anxiety. But we don't lie and cheat and sleep around just because of it. Becky Sharp was a willful woman who knew exactly what she was doing."

"My dear, of course everyone has anxieties," Givens said, exasperated. "But in some people they get out of control and cause antisocial behavior."

Frost wondered mischievously if Givens had perhaps not used the anxiety defense when confronted at home with his own misdeeds.

Then Michael spoke. The silent ones are coming out, Reuben mused. Costas, at earlier sessions, had talked even less than Barbara, though Reuben had never been sure whether this was because he was not very smart—wasn't he too handsome to have any brains?—or because he felt he had to defer to Sherman Deybold.

"You say Becky did what she did for money. Sure, that's part of it. But she wanted to have a good time. She liked showing off at Lord Steyne's, being the center of attention. She liked having him admire her. She liked to dress up. She was a party girl and did what she had to do to enjoy herself."

Tobias reacted to the young man's defense of hedonism by struggling to his feet and excusing himself noisily, muttering that he would be right back. Once again he made a heavy clumping sound as he went upstairs, despite his bunny slippers.

While he was gone, Helena Newcomb steered the group into a dialogue on Becky's assertion, made in an earlier installment, that she could have been a simple country gentleman's wife and a "good woman" if she had "five thousand a year." While the talk went on, Pace Padgett, who had not left the premises after all, cleared away the debris on the table next to Sherman Deybold—Sherman's brandy snifter and the glasses that Tobias had used to mix his rusty nail. He replaced them with a bourbon and water for Sherman and a fresh Scotch for Tobias.

Padgett had put the new drinks down when Tobias returned, almost losing his footing as he bumped into the waiter. Regaining his balance by grasping the back of his armchair, he disrupted the conversation by facing a surprised

Sherman Deybold and thundering out, like a huge, growling bear, "What do you want this time?"

Everyone in the room was startled and puzzled by the irascible question, most of all the pale-faced Deybold, to whom the reeling Tobias seemed to be speaking.

"Sit down, dear," Robyn admonished, firmly but gently. Tobias gave her a disgusted look but did as he was told, breathing heavily as he resettled himself. He drank deeply from the Scotch Reuben had brought him and then took up his needlepoint. His outburst was soon forgotten as Helena Newcomb got the interrupted discussion back on track and Tobias became totally absorbed in adding new stitches to "Pride."

Padgett, who had discreetly moved away from Tobias after their brief collision, now came up and whispered to Robyn. She nodded and gave the young man a dismissive smile, followed by a small wave as he left the room. Frost glanced at his watch. Precisely eight-thirty. No overtime.

While the dissection of Becky Sharp continued, Frost deliberated on the extraordinary kaleidoscope Thackeray had created in *Vanity Fair*, and on the timelessness of his characters. Why, any one of them could step into the Vandermeers' living room now and, with small modifications of speech and dress, be right at home. Or maybe some of them were already present. Surely there was some of Becky in Robyn. Or did she more closely resemble the freethinking and independent Miss Crawley? And didn't Tobias have a bit of Lord Steyne—rich, overbearing and lost in "Red Seas of wine"? Or was he "Mrs. Vandermeer's husband," eclipsed, like Rawdon Crawley, by his wife's prominence? And Wayne Givens, lecturing so pompously, who was he? At this point, Reuben gave up. Thackeray's kaleidoscope had been twisted, and the pattern had changed. Yet Frost was certain that the same colored shards of human faults and weaknesses that were present in the old design were still there in the new configuration now before his eyes.

No one's earlier position on Becky changed as the speculation continued as to whether an adequate stipend would have changed her character. When the dialogue wound down and there was finally a lull, Sherman Deybold asked if anyone else had noticed how "wonderfully deft" Thackeray was in his allusions "to Prince Hal, Macbeth, Ulysses, *The Rape of the Lock*."

"I was particularly struck by the passage in the description of Lady O'Dowd at the Government House ball in Madras," Deybold said, referring to the portion of the night's reading ruled out from discussion earlier. "You remember, it tells how she 'danced down' two aides-de-camp, a major and two civil servants, after which she retired, *lassata nondum satiata recessit*. That, of course, is a direct quote from the passage in Juvenal's *Satires* that tells of the Empress Messalina's return to the palace after spending the night in a brothel."

Of course, Reuben thought, and where did you read that? The slight frown on Helena Newcomb's face confirmed that she shared his view that Sherman had, once again, violated the reading club's rules.

No one took the bait, which caused Tobias to interrupt, looking up from his needlepoint. "Aren't we going to talk about Amelia Osborne tonight? Look what happened to her. Her son-of-a-bitch father-in-law using his money to get her little son away from her. He should've supported her, poor girl."

Now drinking the Scotch the waiter had brought him, Tobias took a satisfied gulp, his needlepoint in his right hand, the Scotch glass in his left. Before the others could comment on Miss Amelia's dilemma, Tobias suddenly dropped both the glass and the needlepoint, freeing his hands to grab at his collar. He made unearthly choking noises as he tried frantically to loosen it, then clutched at his chest as his massive body fell out of the chair and thudded to the floor, upending the table at his right and the coffee table in front of him as well.

Chaos followed. The glass that had been on the table beside Tobias and the ashtray holding Barbara Givens' cigarette had crashed to the floor. The cigarette started to burn a hole in the rug, and Helena Newcomb sprang up to stamp it out, managing to break the fallen glass as well. Robyn Vandermeer screamed in panic and tried to claw her way to her husband. She succeeded only in unbalancing Sherman Deybold, who had leaped up as soon as Tobias had been stricken; he fell back unsteadily into his chair.

Wayne Givens, on his feet, seemed frozen in place, unable to move, until Robyn screamed, "Wayne! You're a doctor! Do something!"

Galvanized by her panicked command, Givens pushed toward the body. He pounded Tobias' chest and took his pulse. Then he dropped the victim's arm and rose slowly.

"It's too late," he announced. "He's dead. Poisoned."

"Poisoned?" Reuben asked incredulously. He was about to ask the doctor how on earth he could know that. Then he looked at the dead man's face and saw the blue coloration around his gaping mouth. "We'd better clear this room," Frost said. "Let's everyone go into the library."

Reuben's command stopped the hysteria. The survivors went across to the library, Reuben with his arm around the sobbing widow. All were stunned to realize that they had been witnesses to a murder. And that the murderer might well be there among them.

IN THE CONFUSION, REUBEN CAUGHT UP WITH HIS WIFE AND told her he was going to call the police. He also asked her to do her best to keep everyone in the library. This admonition given, he hurried upstairs to Tobias' private study.

His first inclination was to call his old friend Luis Bautista, the young homicide detective with whom he had worked in the past. But he decided to go by the book and dialed the emergency 911 number, dutifully answering the terse, businesslike questioner to whom he was connected. He then tried Bautista, both at his office and at home, but could not reach him. Probably out with his permanent girlfriend, Francisca Ribiero, Frost thought. Discussing for the nth time whether he should stay in the Police Department now that he had obtained his night school law degree.

Stymied, Frost sat for a moment collecting himself. He was tired, his fatigue hardly surprising given the appalling event that had just occurred, plus the fair amount that he had eaten and drunk. As he looked around the room, decorated with autographed pictures of jazz musicians and three or four framed examples of Tobias' needlepoint, he spotted a manila folder on the desk, labeled simply "GREAT KILL OPER-ATIONS—Week ending March 3." He could not resist looking inside and examining the summary sheets he found.

The information in the neat folder showed that Great Kill was profitable indeed: cash receipts were $402,000 for the week. Frost calculated that if this was typical it meant annual cash flow on the order of $20 million, or perhaps even more, most of which was pretax profit. Not bad, not bad at all, Reuben thought. And certainly enough money to interest a murderer.

Frost tried to recall the terms of Tobias Vandermeer's will, then remembered that the 50 percent share of Great Kill still in Vandermeer hands was in trust for Tobias' children. But Tobias had not had any children. Who would inherit? The Bloemendael Foundation? Dr. Givens' foundation? Reuben shuddered, trying to repel the nasty speculation that crossed his mind.

But how about Robyn? he asked himself. Again he tried to reconstruct what he knew of Vandermeer family affairs, but could not recall how Robyn was provided for. Certainly she must be, he reasoned, and, based on the figures before him, ruefully concluded that she would be able to pay the servants without his help.

He snapped the folder shut, realizing that he must return to the others, though he first stopped in Tobias' bathroom adjoining the study.

When he went to wash his hands, he saw that the top of a plastic medicine bottle was sitting in the middle of the wash-basin. Looking around, he discovered the topless bottle under the sink. Capsules, each half-blue and half-aqua, were tumbling out onto the floor. He was going to pick the bottle up when he noticed for the first time a peculiar smell in the room that was strongest near the spilled container. He could not decide what the odor was; perhaps burnt almonds, but he couldn't be sure.

Reuben had already decided that if Tobias has been poisoned the lethal substance must have been in one of his manifold drinks. But now he realized that perhaps there was an alternative, and that he might now be looking at the source of the poison. He gingerly got down on his hands and knees and was able to read the label, which described 120-milligram capsules of Inderal-LA, two capsules to be taken once a day.

Shaken, he got up and closed the bathroom door firmly behind him, the pill bottle still in its odd location, and headed downstairs.

The group he encountered in the library was frightened, if not downright terrorized. All eyes turned to him as he entered and announced that the police were on the way.

Robyn Vandermeer sat forward in the armchair in which she was sitting. "Why do we have to have the police, Reuben?" she pleaded. "You're a lawyer and Wayne is a doctor. Can't you take care of the red tape? The death certificate, all that?"

"I'm afraid it's not the simple," Frost said. "After all, Tobias was poisoned."

Robyn sighed deeply; the others stirred uncomfortably. "I can't believe it. I know Wayne says so. But it's ridiculous. Tobias drank himself to death. That's the truth and I know it."

"Robyn, it's distasteful, but there really was no choice but to call the police. I'm sure they will make things as easy as possible," Frost said.

His words were belied by a noisy troupe that invaded the apartment—two radio patrolmen and two paramedics. Reuben, nearest the library door when the doorbell rang, went to admit them.

"Someone's been poisoned?" the taller of the policemen, Patrolman Aurelio, asked brusquely.

"Where's the body?" one of the paramedics asked simultaneously.

"Yes, in there," Frost said, answering both questions and gesturing toward the living room.

"Other people here?" Aurelio asked.

"They're all in the library. Across the hall."

"Who called us? You?"

"Yes, I did."

"And you said it was a poisoning?"

"Yes."

"What's back there?" Aurelio said, pointing in front of him.

"The dining room and the kitchen."

"Come with me."

Frost, with Aurelio on one side and Patrolman McKenna on the other, was gently propelled toward the kitchen and told to sit down at the kitchen table. He gave the two policemen Tobias' vital statistics as best he knew them, a brief account of his host's dramatic collapse and a run-down on the witnesses who had been present.

"How did you know he was poisoned?" Aurelio demanded.

"I didn't. That was Dr. Givens' conclusion. He's a psychiatrist, which I believe means he's an M.D."

"Go get him," Aurelio said to his partner. "Bring him out here."

While they were waiting, Frost remembered the offending bottle upstairs.

"There's one thing I think you ought to do right away," Frost said, going on to describe the Inderal bottle and how he had found it. He remembered his friend Bautista's complaints about ordinary cops messing up evidence, but felt nonetheless that it was important to have it under police control as quickly as possible.

While Reuben was talking, McKenna returned with Dr. Givens and was given the new assignment of securing the medicine bottle and its spilled capsules. Givens seemed shaken in the presence of the police. He started to ask Reuben what was happening, but Aurelio brusquely interrupted him.

"Mr. Frost, could you wait in here, please?" he said, motioning to the maid's room normally occupied by Kathleen Boyle.

"Can't I join the others in the library?"

"No, best you stay here. I want to talk to Dr. Givens and then I'll get back to you."

Frost went into the servant's room without protest, Aurelio closing the door behind him. In the circumstances, the austerity and minuscule size of the room reminded him of only one thing: a jail cell. He sat down in the solitary chair, nervously contemplating the religious iconography assembled by the devout Miss Boyle.

Frost could hear Aurelio and Wayne Givens talking in the kitchen, but could not make out what they were saying. (He prudently refrained from putting his ear directly to the door, though he concluded that it was fair game to stand near it and try to hear.) When the voices disappeared, Frost stayed obediently in his confinement. He was tempted to stretch out on Miss Boyle's chaste single bed but decided against it. Instead he concentrated on the religious pictures on the dresser until the eyes of the Virgin in the largest chromo appeared to him to move, whereupon he fled the room, police orders or not; a murder and a miracle in one night would be too much.

The kitchen was empty, but voices were audible in the dining room. He opened the swinging door, lightly striking Aurelio's arm as he did so.

"Pardon me, officer. I was wondering . . ."

"Okay, Frost. We're almost ready for you. Stay there in the kitchen and we'll be with you in a minute."

"Can I make a telephone call while I'm waiting?"

"Later, sir, if you don't mind."

Was there some new hostility there? Frost wondered. "Frost," not "Mr. Frost." Not that he cared in the least, but why the change in attitude? Or was he simply edgy in the surreal circumstances in which he found himself? And what about the phone call? Even criminals caught red-handed could make one free phone call, or so he had always believed. He wanted very much to reach Bautista, who would not keep him waiting in suspense in Robyn Vandermeer's kitchen.

Reuben's nervous-making meditations were interrupted by a new pair of strangers. He rose from his seat at the kitchen table almost reflexively as they approached.

"Sit down, sit down," the shorter of the two said. "You Frost?"

"Yes."

"I'm Detective Springer," said the short one, an ample, rounded figure fully occupying his composition brown suit, both his shape and clothing making him look older than he probably was.

"And this is my partner, Detective Mattocks," he added, with a jerk of the thumb toward a tall young black wearing a plaid sportcoat and navy-blue slacks. Both showed Frost their police shields.

"What happened?" Springer asked, carefully opening his notebook and pulling a ballpoint pen from his pocket after taking a seat beside Frost at the round kitchen table. Mattocks, who remained standing, leaned against the wall and looked directly at Frost.

Reuben was disconcerted by Springer's vague but direct question and Mattocks' unflinching stare.

"How do you mean, officer?" Frost asked, resorting to the stalling device of lawyers and appliance repairmen of answering a question with a question, and realizing as he spoke that his response must have sounded stupid.

"Let's take it step by step," Springer said deliberately. "There was a call to nine one one at eight fifty-five. You made that call?"

"I called nine one one and that certainly would have been about the time."

"And you said the victim—" Springer glanced at his notebook—"Tobias Vandermeer, was dead of poisoning, right?"

"That's correct."

"How did you know that?"

"As I told your colleague, one of the people in the room was a doctor. A psychiatrist, but a doctor. He said Tobias had been poisoned."

"After he'd examined him?"

"Yes."

"Not before?"

"No, I'm certain not."

"So you had no independent knowledge of the victim being poisoned, aside from what the doctor, Dr. Givens, said?"

"That's right. Except of course that even I could see that something was terribly wrong. Tobias' lips and mouth were blue."

Springer questioned Reuben closely on this. How had he

been able to see Tobias, sprawled on the floor several feet from where Reuben, on further interrogation, placed himself? Where were the others standing or sitting? Who actually touched the body? Who broke one of the glasses that fell to the floor?

Frost answered the detective's queries as clearly and concisely as he could. Working with Springer, the two constructed a diagram of where everyone had been sitting at the crucial moment. As for who touched the body, Frost said he was sure that Dr. Givens had been the only one. And, while cautioning the detectives that he could not be sure, he told them he believed Helena Newcomb had stepped on the glass that had broken.

As Springer and Frost talked, Mattocks remained silent and kept up his disconcerting surveillance of Reuben. Springer's initially gruff and suspicious attitude seemed to vanish as his subject gave patient, straightforward answers to his questions. Frost was nonetheless puzzled by the detective's seeming disorganization. He jumped from subject to subject in no particular order or logical sequence. Surely this was intentional, Frost concluded—some police-academy technique to keep him off base.

Once Springer had established the seating arrangement in the living room, for example, he took up the subject of the medicine bottle found upstairs, pressing Reuben about how he had happened to find it. (The very simple fact that Reuben had gone to the bathroom and had found the spilled bottle in the process seemed to him a completely plausible explanation of the discovery, yet he had the feeling that Springer found it deficient.)

"Did the bottle contain the poison?" Frost asked, turning the tables on the detective.

"We won't know until the lab does its analysis. All we know now is that it had a damn strange smell, like you said."

Springer then took Reuben through a chronology of the evening, starting with the cocktail hour before dinner but concentrating on the sequence of events after the reading club had assembled in the living room.

"How much do you know? Have you talked to the others about this?" Frost asked.

"No, we'll get to them in due course. We're starting with you," Springer said curtly, implying that it was none of Reuben's business who had been questioned.

"Well, I'll try to reconstruct things as best I can."

Prodded by Springer's clarifying questions, Reuben pieced together the happenings of the evening as he remembered them. Now very tired, he told the detective what he could recall, including the mixing of Tobias' rusty nail and his trip upstairs to the bathroom.

"How did you know he was going upstairs to go to the bathroom?"

"I guess I assumed it," Frost replied, a little sheepishly. Springer did not criticize Reuben, but his look said that the latter should keep his assumptions to himself.

Frost then told his interrogators about Tobias' inexplicable outburst shortly before he died.

"What exactly did he say?" Springer asked.

"Something like 'What do you want this time?' " Frost replied.

"Any idea what he meant?"

"None."

"Who was he shouting at?"

"It appeared to be Sherman Deybold. Tobias was looking at him when he spoke."

"Were there any servants around, by the way?" Springer asked.

"The only one I'm aware of was a waiter."

"Who cooked the dinner?"

"The Vandermeers' Japanese cook, I believe."

"Name?"

"I'm not sure. But I don't think he was here at dinnertime. I wasn't paying much attention, but I had the idea he'd prepared the meal earlier and this waiter dished it out and served it."

"The waiter. What do you know about him?"

"Next to nothing. He was a temporary, from a service."

"How do you know that?"

Frost reluctantly told the officers about Robyn's financial embarrassment.

"What did he look like?"

"Black hair. Very green eyes, I remember that. And one of those Mark Spitz mustaches," Frost said. All of his questioners were too young to know about Mark Spitz, so he had to explain who the Olympic swimmer was and describe his mustache, which, Frost suddenly realized, resembled Patrolman Aurelio's and Detective Springer's.

"Did this guy serve drinks after dinner?"

"Yes, he did. I remember distinctly that when Tobias went upstairs, the waiter cleaned up around his chair and brought him a new drink. Brought him and Deybold new drinks. He faded into the woodwork and I really didn't notice his manner or what else he did."

"Was he here when Vandermeer was stricken?" Springer asked.

"No, he left at eight-thirty. On the dot."

"You remember that?"

"I happened to glance at my watch."

"He faded into the woodwork all night, but you looked at the time when he left?"

"You forget my loan to Robyn. She had borrowed enough to pay him until eight-thirty, and I was curious to see if he had gone overtime."

Springer wrote laboriously in his notebook, with what Reuben took to be a look of skepticism on his face. Then, to Frost's discomfort, he went over the whole sequence of events in the living room again. Reuben was sure, or almost sure, that his answers the second time around were the same as the first.

"Did anybody else that you know of go upstairs? The waiter, for example?"

"I don't know about the waiter. Let's see. Sherman Deybold did, before dinner."

"To the bathroom?"

"I don't know that for a fact," Frost said with satisfaction, "but that was my assumption."

"Deybold. He's an art dealer?"

"Yes."

"A friend of the Vandermeers?"

"Yes, though I don't know how close."

"The paintings out there," Springer asked, "were they bought from Deybold?"

"I'm certain some of them were."

"And this fellow Costas. He's, uh, Deybold's assistant?"

"Yes."

"Anything more than that?"

"You'd better ask him."

"I will, Mr. Frost. I just wanted your impression."

"My impression is yes."

"Lovers?"

"I don't know that for sure."

"But a good bet?"

"Yes."

"Did anyone else go upstairs that you saw? Mrs. Vandermeer?"

"Not that I'm aware of."

"Okay, is there anything else we ought to know?"

"Offhand I can't think of anything."

"You're satisfied you've told us all you know?"

All you've asked about, Reuben felt like answering, but shook his head affirmatively instead.

"Okay, there's something else. Art, get that knitting thing from the CSU guys, will you?" Springer asked Mattocks, who went into the living room.

Minutes later he returned with a plastic bag. "Christ, they're still all over the place," he muttered, referring to the Crime Scene Unit personnel who were going over the room where Tobias had died, as he handed the bag over to Springer.

"Recognize this?" he asked, putting the object down in front of Reuben.

"Why, yes, I do. It's the needlepoint Tobias was working on tonight." The scene of the vain woman and her mirror was visible through the transparent bag.

"Kind of odd lettering, don't you think?" Springer asked.

Frost recalled that Tobias, when he had shown his handiwork to the group, had stitched part of the word "PRIDE" at the bottom. Now, examining the object more closely, he saw that he had completed the word "PRICK" instead. He had no idea what to make of the change, recalling only that the dead man had been stitching as furiously as his drunken state would allow, presumably to complete the altered word.

"You agree that it's odd?" Springer pressed.

"Yes, indeed," Frost replied, before relating how Tobias had displayed the needlepoint to the assembled group.

"Did he do this sort of thing often?"

"You mean, change 'PRIDE' to 'PRICK'?"

"No," Springer said impatiently. "Did he do this embroidery stuff, or whatever it is, a lot?"

"Yes, it was one of his hobbies. Eccentricities, you might say."

"Where the hell did he learn it?" Springer asked incredulously.

"He told me once he'd picked it up during the War. He was stationed in New Orleans. He had a desk job and he and some of his buddies started doing needlepoint to drive their commanding officer crazy."

"Needlepcint? That's what you call it?"

"I believe so."

"Damn strange for a man, I'd say. He wasn't, ah, queer or anything, was he?"

"I'd be amazed if he was. As I said, I think it was just one of his eccentricities."

"Well, it's a new one on me," Springer said uneasily.

As they stared at the unusual needlepoint, the kitchen door opened and a man in his mid-thirties, slightly balding, came in. His hair and suit were both disheveled and he peered around the room through Coke-bottle glasses. Frost started when he saw him; he was sure he'd seen him before.

"Springer, Mattocks, can I see you?" he said oblivious to Frost. The three went out, leaving Frost alone.

Who was that fellow? Frost asked himself. Then he remembered—Bautista's nemesis, the assistant district attorney in charge of the investigation of the murder of Frost's godson, the author David Rowan.

Soon the law-enforcement trio returned, and Assistant

District Attorney Joseph Munson introduced himself to Frost, who did not point out their past association (in which he, and not the police or the District Attorney's office, had solved Rowan's murder).

"I take it you've given a full statement to these detectives, Mr. Frost?"

"I wouldn't call it a statement, Mr. Munson, but I've tried to answer their questions as best I could."

"I stand corrected," Munson said. "How long have you known the deceased?"

Reuben calculated mentally—how long had it been since the "bigamy" memo?—and finally replied "Twenty-five years."

"Are you, were you, his lawyer?"

"Not really. My firm represents him. My former firm."

"You retired?"

"Yes."

"And your firm was?"

"Chase & Ward."

"That small, friendly family outfit, eh?"

Frost ignored the crack, directed at Chase & Ward's size— and just possibly its power and prestige.

"Will Chase & Ward represent Vandermeer's estate?"

"I would expect so, yes."

"That's all I have, gentlemen," Munson said. "Who do you want to talk to next?"

"How about the cutie?" Mattocks said.

"Good idea," Springer agreed. "Let's go. Mr. Frost, if you don't mind, would you stay here?"

Once again, Reuben was semi-incarcerated, though he noted with some satisfaction that he was again "Mr. Frost." They must think I'm a cooperative witness, he concluded. Though he could not figure out who the "cutie" might be. Helena Newcomb? Probably. Or perhaps Michael Costas?

REUBEN OBEDIENTLY WAITED IN THE KITCHEN. LIKE A REAL prisoner, he was grateful for a small favor from his jailers—not having to return to Miss Boyle's religious shrine. Given the hour, almost midnight, he was sure her image of the Virgin Mary would not only be moving her eyes, but talking to him. What he knew about such things was largely based on that movie starring Norton Simon's wife, *The Song of Bernadette*, and now, even with the confused troubles around him, he could not help but fantasize over a new Lourdes shrine on upper Park Avenue. The deluge of pilgrims would certainly delight the neighbors.

His outlandish fantasy did not last long; new feelings of nervous anxiety overcame him as he sat alone staring at the gigantic, even ominous, black stove.

After what seemed an interminable wait, Munson, Springer and Mattocks returned. Their grim faces did not bode well, and Munson's stiffly formal "Mr. Frost" unnerved Reuben still further.

"I know it's late," the assistant district attorney said, "but I'm afraid we have a few more questions for you."

"Fine," Frost replied without much enthusiasm.

"First of all, that medicine bottle upstairs. How did you happen to see it?"

"I didn't see it at first," Reuben explained again. "I saw the top of the bottle in the basin when I went to wash my hands. Naturally that made me curious and I looked around. It was then I saw the spilled bottle under the sink."

"Would it surprise you to know that Mr. Deybold, who used the same bathroom before dinner, did not see any bottle?"

Reuben was perplexed. "Maybe it wasn't there," Frost offered. What were they implying? he wondered. That he had put it there? Don't be silly, he told himself.

"Maybe it wasn't," Munson echoed, with perhaps a tinge of sarcasm.

Springer took his old seat beside Frost and turned to look directly at him.

"Mr. Frost, if you don't mind, we'd like to run through again what happened while you were in the living room after dinner. Please reflect carefully and try not to leave anything out."

Once again Reuben went over the chronology, starting with the serving of drinks and coffee and Tobias' attending to the mixing of his rusty nail.

"Are you sure that's all?" Springer asked, when he had finished.

"I believe so, yes."

"Mr. Frost, would it surprise you to know that all the other guests recall that at one point you got yourself and Vandermeer new drinks?"

Springer's question caused Frost's stomach muscles to tighten. Of course, he had gotten Tobias a drink. And why in the name of God had he not remembered it? What an embarrassment!

"Yes, you're quite right," Reuben said very quietly. "I apologize to you gentlemen."

"Will you tell us about it?"

Frost did so, trying to place his deed in the proper sequence.

"Why didn't you mention this before?" Munson asked.

Frost thought of pleading old age, but that would be cheap. "I'm embarrassed to say I simply forgot it." Never complain, never explain, as his old legal mentor, Charles Chase, had always been fond of saying.

"If Vandermeer was poisoned, don't you think that was a pretty important fact to leave out?"

"I have to agree with you. All I can do is apologize."

"Another matter, Mr. Frost," Munson said. "You said that your firm represents Mr. Vandermeer?"

"That's correct," Reuben said, puzzled at the abrupt change of subject.

"Are you still a partner in the firm?"

"No, I'm retired, as I told you."

"Are you of counsel?"

"Yes, I am, though I'm really not active these days."

"How are you compensated?"

"I get an annual retirement payment."

"Based on firm income?"

"No, it's a fixed amount."

Munson seemed disappointed. "But you still are dependent, shall we say, on the financial well-being of the firm?"

"Well, yes, of course. If Chase & Ward went belly-up, it's unlikely I'd get paid. I'm reasonably certain you can dismiss that possibility, however," Frost retorted, peeved at Munson's questions, which he regarded as highly personal.

"And your firm, Chase & Ward, I assume will get a fee for handling Mr. Vandermeer's estate?"

"I have no idea what the fee arrangement with Mr. Vandermeer was. But I'm sure you're correct, yes."

"Just a minute, Mr. Frost," Munson said, as he led the two detectives to the back of the kitchen and talked to them in a low voice.

Frost, left alone, was in a state of confused panic. Did these young men think *he* had killed Tobias? It was entirely possible. Suspicious of everything he said—or didn't say, in the case of his cursed lapse over the drink he had poured for Tobias. And now this myopic, self-important ADA fitting him out with a motive—benefitting from the fee Chase & Ward would get for representing Tobias' estate.

"That's all, Mr. Frost," Munson said perfunctorily when his sidebar conference had ended.

"What now?"

"You can go home. Your wife's waiting for you in the library."

"Thank you."

"There's just one thing," Munson said, handing Frost his card. "If you decide there's anything else you should tell us, give me a call. And I would ask that you don't leave town without letting me know first."

At least they don't want bail, Frost thought, as he went to pick up Cynthia.

In the living room the police technicians were still at work. Tobias' body had been removed, though a large chalk mark showed where he had fallen. Frost hurried across to the library; seldom had he been so glad to see his wife.

"Reuben, where have you been? I thought they had arrested you," Cynthia said.

"For God's sake shut up! They're still here!" he hissed at his wife.

Startled, she put her hand on his arm and squeezed it.

"Let's get out of here," he said. "Where's Robyn?"

"I made her go to bed around fifteen minutes ago."

"And the others?"

"They've all left except Helena Newcomb. She's staying over with Robyn. We had to wait until the Medical Examiner came and they took away Tobias' body."

"Like being at a party with the goddam Queen," Frost said, his mood dark and not a little desperate. "Can't leave until she leaves. But she's—he's gone, so, dammit, let's go home!"

"This whole business is incredible," Reuben said, as he and Cynthia walked down Park Avenue. "I don't mean to worry you, but they suspect *me*!"

"That's preposterous."

"Is it? What do they say? Look for someone with a motive, an opportunity to commit the crime and the means to do it. That's me."

"Reuben, you must be tired. I've never heard such nonsense."

Frost kept talking as they walked, continuing as they entered their townhouse and as they sat in the living room on the second floor. He told his wife about the odd lettering on Tobias' needlepoint and the open medicine bottle with the peculiar smell. And his terrible gaffe in failing to remember that he had gotten Tobias a drink.

"Oh, dear, I told the police about that," Cynthia interrupted.

"That's all right. It's my own stupid fault. But the police certainly acted as if they were on to something when they questioned me the second time."

"All right, dear, so you had the opportunity to kill Tobias—either by slipping poison into his Inderal bottle or into his drink. Which was it?"

"Very funny."

"What about a motive? You thought Tobias had become a disgusting drunk. So did everyone else, including me. Surely the police don't think that's a motive for killing him? Unless you had to live with him."

"Believe me, I considered that angle while I was waiting. But it's too late at night—or too early in the morning—to speculate about Robyn. Let's stick with *me*."

"Sorry, dear."

"The little twerp ADA on the case thinks he's found a motive, I'm sure of it. Chase & Ward will get a large fee for handling Tobias' estate. Chase & Ward pays me my retirement. Q.E.D., I stood to benefit from Tobias' death."

"But you're not a partner any longer; you won't get a percentage of that fee."

"Quite right, Cynthia. Just try and tell Mr. Smarty-Pants that. If Chase & Ward were going broke—which it most certainly is not—there could be a link between getting a big fee from Tobias' estate and my fixed retirement payments."

"I hate to say it, but you seem a trifle paranoid, Reuben."

"I'd like to think that's all it is. But this guy Munson was pick, pick, picking about the firm, what I got out of it, and on and on. He's probably a great prosecuting attorney but he doesn't know a damn thing about law firms, at least mine. Do you want a drink, by the way?''

''No. I'm exhausted. A Perrier would be nice, though.''

Reuben got up to do his errand, fixing a light Scotch for himself in the process. He winced when he thought of his earlier drink errand at the Vandermeers.

''So you had a motive, Reuben,'' Cynthia said, when he returned. ''That leaves the means. Where did you get the poison? What was it, by the way?''

''They don't know yet. The police said the almond smell upstairs was a sign of cyanide. Wayne Givens said the blue color around Tobias' mouth was a symptom of cyanide, too.''

''Don't remind me of Tobias' face,'' Cynthia said with a grimace. ''I don't want to think about it.''

''Let's say it was cyanide. I grant you I'm not in the business of buying poisons, but I remember what Luis once said to me—with a little looking, and enough money, you can buy anything in this town. And if teenage kids can make crack, surely an intelligent adult can cook up cyanide.''

''At least you're not a doctor, like Wayne, who surely would have access to such things.''

''My dear, that thought crossed my mind, too.''

''Reuben, we're both very tired. But it's folly for anyone to believe that my darling husband would, or even could, commit murder.''

''All I can say is I was told not to leave New York.''

''That's serious. What about our trip to Rio?'' Cynthia said, referring to a long-planned visit the Frosts were scheduled to make at the end of March. ''The Herculanos will be very amused if you are under house arrest in New York.''

Frost groaned. His Brazilian friend, Alfredo Herculano, was a great kidder. The idea of the ultra respectable Reuben Frost as a murder suspect could fuel his teasing for years.

''Let's hope that everything is resolved by then. But enough about me, thank you. What happened where you were?'' Frost asked.

''After they took you away, you mean?''

''Yes.''

''Let's see. You went to the door to meet the cops and that

was the last we saw of you. Why did they separate you from the rest of us?''

"I'm just guessing, but I seem to recall Luis telling me that if somebody at the scene of a crime is making a serious allegation, you peel him off from the rest. Since I called the police and mentioned poison, I think that was the reason.''

"Then that explains why they took Wayne Givens away, too?''

"Probably.''

"They left the rest of us in the library. That is, until the two detectives came and put each of us in a separate room.''

"Where were you?''

"In one of the guest rooms upstairs. Ghastly. It smelled of vomit.''

"Oh, God. Tobias again. Remember that tale his cousin told us last year, that when he's drunk he sleeps in whatever room he falls into—and throws up in his sleep?''

"Yes, of course I remember. Who could forget a story like that?''

"Lord. Lifestyles of the rich and famous,'' Frost said. "Tell me, though, before you were isolated, what happened in the library?''

"Everyone was completely stunned—and frightened. Robyn was really the only one who talked, babbling on about how absurd it was to think Tobias had been poisoned.''

"I got some of that, you remember, when she found out I'd called the police.''

"Well, she went on with it, insisting that drink had finally caught up with her husband.''

"How was she otherwise?''

"As calm as could be. Eerily so. She was back to playing the Principessa, the grande dame. Apologizing for the inconvenience, asking if everyone was comfortable.''

"Not exactly grief-stricken?''

"Not exactly,'' Cynthia said. "I must say, dear, if and when I keel over, I would hope there would be a few tears.''

"And vice-versa,'' Frost replied. "Did she say anything about money?''

"I'm sure she didn't. Robyn may be crass sometimes, but she's not *that* crass."

"I was just asking. I can't for the life of me remember, if I ever knew, what Tobias' arrangements for her are. What about the others?"

"Everybody was too shocked to talk much. Mutterings and inane small talk, and not even very much of that. Except for Barbara Givens, who was in hysterics much of the time. Robyn had to calm *her*.

"We all knew that Wayne had brought up the matter of poison," Cynthia went on. "Helena Newcomb started to speculate on how Tobias could have been poisoned. We didn't know about the pill bottle upstairs, so when she said it must have been in Tobias' drink no one disagreed. We got off the subject fast when it dawned on us that one of our group—or you or Wayne—must have put it there."

"Or, I suppose, that waiter Robyn had hired," Reuben said.

"You mean the butler did it?" Cynthia asked. "I suppose in real life you don't have to follow the conventions of the murder mystery."

"My dear, we've reached our limits. We've got lots to chew over, but I can't stay awake another five minutes. I need a good night's sleep, and we can talk to our hearts' content tomorrow."

"You're absolutely right. Good night, dearest. And despite Mr. Munson, I hope you sleep the sleep of the just."

PIECING THINGS TOGETHER

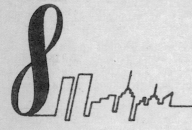

DESPITE HIS LATE NIGHT, AND DESPITE A KAFKA-ESQUE nightmare in which he was tried for the murder of Tobias Vandermeer without being able to prove his innocence, Frost rose early Monday morning and was immediately on the telephone.

His first call was to Luis Bautista. After much switching around, he was informed that Bautista was out of town and not expected back until the next day. Frost cursed to himself silently—there would be no way to get Springer & Co. under control until he could speak to Bautista—and left a message stressing his urgency.

Then he called his doctor, Martin Odenson. It was early in the morning; Cynthia was still in bed and had not squeezed him his customary fresh orange juice. So it was with a dry throat that he undertook the task of getting past Dr. Odenson's receptionist.

Marian Gaylord would have done well as a switchboard operator at the White House, screening crank callers and bringing the majesty of the Presidency to bear to intimidate them. Frost knew from past experience that one could not get through to Dr. Odenson without giving Ms. Gaylord a thorough description of one's symptoms, often receiving back a diagnosis and a prescribed course of treatment from the confident receptionist herself.

This time, Frost was ready.

"Yes, the doctor is in," Ms. Gaylord informed him, "but he's with a patient right now." ("He's with a patient," Frost was sure, being a dodging euphemism comparable to the "He's in conference" favored by legal secretaries.)

Then the dreaded question: "What's the matter, Mr. Frost? What's wrong?"

"It's not about me, Ms. Gaylord. I'm calling on a personal matter. A homicide that occurred last night."

"Oh, I see," said the receptionist, adding, after a pause, "Just a minute."

"Reuben, what the hell is this about a homicide?" the doctor asked when he came on the line.

Frost explained the circumstances of Tobias' death.

"How can I help, old friend? It sounds to me like Vandermeer is quite dead."

"I have a couple of questions regarding poisoning. Wayne Givens—you know, Dr. Wayne, the TV doctor—was there and said that he thought it was cyanide poisoning."

"Sounds reasonable from what you said."

"My question is this—how long does it take for cyanide to work?"

"Around two seconds, I'd say. Remember fat old Hermann Goering at Nuremburg? Someone sneaked a cyanide pill into his cell. He was under twenty-four-hour surveillance, but he bit into that pill, swallowed it and was dead before the guards could do anything."

"So if someone put cyanide in Tobias' drink he would have keeled over as soon as he drank from it?"

"Right. If the dose was strong enough."

Frost then explained the alternative theory that cyanide may have been put in his Inderal capsules. "What's that stuff for, by the way?"

"That depends. Was it Inderal or Inderal-LA?"

"The latter."

"And what was the dosage? Once a day?"

"Yes. Two capsules once a day."

"Okay. Inderal is the brand name of a so-called beta blocker, the generic name of which is propranolol. It's used to treat hypertension, angina, abnormal heart rhythms. Inderal-LA is the slow-release form. What were the capsules, eighty milligrams or one-twenty?"

"One-twenty."

"Sounds like a maintenance dosage. Your fellow probably had some angina complaints, or a funny heartbeat, and the Inderal was supposed to keep things under control."

"I see. If somebody put the cyanide in those capsules, would it have worked just as fast as if it had been in his drink?"

"Yes. Just as soon as the capsules began dissolving. That would happen right away. But there's another possibility. Let's assume some fiend replaced the Inderal in the capsules with cyanide. He or she could have coated them on the outside so that they would dissolve slower."

"Very interesting. So Tobias could have taken capsules in his bathroom, returned to the living room and not been stricken until a few minutes later?"

"I'm no expert, Reuben. Poisoning is a little out of my line. But I think the answer to your question is yes."

"Martin, thank you very much."

"Not at all. How are you feeling by the way?"

"No big complaints."

"Good. Just remember what I told you the last time you were in here. You're a *bon' vivant*, no doubt about it. But the time has come for you to concentrate on the *vivant* and ease up a little on the *bon*."

"Thanks, Martin."

"One more thing, Reuben. Cyanide's awfully, old-fashioned. Next time keep in mind that there's only one way to commit the perfect crime."

"Really?"

"Yes. Injecting digitalis through a hemorrhoid."

"I'll keep that in mind. Thanks and good-bye."

Frost was grateful for the information obtained from his old friend; less thrilled, given his situation, with Odenson's facetious advice about the perfect crime. Medical humor would never cease to baffle him.

Cynthia, fully dressed and ready for work, appeared at her husband's side as he made the next call, to the Bronxville home of Bob Millard, the trust and estates partner at Chase & Ward in charge of Vandermeer matters. She waited, a glass of orange juice in her hand, while Reuben recounted to Millard the events of the previous evening, which he had already heard about on the morning news. Frost arranged an appointment with his former partner for later in the morning.

The call completed, Reuben grabbed for the proffered orange juice and drank it with ravenous pleasure.

"Thank you," he said gratefully. "Have you solved Tobias' murder?"

"Not quite. There are nine possible suspects, and I only eliminated two while I was tossing and turning last night."

"You certainly were."

"And so were you, might I say?"

"Of course. I was on trial for murder."

"Well, it was a miscarriage of justice, my dear. The two suspects I eliminated were thee and me."

"Thanks. That's as far as I got."

Cynthia started to leave the room.

"Where're you going?" he asked.

"Since I'm so wide-awake I thought I'd go to the office. Get an early start on the week."

"I've got a better idea. While our memories are still working—or partially working in my case, I'm afraid to say—let's try to reconstruct *every* move we can remember from last night, before Tobias died."

"That's a bother."

"Not with my new PC," Frost said, patting his new toy and turning on the switch. "I'm going to put it all on here. Very easy."

"All right," Cynthia said dubiously. "How do we begin?"

Frost deftly pushed the keys on his machine and came up with a blank screen, ready to receive their input. He related his conversation with Dr. Odenson to his wife.

"We won't be sure until they get the lab results, but it looks like Tobias could have taken the poison himself when he went upstairs to the bathroom—or his drink could have been poisoned."

"There's another possibility," Cynthia said.

"Oh?"

"Maybe Tobias spilled the medicine bottle. Given the state he was in, that's entirely plausible. Or maybe the person who poisoned his drink left the bottle there on the bathroom floor, where it was certain to be found. A red herring."

"Hmn," Reuben grumbled. "From what Martin said, either the drink scenario or the pill-bottle scenario is conceivable. Let's do the upstairs first. Who could have planted the cyanide capsules in Tobias' bathroom?"

"The Givenses were there when we arrived. Either one of them could have gone upstairs. And Robyn must have been upstairs getting ready," Cynthia said. "And she almost certainly knew when Tobias was supposed to take his Inderal."

"Hmn. Hadn't thought of that," Frost said, while entering the names of Wayne and Barbara Givens and Robyn under the heading "Upstairs." "Who else?"

"Sherman and Michael both arrived from another party and had to go to the bathroom at once. Robyn directed Sherman upstairs. And I saw him go up the stairs," Cynthia said.

"Anyone else?"

"Not that I recall. Except you, my dear."

"But I was there only after Tobias was dead."

"Remember my red herring theory. You could've poisoned Tobias' drink and left the pill bottle later."

"You're damn little help," Reuben said, reluctantly entering his own name in the interest of completeness. "Now, isn't it true that one or the other of us had everyone in view during the whole evening?—I didn't myself, because I went off with Robyn to conclude our little loan transaction—and no one else went upstairs? With the possible exception of the Givenses and Robyn?"

"And Tobias himself. And we don't know what that waiter did."

"Ah, the waiter. You're right, he could have snuck up the stairs anytime."

"The only question is, how would he know his way around?"

"That's easy. I'm sure we've seen him at the Vandermeers before. Let me put him down."

"How about the maid, what's her name, Miss Boyle? I'll bet she was around before the party."

"Probably so. I'll add her. And that's it for the upstairs, isn't it? Six people—Wayne, Barbara, Robyn, Sherman and the waiter and the maid. Plus me, dammit. So on to the downstairs possibilities."

"There's the waiter again. He brought the first drinks after dinner," Cynthia said. "And a second round later."

"All right." "Waiter" was entered under the heading "Downstairs."

"We want this as complete as possible, don't we?"

"Definitely."

"Then there's you."

"Hmn." Reuben added his own name to the list once again. "Who else?"

"I suppose Sherman and Helena, who were sitting on either side of Tobias."

"We didn't actually see them do anything, like stick poison in Tobias' drink. Or one of his drinks."

"No, but they could have."

"Agreed. So on the list they go. Let's see what we've got," Reuben said, turning on his printer and producing a sheet that showed the following:

Upstairs
  Wayne Givens
  Barbara Givens
  Robyn
  Sherman Deybold
  Waiter
  Maid (Boyle?)
  Reuben

Downstairs
  Waiter
  Reuben
  Sherman Deybold
  Helena Newcomb

"All of which leaves you and Michael Costas in the clear," Frost said.

"One suspect to a family," his wife observed. "That's only fair."

"Very funny. We're left with eight possibilities. Seven, if you agree I have no business on the list."

"I do agree, dear. Are we finished?"

Reuben sighed. "Unless you can figure out who the 'prick' was. Or why Tobias was yelling at Sherman."

"Haven't a clue. So let me leave you to your thoughts. The world's work must go on, Tobias or no Tobias."

"And my work must go on until I get my name off that list."

"You should have injected Tobias through a hemorrhoid."

"Goddammit, Cynthia. Martin Odenson's kidding was bad enough. I don't need yours."

"I'm sorry, dear. I'll see you this evening. Call me at the office if you get an inspiration."

"You'll be the first to know. But don't hold your breath."

THE VANDERMEER FORTUNE

REUBEN CONTEMPLATED THE UPSTAIRS-DOWNSTAIRS LIST long after Cynthia left him. It yielded no secrets, so he looked forward to his meeting with Bob Millard. Perhaps there was something in the tangle of legal arrangements governing the Vandermeer fortune that would offer a clue.

Contrary to his usual practice, Reuben took a taxi to the Chase & Ward offices at One Metropolitan Plaza. The events of Sunday night had taken their toll, and he simply did not feel up to his normal subway ride.

Grateful that he had hailed a driver who spoke English and at least purported to know his way to the bottom of Manhattan, Frost sank into the back seat of the taxi and thought about his former partner, Bob Millard.

Millard was a serious forty-year-old with just enough sense of humor to keep him from appearing severe. A thin, lanky jogger, he was the epitome of suburban conventionality: well-groomed house in Bronxville, complete with well-groomed wife and two well-groomed young children, a boy and a girl. Life consisted of the daily train commute to Chase & Ward and escape on the weekends to a reconverted farmhouse an hour north of Bronxville, in Dutchess County, though Reuben for the life of him could not understand what there was to escape from, Bronxville being quite bucolic enough for him.

Frost reflected that he had seen far too much of trust and estates lawyers in recent years, the sad and inevitable consequence of growing old and having one's contemporaries die off. He had concluded that the T&E advisers to wealthy New Yorkers fell into three categories. One consisted of the drudge technicians obsessed with minimizing estate taxes, to the exclusion of common-sense dispositions of individual estates. Their obsessions usually coincided with those of their clients, for whom the thought of sharing even a portion of their amassed wealth with the government was repugnant.

A second group was made up of society lawyers with the appropriate school and club pedigrees and, very often, a refined hot-potato accent. But in many instances not overly generous endowments in the brains department. Most of these social worthies kept bright but less prepossessing young men and women tucked away in their offices, insurance against making damaging mistakes in complying with the intricate and highly technical laws of inheritance.

Finally, there were the solid citizens like Bob Millard, adept enough in the social graces, yet not natural denizens of the Brook or the Links. They did have brains, however, and dispensed intelligent, sensible advice in comforting midwestern voices akin to those of airline pilots or easy-listening radio announcers.

Millard had succeeded to responsibility for several of the firm's more important personal clients three years earlier, when Arthur Tyson, the firm's senior T&E partner, had died suddenly of a stroke. A belligerent Type A personality (except with his well-heeled clients) and no favorite of Reuben's—they had clashed violently at the time of the murder of their colleague, Graham Donovan—Tyson had left behind a practice that any lawyer would envy. Bob Millard, through diligent and careful work, had kept Tyson's impressive roster of clients, including Tobias Vandermeer and the Vandermeer Trust.

Frost had felt an affinity for Millard from the time he'd first worked with him, both of them having come originally from small towns. The elder lawyer, like Chase & Ward's clients, had found Millard both smart and reassuring; he and Cynthia had both been quite content to have Millard draw their own most recent wills.

Now eager to see what he would uncover by talking to his erstwhile partner, he went immediately to Millard's office on arriving at the fifty-first floor of One Met Plaza.

"So you're back in the murder business, Reuben," Millard said as he stood up behind his desk to shake hands.

"I'm afraid so. Can't seem to avoid it."

"Tell me exactly what went on."

Frost filled in the details that Millard did not already know.

"How's Robyn taking it?"

"Very calmly, according to my wife, though I haven't talked to her this morning. As I told you, I was pretty much in solitary confinement after the police arrived."

"She's a pretty cool customer."

"That's your impression?"

"Definitely. A very businesslike woman. Very determined. Most of my dealings were with Tobias, but we did her will as well."

"Anything special about it?"

"Very routine. Everything she owns at her death goes to READ. Her big concern has always been that no one else could get anything from her estate."

"Like who?"

"She's never said. She did admit once that Tobias was her fourth husband, so I assume she may have been worried over the other three."

"*Four* husbands! I knew about the Italian prince, but who were the other two?"

"Again, she's never told me."

"That's a new one on me. What about children?"

"I asked her that specifically. She said there never had been any. I seem to recall something about a miscarriage, but she was very definite that she'd never had children. And didn't want any."

"Hmn."

"As I say, she's a very astute businesswoman. You remember when the Tax Reform Act was passed back in eighty-six, our tax department put out a memo on it to our clients. Even before they'd done that, Robyn was on the phone wanting to find out how the act affected her *and* the Vandermeer family. Not so exceptional, I suppose, but her interest in money is not limited to philanthropy, as you might be led to believe by all that favorable press coverage she receives.''

''Interesting.''

''Now, Reuben, I got the Vandermeer files out when I got in, as you can see,'' Millard said, gesturing to the pile of folders beside his desk. ''There's a lot of curiosity over Tobias' estate. I've had a call already this morning from Mark Small at the Rudenstine, Fried firm, requesting a copy of Tobias' will. Also inviting me to a meeting of the Bloemendael directors on Thursday.''

''Small's still counsel for the Bloemendael Foundation, isn't he?''

''That's right. I suppose he wants to check up on what his client will get. But now, what can I tell you?''

''I'm not quite certain, Bob. I guess it would help me to have fixed in my mind precisely how the Vandermeer estate is set up.''

''Okay. I'm sure you're familiar with most of the story, so stop me if I'm going over old ground.''

''Please go ahead.''

''You have to start out with the will of Hendrik Vandermeer, Tobias' father,'' Millard said, searching through the folders. ''Here's a copy, dated October seventeenth, 1964. Basically, it left one-half the stock in Great Kill Holdings to the Bloemendael Foundation, the rest of the Great Kill stock and everything else Hendrik owned to the Vandermeer Trust, for the benefit of Tobias' children, with a life estate in the Trust income for Tobias.''

''In other words, it cut out Tobias?''

''Except for the income for his lifetime.''

''And since Tobias didn't have any children, what happens now?'' Frost asked.

''Everything goes to the Foundation, with one twist. Hendrik executed a codicil to his will in 1968, authorizing Tobias to appoint a life estate in the Trust income to Robyn, beginning after Tobias' death and for the rest of her life. Here's the codicil, take a look at it.''

Frost read the operative provision:

ONE: I amend Article ELEVENTH of my said will to the extent necessary in order to grant my son, TOBIAS, the power to appoint the income from all or part of the principal of the Vandermeer Trust to his wife, ROBYN VANDERMEER, for her life. No appointment by my son shall be effective to exercise such power unless it shall specifically refer to such power and express the intent to exercise it. If such an appointment shall require that the trust principal continue in trust for the benefit of my son's wife, upon her death my trustees shall distribute such principal to my son's issue who shall survive her, *per stirpes*, or in default of any such issue, to the Bloemendael Foundation.

''I assume he exercised this power?'' Frost asked.

''That's the problem, Reuben. As far as our records show, he didn't. He could've done it by executing and delivering an irrevocable deed in Robyn's favor, or in his will. His will is silent on the subject and we don't have evidence of any deed being executed during his lifetime.''

''So Robyn doesn't get anything from the Trust? And the Bloemendael gets everything right away?''

''That's the way it looks.''

''Hmn. So Tobias provided for Robyn in his will, I assume.''

''No, he did not. She gets nothing. The art collection goes to the Metropolitan, and the balance of the estate is divided up among the Jazz Center, whatever that is, the Museum of the City of New York and Marble Collegiate Church. When I took over after Arthur Tyson died, I reviewed all the operative papers in our file and I remember very clearly calling to Tobias' attention that he hadn't exercised the appointment to Robyn so that she could get the Trust income after he died.''

''What did he say?''

''He said she'd already been taken care of.''

''But as far as you can see she hasn't been?''

''That's right.''

''She can elect against his will, can't she?'' Reuben asked.

''Yes, she could do that. In New York, and since there aren't any children, she could elect and take half of Tobias' estate.''

''But that's not where the big dollars are,'' Frost said.

''That's right. Getting the Trust income would be the most important thing for her.''

''Hmn. What's Tobias' estate worth?''

''Well, it's not nothing. Except for his plunges in the art market, he was very frugal, as you're aware. And it would've been hard for him to drink up the dividends he got from Great Kill, though sometimes I thought he was trying to do that.''

''What's a rough figure?''

''Probably fifteen, eighteen million after estate taxes, depending on what the paintings are valued at.''

''Hell, that Jasper Johns he owned they say is worth ten million alone,'' Frost said.

''Then I may be low.''

''Whatever it is, half isn't too bad. Robyn could certainly get by on the income from, say, eight million. Maybe not as well as she'd like, but she wouldn't starve. Did Tobias say anything else when you spoke to him?''

''No. He seemed annoyed that I'd brought the subject up and clearly didn't want to talk about it. So I dropped the whole matter.''

''It sounds to me like the Bloemendael's pretty lucky. Wayne Givens will be in pig heaven.''

''He already is. Didn't you see that *Times* Magazine article on the 'Medical Medici' three weeks ago?''

''Oh, yes, I did.''

''He plays the Bloemendael like an accordion. It's his soapbox for making all his statements on drug addiction in the press, the testimony in Washington, the television stuff.''

''You don't know the half of it, Bob. I was the one who set up the Bloemendael for Hendrik. The original purposes of the Foundation were threefold—to promote the education of Negroes, as we said back then, the study and prevention of drug addiction and the study and prevention of alcoholism.''

"That's a pretty odd combination.''

"Yes, it is. We were curious, and one of my seniors finally asked Hendrik about it at the time. The answer turned out to be simple—in some ways he was trying to atone for the Vandermeers' nineteenth-century involvement in the slave, opium and rum trades.''

"Where does 'Bloemendael' come from, by the way?'' Millard asked.

"It's the Dutch form of Bloomingdale, which referred to the area north of Fifty-ninth Street where the family owned considerable property. Hendrik was too publicity-shy—modesty isn't the right word—to call it the Vandermeer Foundation.''

"I see.''

"Anyway, Givens is the one who got the Foundation zeroed in on drug addiction. It's his specialty, of course, and he managed to work the trustees around to agreeing to concentrate exclusively on drugs. I'm convinced he's determined to be the country's leading authority on the subject—running treatment centers, appearing on television, giving out research grants to others, being a rival of the President's drug 'czar'. And now, with the Bloemendael immensely richer, he'll be able to send up even bigger rockets from his launching pad.''

"The Bloemendael will be richer than you probably imagine, Reuben. Under the Internal Revenue Code, the Foundation's got to get rid of practically all its Great Kill stock two years from now. Not to be technical, but the stock they owned was 'grandfathered' under the IRS's disposition rules for fifteen years from the time Hendrik's estate was settled. Now the time's almost up, and they have to unload it. And I'm sure they'll get a better price per share if they can deliver *all* the Great Kill stock free and clear, rather than just fifty percent.''

"Hmn. What's Great Kill worth, do you suppose?''

"My guess would be somewhere around three hundred million."

"God, the Bloemendael will be a real heavy hitter."

"Yes. Not one of the billion-dollar babies, like the Rockefeller or the Ford, but right up there in the top ten or twenty. And certainly the biggest private foundation concentrating on drugs."

"Going back to something you said earlier, Bob, about Robyn taking a great interest in Vandermeer family affairs. Didn't she ever ask whether Tobias had exercised his power of appointment?"

"Not that I recall."

"Certainly she must have been aware of it?"

"I'm sure she was."

"I think it's odd she never asked."

"Yes, it is. There're some other oddities, too. Tobias made a new will in April 1985. It left everything to the charities I mentioned and cut out Robyn."

"Had she been mentioned in his old one?"

"Yes, he'd made a will shortly after they were married, and she was to get half of everything Tobias owned."

"Was there any provision in that will for a life estate in the Trust?" Frost asked.

"No, Hendrik wasn't dead yet, so the Trust didn't yet exist."

"Oh, sorry. Of course."

"The other thing about the 1985 will was that Tobias left out two specific bequests that had been in before."

"Like what?"

"That Jasper Johns you mentioned. He left that to his former wife in the old will. Not in the new one."

"It's become so valuable he probably had second thoughts."

"I don't know."

"You said there were a couple of bequests."

"Yes," Millard said. "Let me see here. Yes, in the old will there was a bequest of two million dollars to a Grace Alice Rourke. Not a huge amount, but certainly more than a thousand bucks to a good and faithful servant."

"Who on earth is she?"

"Damned if I know. Arthur Tobias drew up the 1985 will and discussed it with Tobias. Arthur never mentioned her to me. Nor did Tobias."

"Any other information? An address, for example?"

"Nope. Just the simple statement that he leaves two million to Grace Alice Rourke."

"Hmn. Let me write down that name," Frost said, taking out the small notebook he habitually carried. "Rourke, R-o-u-r-k-e?"

"Correct."

"Any other surprises in the files?" Frost asked.

"Not really. Your superconfidential memorandum on bigamy."

"A masterpiece, if I do say so myself."

"Oh, and a memorandum by one of Arthur Tyson's associates on adoption."

"Adoption? That's curious."

"It's pretty routine. A bread-and-butter memo that Arthur sent on to Tobias regarding adoption—how a child, when legally adopted, acquired all the rights of an offspring of his adoptive parent or parents, but loses any legal rights against a natural parent."

"Do you think Tobias and Robyn ever considered adopting?"

"I certainly never heard of it. And again, I never heard Arthur mention it."

"It seems unlikely. Robyn's always been so taken up with her good works and Tobias was too busy drinking to be much of a parent. When was the memo written?"

"Let's see here. Hmm, March 1985. Just before Tobias revised his will."

"That makes it even more unlikely, it seems to me. They would have been too old to adopt by then."

"It would seem so."

"Maybe Tobias was thinking of beating the Foundation out of its legacy. It is true, isn't it, that if Tobias had adopted a child that child would ultimately get the corpus of the Trust—and not the Foundation?"

"That's right. In New York a legally adopted child has all the rights of a natural heir."

The two men were silent for a moment, pondering Tobias' puzzling interest in adoption, before Frost asked another question.

"Bob, I've told you the cast of characters that was present last night. Which one poisoned Tobias?"

"Reuben, I've no idea. Robyn's tough, as I said, but just being tough doesn't make you a murderer. And even if she were homicidal, I would've thought she'd have waited until Tobias had fixed her up with a life interest in the Trust income.

"We've already decided that the Bloemendael's good fortune is a big plus for Wayne Givens. But would he kill to bring it about?" Millard went on. "I just don't see it. I think the butler did it."

"Cynthia thinks so, too. But why? The only reason is because he's a stranger to us—if he did it we don't have to face up to the possibility that someone we know was the killer. It's too convenient."

"Well, Reuben, it's really your department, and I'm sure you, or the police, will come up with the answer."

"God, I hope so," Frost replied, continuing to keep from Millard the police suspicions about Frost himself.

"Just to finish, Bob," he continued. "Will the firm get a big fee now that Tobias is dead and the Vandermeer Trust gets wound up?"

"Oh, absolutely. There'll be a final accounting for the Trust and the fee for acting as counsel to Tobias' estate."

"Who's the executor, by the way?"

"Bill Kearney."

"I see. But getting back to our—your—fees. What are we talking about?"

"Hard to say. Three to four million, probably."

"I'm glad, for the sake of my old partners," Frost said. Not so glad, he could have added, for what suspicious Assistant District Attorney Munson might make of Chase & Ward's windfall.

THE WIDOW

AFTER A LATE LUNCH AT THE GOTHAM CLUB, FROST LEI-
surely walked the fifteen blocks to his house, stopping to
browse several times along the way. He knew that the com-
puterized list he had made earlier was still sitting on his
library table, and his instincts told him that it would continue
to fail to produce any new insight into the identity of Tobias'
murderer.

He was right, and after staring at the list for some time
falsely concluded that a stiff martini might inspire him. All
the carefully prepared drink did was make him sleepy, however, and he was in a state of semi-drowsiness when Detective Mattocks called. Could he come by? the detective asked.
Reuben, with fresh memories of Sunday's interrogations, was
not delighted, but saw no practical way of avoiding him.

Mattocks, now without his partner, turned out to be surprisingly amiable, though Frost continued to have a vision
of a giant muscular black man giving him a penetrating stare
in the Vandermeer kitchen. Except for the amiability, there
was no new thrust to the officer's questions; he merely wanted
to go over once again the movements of those in the Vandermeer living room prior to Tobias' death.

Mattocks exhorted Frost to search his memory for any
additional information. The exhortation produced nothing,

although Frost finally gave him the computer list (not before thinking twice about it, given the double inclusion of his own name).

"Hey, this is great!" Mattocks acknowledged, with something almost approaching enthusiasm. The enthusiasm waned, however, when he realized that the piece of paper he had been handed did not contain anything new. And the officer became more guarded as Frost sought to find out from him what was going on.

"Do we know yet how Tobias was killed? Was it cyanide in his drink, or from a capsule, or what?"

"I haven't seen anything," Mattocks answered ambiguously, not making clear whether a medical report yet existed.

"What about the others? Have you talked to them again?"

"Some of them."

"Mrs. Vandermeer?"

"We tried, but she was too broken up to talk."

"And the waiter? Have you found him?"

"We're working on it."

Frost could tell he was not going to find out any news, so he asked Mattocks if there was anything more he wanted to ask.

"No, but where's Mrs. Frost? Is she here?"

"Speak of the devil," Reuben said, as Cynthia entered the room, home from her day at the Foundation.

"A nice way to address your wife," she said, going over to kiss her husband on the forehead, then turning to Mattocks, who had gotten to his feet.

"Good evening, ma'am. I was just asking your husband if I could see you for a few minutes."

"Good evening to you. Of course."

There was an awkward pause, during which it became evident that Mattocks wanted Reuben to leave the room, which the latter confirmed by asking the question directly.

"If you don't mind, sir, yes, I'd like to talk to your wife alone."

"Still trying to divide and conquer, Officer," Frost said.

"I'm sorry, sir. It's Standard Operating Procedure."

Frost went out, his empty martini glass in hand, and shut the library door behind him.

Cynthia and Reuben compared notes after Mattocks had left, concluding that they had learned nothing and that Mattocks had merely been plowing what was by now old ground.

"I was sorry to hear that they couldn't speak with Robyn," Frost said. "We really should call her, don't you think? I've been putting it off all day."

"You or me?"

"Why don't you start?"

Cynthia did as she was told, and soon was gesturing to her husband while talking on the telephone. "She wants us to come over," she whispered to her husband. Reuben extended his arms in a gesture of resignation.

"Fine, we'll be there in a few minutes," Cynthia told the widow.

"Before we go," Reuben said to his wife, "I ought to tell you what I learned about the Vandermeer estate today." He summarized his conversation with Bob Millard; neither he nor Cynthia could fathom what Tobias' actions, or his inaction, meant.

Kathleen Boyle admitted the Frosts to the Vandermeer residence.

"Wait in here, please," she said, gesturing toward the living room. The Frosts entered skittishly, reenacting in their minds the terrible scene of the night before, though the room had been completely tidied up and no evidence of the murder remained.

"The Missus is upstairs. I'll call her," Kathleen said.

"How is she?" Cynthia asked.

"Carrying on something terrible," Kathleen said. "She had a little nap earlier and I hope that calmed her down. Death is a terrible thing when it comes, Mr. Frost."

"Yes, indeed, Miss Boyle."

"Think of him being poisoned—and in his favorite chair yet!"

"When did you come back here?" Frost asked.

"Not till this morning. I stayed overnight with my cousin in Astoria and got back here just in time to clean up the mess left by New York's finest. The living room a mess, the kitchen a mess, and the Missus in hysterics. It's been a day to test the blessed, Mr. Frost."

"Miss Boyle, can I talk to you for a minute before you call Mrs. Vandermeer?" The Frosts sat down on the sofa they had occupied the night before. It was hard to imagine Miss Boyle, the small, almost birdlike woman now sitting uneasily on the edge of Tobias' "favorite chair," as a suspect in the crime, but they knew that seemingly innocent and devoted maids and nurses had more than once turned out to be ruthless poisoners.

"Miss Boyle, Mr. Vandermeer's death was a great shock for us, as I'm sure it was for you. Doubly shocking, because we haven't the faintest idea of who might have killed him. My question to you is, do *you* have any idea, any notion of who it might have been?"

"None, Mr. Frost. That's the frightful thing. Poor Mr. Tobias had his faults, the whole world knew that, but I can't imagine what worm might have killed him."

"There were seven people here last night, in addition to Mr. and Mrs. Vandermeer. Eight if you include the waiter. You know who they were, Miss Boyle?"

"Some of them. The Missus mentioned some of them."

"Let me go through the list," Frost said. The exercise proved futile. It was clear that Miss Boyle did not take to Dr. Givens or Sherman Deybold, or "the pretty boy who's always with him," but when pressed, disclaimed suspicion of any of them.

"How about the waiter?" Frost asked.

"Mr. Padgett?"

"That's his name?"

"Yes. Pace. Pace Padgett. He's become an old hand here. He's all right, as temporary people go. I wouldn't say he's the murdering type, myself. And why in the name of heaven would he want to kill Mr. Tobias?"

"If I had the answer to that question, the whole puzzle

might be solved,'' Frost said. ''I take it you can't think of any reason?''

''None at all. He's just a poor actor earning some extra money as far as I could see.''

''You saw him yesterday?''

''Oh, yes. I was here when he came, around four o'clock.''

''And there was nothing suspicious, nothing out of the way?''

''Nothing at all. He went off to make a couple of telephone calls while he should have been helping me, and he didn't finish the dishes, but those are just my complaints, nothing to do with being a murderer.''

Frost wanted to ask the woman about Robyn, but decided there was nothing to be gained, at least at the moment, in doing so; better to see and talk to the lady herself.

Robyn Vandermeer was weeping as she came down the stairs and entered the living room, her tears increasing as she rushed to embrace Cynthia and then Reuben. ''Recourse to the water works,'' Reuben thought, recalling Thackeray's phrase.

''Let's not stay here,'' she said, trying to compose herself. ''I'm not sure I'll ever be able to sit in this room again.''

Robyn steered her guests to the library, where she noticed that the message button on the telephone answering machine was blinking.

''My God, it's so awful,'' she said. ''People have been calling all day. Everyone I ever knew, it seems. They all mean well, but what a strain! I turned the phone off an hour ago and put the machine on—now look, one, two, *five* messages in that short time.'' She pushed the replay switch and the new accumulation came forth as Robyn and her two guests stood around it.

''Mrs. Vandermeer, this is Sarah Cromer of the New York Press. *Please call me as soon as you can. . . .''*

''The reporters are shameless,'' Robyn said. ''There's no respect for one's privacy. Ms. Cromer must be the tenth one to call today—everything from cable news to the *Enquirer*. It's utterly tasteless.''

''Robyn, it's Norman, the Mayor. I just heard the news and

I'm horrified. Please call me if there is anything I can do. And we must talk about your award later this month. So long."

"Dear Norman," Robyn commented. "What shall I do about that ceremony at Gracie Mansion. Ssh—we can discuss it later, here comes another one. . . ."

"Robyn, this is Wayne Givens. It is five-twenty in the afternoon on Monday and I was just calling to see how you are. No need to call back unless you want to talk. Barbara and I both send you our love. . . ."

"Poor Wayne, that's the second time he's called."

The tape in the answering machine gave off a shrill whistle, which then disappeared as the next message came through:

"Robyn, carissima! I just heard the news . . ."

"My God, it's Enrico, my ex-brother-in-law!"

". . . here in London and wanted to call you right away! I'm so sorry about . . . Tobias. Will you call me if there's anything I can do? I'm at double four one, six zero six, one double two one. My love to you, dear Robyn."

The recipient of Enrico's message—"Robeen"—seemed genuinely moved at what she heard, but did not have time to speak before the last message began:

"Hi, Mr. Vandermeer, this is Betsy Goodridge of Shearson Lehman. We have some very special bargains in tax-free municipals—triple-tax-free . . ."

Robyn snapped off the answering machine before Ms. Goodridge could complete her sales pitch. "Indecent!" she spat out loudly. "How dare they!"

"There's no honor any more," Reuben observed. "It used to be only the bucket-shop operators that made 'cold' calls like that, between stays in jail. Now even the respectable houses do it."

"Well, I guess she had no way of knowing that Tobias was dead."

"It's still indecent; you were right the first time," Reuben said. "Calling complete strangers at home during the dinner hour to sell them securities."

"Who was the caller before that, Robyn?" Cynthia asked. "Did you say it was your brother-in-law?"

"Ex-brother-in-law. Gianfranco's younger brother. And the only member of the noble family of Montefiore del'-Udine that you could call anything close to being honest."

Cynthia would have loved to pursue the subject of Gianfranco; all she really knew about him was that he had converted Robyn into a Principessa through their brief marriage. But this was hardly the time to discuss Robyn's penultimate husband.

"See what I've been through? Calls like that all day," Robyn complained.

"If you want to return any of them we'll be happy to wait," Reuben said.

"No. I'd just like to sit for a few minutes with my old friends. Tell me what you've heard. The police have told me nothing. That black detective was here, going over every move people made last night. But he was closemouthed about everything."

"We saw him, too," Reuben said noncommittally. "I know they're still operating on the theory that Tobias was poisoned, but they claim they're not sure how."

"You mean by whom?"

"No. They're not sure whether the poison was in one of Tobias' drinks or whether it was in capsules he took upstairs."

Frost's simple declaration set off a new round of deep sobs. Then, as they talked, it became clear that the police had not spelled out for her the possibility of Tobias taking poisoned capsules.

"Reuben, I'm sorry," she apologized. "I thought for a minute you were suggesting that Tobias had killed himself. I couldn't believe it when Wayne Givens said Tobias was poisoned last night. But he must know what he's talking about, and the police certainly believed him. My first thought was that Tobias had at last destroyed himself with drink, which the Lord alone knows he tried to do."

Frost seized his opportunity. "I'm afraid we all noticed that Tobias was drinking more lately—"

"Lately? He was on one long binge for almost five years, drinking morning, noon and night. Of course he'd always been a drinker, ever since I first knew him. It used to be steady, quiet drinking, but for the last few years he's tried to absorb just as much alcohol as his system could take."

"You say it's been five years, Robyn?" Frost said.

"Yes, almost. I remember exactly when it started. Our twentieth wedding anniversary came up in December of eighty-four. It was a very busy time—the President gave a wonderful lunch to honor READ at the White House early that December—but I pleaded with Tobias to go to Paris. We hadn't been for over two years and I remembered very fondly the good time we'd had there on our tenth. And Tobias loved Paris. He'd been there in the mid-fifties—it's where he met the dear Ines, in fact—and always said it had been the happiest time of his life, exploring the jazz clubs and being out from under his father's thumb.

"This time, he suddenly started behaving horribly midway in the trip," she continued, then broke off into crying. "I'm sorry. It's a painful memory. Tobias had to be physically carried out of the Grand Véfour. Passed out with his face in his plate."

Frost tried to imagine panicked waiters trying to cope with Tobias' giant deadweight amid the splendor of Le Grand Véfour.

"That was just one incident. I won't bore you with the others. It was a ghastly trip, and things never got better when we came home. Except for the nightclubs, he seldom went out. Just sat here drinking, or playing the piano, or trying to. You heard him the other night. Drink finally dissolved whatever talent he had. Or he would fiddle with that damnable needlepoint. Occasionally he would show some interest if Sherman came up with a new painting to buy, but that was rare. Drinking was his vocation, everything else was a hobby.

"I was desperate. I wanted to have an office. There was no room for one at READ, and I didn't want to impose on anyone else. I asked Tobias over and over if there wasn't some space in the Great Kill empire I could use. He refused absolutely, and clearly had instructed Bill Kearney never to talk to me about it.

"It wasn't just the money for the office, either. *I had no money at all!* Oh, yes, I had a free hand with my charities.

All I had to do was call up Kearney and a check would be sent to READ or your National Ballet, Cynthia, or whatever the cause might be. And the American Express card I had was supposed to take care of all of my needs. But ever since the start of Tobias' decline, I haven't had a *cent* of cash except exactly one hundred dollars a week—practically a child's allowance. Kearney had stopped all my charges and I had to close my checking account at the Bank of New York—there was no money, and I kept running up penalties. Can you imagine, being married to a multimillionaire and having *no* money, *no* bank account, *no* charge accounts?

"You say you had an American Express card," Cynthia said. "Can't you get cash advances with that?"

"Not with the one I have. It's the lowest form of card they issue."

"What about things like taxi fares?" Cynthia asked, both appalled and curious.

"There was always the limousine. That was crazy, too. If I was going out at night, I'd have to keep Justin and the car for the whole night because I didn't have the money to get home in a taxi! It was madness. Awful madness."

"How do you account for it?"

"Paranoid, drunken jealousy. That simple. Drink made Tobias crazy and inflamed his worst thoughts about me. Starting on that trip to Paris, he abused me terribly. Said I was only interested in READ and the glory I got from it. It was all so startling. He'd been an angel at the Reagans' lunch in Washington, and even stayed sober for it. Then the awful change, without any warning, and after our trip had started beautifully. When we got back, just before Christmas, things didn't get any better, and all the troubles over money—pocket money—started. And every time I was mentioned in the press, or got an award, or made a speech, he would ridicule me without mercy.

"Somehow, Tobias felt that if he could control the cash I had, he could control me. It was insane, but Reuben, you saw last night the kind of trivial, humiliating problems it caused. I'm going to pay you back, by the way, just as soon as—"

"—Don't think anything of it."

"There's one thing I don't understand, Robyn," Cynthia said, as gently as possible. "You said that Tobias was willing to continue helping READ and your other charities, yet he wouldn't give you pin money. How do you explain that?"

"That's easy. Deep down, he was pleased with our public image as philanthropists. He liked that. And he knew—I told him so—that if the philanthropy stopped I would have no choice but to leave him. He didn't want that, he didn't want another domestic battle, like the one with Ines.

"It's awful to speak this way about someone who's only been dead for a few hours, but you asked, Cynthia, and that's my candid answer. I shouldn't run on like this, but I feel as if a bubble has burst and I have to talk to someone."

"We're here to listen, my dear," Reuben said, though in his own mind he was steeling himself to ask Robyn what she knew about her financial situation now that she was a widow. Before he had formulated a discreet way of introducing the subject, Robyn's new basenji, Neil, came into the room. Reuben, no dog lover, had to admit that he was an attractive animal, though his muteness was rather pathetic.

"You all remember my lovely retriever, Dolly," Robyn said. "She was gentle, and as quiet a dog as you could want. But she wasn't quiet enough for Tobias. For months there was a war of nerves in this house as he became more and more hostile to Dolly. If she barked, Tobias would scream at her to be quiet. That made her all the more nervous, so that four or five times a day there would be these wild confrontations between the barking dog and my screaming husband.

"Finally, almost two months ago, I had to do something. Had to get rid of the beautiful dog I'd owned for ten years. I'd always had a dog for as long as I could remember, so I was very sad. Then someone told me about basenjis. I got one immediately, up in Connecticut. And now I have my silent little Neil," she said, reaching out to the dog and patting him affectionately.

"He's really very nice," Cynthia said.

"I probably won't keep him, now that I can have a real dog again. Now that I can *afford* a new dog."

"Yes, I suspect you'll have enough to get by," Reuben

said, though thinking how sad it was that the widow would have to go through the embarrassment of electing against her late husband's will—Tobias' final humiliation.

"Whatever my problems, I don't believe that's one of them," Robyn said. "I assume, Reuben, that the Vandermeer Trust still goes up in value every year?"

"I'm sure it does, but . . ."

"Fortunately, that all got settled before Tobias went crazy."

"How do you mean?" Frost asked, puzzled.

"That was *another* trip to Paris. A second honeymoon for our tenth anniversary. Tobias did have a romantic side, at least in happier days, and he completely bowled me over on that stay in Paris.

"I'll tell you the story. Around the time we got married, Tobias' father made a will that cut out Tobias from the Vandermeer fortune. Tobias was to get the income for life, but everything else was left to the Bloemendael Foundation or in trust for Tobias' children. You must know the details of all that, Reuben."

Frost nodded.

"Hendrik Vandermeer very much disapproved of Tobias' messy divorce from Ines, and also disapproved of me. He himself made it very clear to me that I could expect nothing from the trust fund. I think it was a test to see if I really loved Tobias, and was not just after the family money.

"Luckily for me, dear old Hendrik changed his mind—and his will—so that I could get the Trust income, if Tobias was willing to give it to me. Hendrik died in the summer of 1974, and his estate was still being settled when our anniversary came up and we went to Paris.

"I'll never forget it. We were having dinner at an intimate, tucked-away table at Taillevent. Once we'd finished and were toasting our anniversary, Tobias produced a legal document from his jacket pocket and handed it to me with a flourish. 'I've always loved you, Robyn, and now that we can lead our own lives, now that my father is gone, I want to make sure that you're taken care of if anything happens to me,' he grandly announced.

"He made me read the legal language. I didn't fully comprehend it, but he explained that it was a deed irrevocably granting me the right to the Vandermeer Trust income from the time of his death to my own. 'The lawyers tell me I could do this in my will,' he said. 'But you can change a will. This document you can't. It's forever, and its yours.'

"I was overwhelmed. It was about the most romantic thing Tobias ever did."

Reuben, glancing at his wife, asked Robyn if she had a copy of the deed.

"It's in my safe-deposit box at the bank."

"You're sure it's there?" Frost asked cautiously.

"It was at two o'clock this afternoon."

Frost was uneasy, though uncertain whether his discomfort arose from the surprise Robyn had sprung on him or Robyn's calculation in visiting the bank almost immediately after being widowed. Or from thinking that the autographed picture of President Reagan across the room, showing him shaking hands with Robyn at the White House, was like the portrait of King George that Becky Sharp had bought at Colnaghi's after being presented at court.

"I'm glad for your sake that was taken care of, Robyn. You see, I didn't know about your deed."

"No, that's right. Tobias said it was nobody's business but ours. He didn't even have it drawn up at Chase & Ward, so that your people wouldn't know about it."

"Well, it's a happy surprise," Frost said. "Bob Millard and I were afraid that Tobias had never exercised his power and the Trust would terminate without you getting anything."

"What exactly does happen, Reuben? Let me make sure I understand."

"If the deed we're talking about says what I think it does, you'll get the income from the Vandermeer Trust as long as you live and the Trust won't terminate until you die. Then the Bloemendael will get everything, assuming that Tobias didn't have any children."

"I can assure you of that. Having children was something we never quarreled about. You two are probably not aware of it, but I was married when I was very young. I had a miscarriage—a bloody, horrible, painful miscarriage. I never had the slightest desire after that to have a child. And Tobias simply didn't care one way or the other.''

"And you never thought of adopting, I suppose?"

"Never. Children, or the desire for children, were just not a part of our lives."

"Have you talked to Bob Millard?" Reuben asked, shifting the subject.

"I talked to him this afternoon and am going to see him tomorrow."

"I'd take that deed of appointment with you," Frost advised.

"I will. I'll get it out of the bank first thing tomorrow. Your Mr. Millard is very nice, by the way."

"Yes, he's both nice and competent. A good man."

"My only regret is that I'll still have to deal with Bill Kearney. I've never liked him, you know—how could you like such a sycophant? His whole life's been nothing but catering to Hendrik and, later, Tobias. I used to tease him about not having any personal life, but that didn't seem to bother him at all, as long as he stayed on their good side. He's like some sort of spooky priest, giving up the world, not for God, but for the Vandermeers and the Almighty Dollar. And in spite of the sadistic way Tobias treated him. Like making Kearney report to him every Sunday afternoon, for example. There was no excuse for that."

Frost now recalled the folder he had surreptitiously examined in Tobias' study. "I didn't know about this. Kearney came here on Sundays?"

"If Tobias was in town."

"Including yesterday?"

"Yes. Kearney was here yesterday."

"What time?"

"Two o'clock. Always two o'clock."

"And what time did he leave?"

"Yesterday, I'm not sure. Their meetings never lasted more than two hours, so he must have been gone by four."

Frost darted a glance at his wife, sitting beside him. She saw it and returned it. Their brief eye contact signaled a mutual recognition of a new fact: Kearney could easily have left poisoned capsules in the dead man's bathroom.

"Were Bill Kearney and Tobias getting along?" Reuben asked.

"Oh, yes. Kearney was Tobias' only real confidant. Tobias was also grateful not to have to spend any time on the business. Even though he's a pain, Kearney ran Great Kill very well. And if he wants to be, he can be very helpful. Like today, when he took complete charge of the funeral arrangements."

"What are they, by the way?" Reuben asked.

"If the morgue releases the body in time, it will be at Frank Campbell's tomorrow. The funeral will be Wednesday at Marble Collegiate, downtown. Tobias was never a churchgoer, but he gave them money, so it's the obvious place to go."

"One more thing, Robyn. What's your maid's name—Miss Boyle?"

"Kathleen Boyle, yes."

"You think there's any chance she might have poisoned Tobias?"

"That little mouse? Preposterous! She can complain and be sullen, but she's much too holy to commit murder."

Thinking of the religious artifacts in the maid's room, Frost was inclined to agree. Now, deciding that he could only absorb so much information at one sitting, and being eager to talk over what had been learned with Cynthia, he decided it was time to leave, though he did ask Robyn if she wanted to join them for a quick supper.

"No, Reuben, thank you," she said. "Mr. Obuchi has prepared a nice light meal for me here. But thank you both for coming over and hearing my troubles."

The Frosts insisted that they had been glad to listen to her, and hoped that their exit to a private table in a nearby restaurant where they could talk was not made in unseemly haste.

A WORKING SUPPER

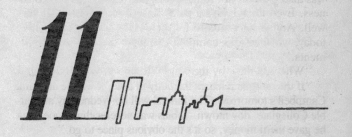

CYNTHIA AND REUBEN, TIRED AND VERY HUNGRY, HEADED immediately down Lexington Avenue to the City's newest stylish Italian restaurant (new French restaurants being almost unheard of), Sette Mezzo, owned by their old friends Nino Esposito and Gennaro Vertucci, and efficiently precided over by Oriente Manìa.

True to their usual form, the Frosts each ordered the simple grilled chicken, accompanied by glasses of the superior house Trebbiano.

"What a weird story," Reuben said, when they turned to the subject preoccupying them.

"It's clear she's going to have a good bit more than a hundred dollars a week to spend."

"By about two thousand times," Reuben said. "Which just might have been a sufficient amount to make a murder seem worthwhile to her. Not that Tobias' conduct wouldn't have been motive enough, without regard to the money."

"That was a real tirade," Cynthia said. "I had no idea what that woman has been going through. Tobias had become a monster. That business about her dog was horrifying."

"Absolutely, though her plans to get rid of that poor little speechless creature are pretty cruel, too. And how about

checking up on her deed of appointment at the bank before
his body's even cold?'' Reuben asked, enthusiastically carv-
ing up his half-chicken as he spoke.

"Okay? Everything okay?" Alfio, their favorite waiter,
inquired solicitously.

"Perfect, as usual," Frost replied.

"I'm afraid, my dear," he said, turning to Cynthia, "that
Robyn Vandermeer doesn't drop off our computer list."

"I'm glad you said it first. Can there be any doubt, Reuben, after what we heard?"

"I don't think so. She had both the opportunity—to put
poison in Tobias' bathroom—and the motive."

"I do believe we can get rid of Miss Boyle, though."

"I agree," Reuben said. "But getting back to Robyn. I
wish I had more of a fix on her. Hell, I don't even know
where she comes from, do you?"

"I believe the Midwest somewhere. She's never said, but
I'm sure I read that once. By the time we first knew her,
she was already the Principessa Montefiore del'Udine—
correction, the *former* Principessa."

"It sounded like she may have left a pig farmer or some
such out wherever it was."

"You mean the miscarriage business?"

"Yes."

"She certainly was definite about never wanting children."

"I'll say. Which makes that memo on adoption—
remember I told you about that, the memo Bob Millard found
in our files—even more curious."

"I suppose Tobias could have had some passing thought
of adopting a child at some point—part of his 'romantic
streak.' He probably dropped the idea fast when he got her
reaction."

"Very odd."

"You're not having dessert, are you?" Cynthia asked,
knowing that Reuben usually passed it up.

"No, but you go ahead."

"I can't resist the tartufo."

"I'll have coffee. Against my better judgment, but I will."

Frost placed the order and returned to the subject of Robyn.

"How are we doing on the husband count?" he asked. "There's Tobias, of course, and the Principe. And now the pig farmer, we think. Who was the fourth?"

"I have no idea. You sure there were four?"

"So Bob Millard says. He claims she told him that."

"And what are we to make of Tobias?" Cynthia asked. "She made it sound as if he went from Cary Grant to Boris Karloff overnight—in the middle of their anniversary trip to Paris. Their twentieth, no less."

"It could be as simple as his alcoholism getting progressively worse. But I agree it was a strange tale. Giving her a life estate worth millions and ten years later begrudging her any money at all."

"You've always said the Vandermeers were tightfisted," Cynthia observed.

"Yes, that may be part of it. But I can't help thinking there's more to the story than we know."

"Do you suppose there could be another man involved?"

"Like Becky Sharp's Lord Steyne, you mean? But look what happened to her—her husband threw her over when he found out. Difficult as her life was, I don't believe Robyn would have run that risk."

"I had Wayne Givens in mind," Cynthia said.

"Doubtful. Givens' fly is open more than any philanderer's in New York, but I don't see him messing around with Tobias' wife. The Bloemendael Foundation is too important a base of operations to him for that. Never dip your pen in company ink."

"Oh, Reuben, please, not that old chestnut. I must have heard that four hundred times when that partner of yours, Tommy Rabb, went off the deep end with his secretary. It was a stupid expression then and it still is!"

"I'm sorry, dear. But however you want to phrase it, I think your suspicion is wrong. Dare I have more coffee?"

"You'll be awake all night."

"I will be anyway," Frost said, gesturing for more.

"Where do we go from here, my dear?" Cynthia asked.

"I wish I knew. I also wish damned Bautista were back. I could talk to him, tell him our feelings about Robyn. I can't do that to Mutt and Jeff."

"He's due back tomorrow, isn't he?"

"That's what they told me."

"What else?"

"Just one other thing. On the theory that Robyn may *not* be Lucrezia Borgia, I just may pay a visit to Mr. William Kearney, Tobias' Sunday caller."

"Now *there's* a nugget you could pass on to Mattocks and Springer and get points for doing it."

"The thought has occurred to me. But I want to talk with him first. Now, finish that appalling dessert and let's go home."

BILL KEARNEY

12

THE OFFICES OF GREAT KILL HOLDINGS WERE IN A REFUR-
bished office building just north of Grand Central Station.
Reuben had made an appointment to meet Bill Kearney there
at eleven o'clock on the Tuesday morning after Tobias' murder.

The day was unseasonably warm for March, so Reuben
set out from his townhouse half an hour early to walk to his
destination. He was proud that his speed was still a city block
a minute and calculated that thirty minutes would be right to
get him to Kearney's office on time.

As he went down Park Avenue, dodging several dogs being exercised and the occasional errant child (*"Roscoe! Roscoe! Come back here this minute!"*), he tried to assemble
in his memory what he knew about the man he was on his
way to see. He concluded that it wasn't very much.

As long as he had been involved with the Vandermeers,
Kearney had been the President of Great Kill. In the old days,
before Hendrik Vandermeer's death, he had distinctly been
the dutiful subordinate, Hendrik himself being the unquestioned number one up to the day he died.

The old man, whenever he had mentioned Kearney to Reuben, had praised him elaborately, yet always with the scintilla
of condescension establishment Protestants like Hendrik

could convey by adding an ethnic tag to their descriptions. "My good Irish right arm" Hendrik often called Kearney, in straightforward admiration, but nonetheless with an implication that it was perhaps surprising to find an Irishman capable of functioning so well. (Democracy did progress, Reuben thought. Hendrik's words of a generation ago would probably now be "my clever black assistant," emanating from the mouth of a not necessarily Protestant, and maybe even an Irish, boss.)

Kearney had started life in real estate in Queens, after graduating from the business school at Fordham University. "I got him and trained him before he learned all the bad habits you can pick up in this racket," Hendrik had once boasted to Reuben. The elder Vandermeer had obviously been pleased with the results, naming his protégé as his representative on the board of directors of the Bloemendael Foundation and as one of the co-trustees of the Vandermeer Trust, in the latter case to the exclusion of his own son.

Frost's own dealings with Kearney had been limited. The sort of operating legal problems Great Kill encountered—tax-assessment contests, zoning fights, even the writing of the company's leases—were handled by in-house lawyers and the firm of Quinn & Kallman, which specialized in the black, esoteric and often political art that constitutes a New York City legal practice in real estate.

He did remember that Hendrik, shortly before his death, had consulted Reuben about drawing up a long-term employment contract for Kearney. He had done so, and now recalled that it had been a financially generous one, guaranteeing Kearney's job as President of Great Kill for ten years, unless dismissed for cause. There had been little negotiation of the agreement; it had been signed practically as Frost (or more precisely, a Chase & Ward associate) had drafted it.

By his reckoning, Kearney's contract would have run out roughly five years earlier. Had it been renewed, he wondered? Or renegotiated? It might be interesting to find out.

Then there had been the incident several years back that still rankled with Frost. When Hendrik had established the Bloemendael Foundation, Chase & Ward, hardly surprisingly, had acted as its counsel. Later, after Hendrik's death, the directors decided to retain the firm of Rudenstine, Fried & D'Arms, and Mark Small in particular, as lawyers for the Foundation, the reason given being that they felt it should have counsel that did not represent the Vandermeers in other capacities, as Chase & Ward most certainly did.

In Reuben's mind there had not been any conflict of interest, and Wayne Givens had hinted to him privately that Kearney had been behind the switch to Rudenstine, Fried.

All this occurred in the days before lawyers could advertise, though this had not stopped attention-getters like Mark Small, who touted his expertise as an expert on not-for-profit institutions by writing frequent articles in legal periodicals and appearing ubiquitously at seminars where their problems were discussed.

Frost had never liked Small, whom he regarded as a pompous, self-promoting little bantam. He and his partners had begrudgingly, yet gracefully, acceded to Small's ascension at the Bloemendael, though Frost was sure he, or his successors at the firm, would be less magnanimous if Small ever tried to grab off more of the Vandermeer legal work.

Frost admired the elegant and newly restored Art Deco paneling in the elevator of the building he now entered. (How lucky some real estate barons were, he thought. Twenty years ago, commercial tenants wanted steel and glass; an Art Deco interior like this one would have been considered hopelessly dated. Now old Art Deco spaces were a positive selling point with tenants.) He got out on the twenty-eighth floor and entered the discreetly, even obscurely, marked entry door to the Great Kill offices.

A pretty but overly made up receptionist—one of the little shop girls who delighted the American cosmetic industry—greeted him, called Kearney's secretary and motioned him through the closed door behind her that led to the active office space. The reception area was paneled in dark oak, not seedy but not exactly luxurious either. The offices behind, ranged around the edges of an open zone of desks occupied by clerks busy at calculators and computer terminals, were utilitarian and decorated without distinction.

Most of the offices had glass windows facing the open work area. Kearney's was the exception. Larger than the others, it filled the northeast corner of the floor and was reached only through a secretary's office.

Kearney came out into the public space to greet his guest.

"Hello, Reuben. It's nice to see you again, even under the sad circumstances." His greeting was warm enough, but tempered by his austere appearance. Reuben, unlike Kathleen Boyle, inexperienced in the ways of Catholic monsignors, thought Kearney resembled an old-fashioned, middle-aged schoolmaster with his unfashionable crew cut and rimless octagonal glasses.

In Kearney's office, a glass-topped desk was the only break in the austerity projected by the room and its occupant. The cloth-covered easy chairs and sofa surrounding a plain black coffee table that constituted the "sitting area" could have come from a young bachelor lawyer's walk-up apartment and been purchased at the Door Store. The Currier & Ives print of downtown New York, behind Kearney's desk, seemed a purely functional piece of decoration, though conceivably it depicted a parcel or two of Vandermeer real estate.

"Bill, I'm sure you're wondering what the hell I'm doing here," Frost said, once seated. "You probably think I'm meddling in something that should be left to the police, and you may be correct. But I do have an interest in finding out who killed Tobias. My wife and I were present when it happened, after all. Which means, until the murderer is found, we are under a cloud personally. While I'm sitting here, the police are undoubtedly out there fishing around about me and Cynthia. I would like very much to put a stop to it."

"I can't blame you."

"I also have a purely intellectual interest in seeing this puzzle to a conclusion. Once bitten with the detective bug, as I unfortunately have been, it's hard to shake off the infection. For better or worse, I'm a curious old man."

"I understand that, too. Your exploits may not have made the newspapers, but your reputation has gotten around, ever since your partner was murdered at Chase & Ward. I'm not sure how I can help you, though.''

''I have a feeling—and it's only a feeling at this point—that if I learn more about Tobias some light may be shed.''

''Or Tobias and Robyn perhaps?''

''Why do you say that?''

''God knows I'm not going to cast suspicion on anyone. But she was present when he died, wasn't she?''

''Indeed. I want to ask about her and several other things as well. Any help you can give, Bill, will be appreciated.''

''I'm not going anywhere.''

''Before we get to Robyn and Tobias, let me ask you how Great Kill is doing.''

''Same as ever. Making money.''

''No downturns? No recent changes or developments?''

''No, sir. Just a steady climb in asset value and income. You know, Reuben, I had a kid from the Harvard Business School in here the other day. Wanted to find out all about us. I told him it was like having a cable-television franchise. When you've put it in place, the only thing you need is a girl to open the checks that come in every month. That's what we have. All our properties except a couple of small ones are leased out. Those people you saw outside my office really do it all—keep track of the lease payments and deposit the checks in the bank when they arrive.''

''Nobody's agitating to make changes?''

''Change means risk, Reuben. Great Kill has always avoided the swinging part of the business, the developer's part. That means we haven't made as much money as the Trumps or the Rudins. But we haven't had losses or bankruptcies either. We just lease out our land on nice, steady triple-net leases. Our tenants have all the risk and expense—and the big profits, if there are any—and we have our stream of ground rents. Do you realize we have properties that Tobias' grandfather bought? We haven't sold a single parcel since the day Great Kill was formed. I don't like the expression 'money machine' but let's face it, that's what Great Kill is.''

''How about selling Great Kill?''

"Well, the Bloemendael Foundation's going to have to sell its part fairly soon, but they think they can do it in a single private transaction that won't make waves."

"And they'll have the other half to sell after Robyn dies," Frost said.

"I believe so," Kearney replied, though there seemed to be a trace of doubt in his voice.

"You're Tobias' executor and a trustee of the Vandermeer Trust. Is there any doubt about it?" Frost asked, somewhat impatiently.

"No, no. You've got it right," Kearney said hastily.

"Let's go on to Robyn and Tobias, as you suggested. You must have seen a lot of them. How would you say they were getting along?"

"Actually, you know, I didn't see a lot of them. Tobias had an office here, but he almost never used it. We got together to talk business at his house once a week and that was it." Kearney did not mention that the weekly meetings were on Sunday, and Frost let the point go by for the moment.

"How about Robyn? Did you see her regularly?"

"I'd talk to her on the phone when she needed money."

"Was that often?"

"You could say that. You see, I write the checks. She'd call and say READ or some other outfit was to get such and such and I'd cut the check."

"After talking with Tobias?"

"Oh, yes. We had an understanding. I was never to disburse anything without telling him first."

"And her personal expenses? What about cash?"

"She had an allowance and a credit card."

"How did she get her allowance?"

"We sent it up to her in cash. By messenger."

"How much was it?"

"I forgot offhand," Kearney said uneasily. "It was nominal. She was supposed to use her American Express card. Tobias always wanted a record of everything, and forcing her to charge her purchases to one card made it easy."

"Her allowance—a thousand dollars a month? Ten thousand? More? Less?"

"Less than a thousand. As I told you, she was supposed to charge things."

"Did you and she ever fight over money?"

"Not to speak of. I was only the bookkeeper."

"It appears that she's going to need more bookkeeping now," Frost said. "She told me about the deed of appointment Tobias gave her."

"A very sore point," Kearney replied.

"What do you mean?"

"Look, Robyn Vandermeer is a very clever woman. She's done a lot of good, no question, but she's been quite capable of looking out for herself.

"When she married Tobias, his father was dead set against the marriage, and deliberately wrote his will so she'd never get her hands on anything except what Tobias chose to give her out of his own estate. She went to work on the old man and sweet-talked him into changing that. And then she sweet-talked Tobias into giving her that deed."

"Are you saying he didn't want to do that?"

"No, he did. He was still infatuated with her when his father died, and she was able to persuade him to execute it very easily."

Frost was taken aback at Kearney's account, which did not square with what Robyn had told him. Had the gift of the deed of appointment been a romantic gesture, as she had said, or a scheme on her part to ensure her future?

"It was a terrible mistake," Kearney went on. "When she got that deed in her hands, she started going her own way, with her own friends, her own interests. The same as happened with Tobias' first wife. Their marriage became a living arrangement, nothing more. Tobias became increasingly depressed about what he had done and finally asked her to give the deed back."

"She refused, of course."

"Of course. And there was nothing he could do about it."

"When did this happen?"

"I don't recall exactly. Four, five years ago."

Frost reached for a pencil from the holder on Kearney's coffee table and began doodling on a pad in front of him, uncertain about what he was hearing, uncertain how to proceed with his questioning.

"Would it surprise you if I said Robyn tells the story a little differently?"

"No. She knows how to put a good front on things."

"You don't like her."

"We get along. But Tobias was my boss, not her."

"One thing puzzles me," Frost said. "You say Tobias wanted to revoke Robyn's life estate. And from what she says, and I don't think you've really denied it, he kept her on a pretty short string. So why did he continue to give money to READ and the other benefits and charities Robyn supported?"

"That's simple. Or maybe it isn't. You have to understand, you must know this, that a man as rich as Tobias is fair game for every cause going, from the Red Cross to amateur string quartets. We're not talking boxes of Girl Scout cookies, either, but demands for big money. He was tightfisted in many ways, but he was not against charitable giving. He had to limit the things he supported in self-defense. He had his own charities, the Jazz Center and the Museum of the City of New York, and it made sense to include Robyn's as well. They were worthy causes, after all."

"If he was in a bloody battle with her for her interest in the Trust, why wouldn't he just cut off everything?"

"He'd been through one messy divorce and I don't think he wanted another one. Which he'd certainly have had if Robyn couldn't play the social lion any longer."

"If he was afraid of a divorce, why did he restrict her personal spending?"

"That's Robyn's version. She wasn't lacking anything. Tobias wanted to keep tabs on the amount she spent, that's all."

Frost characterized Tobias' behavior as "irrational" and received a noncommittal "maybe" when he asked if Kearney thought drink was at least a partial cause of it. Kearney was equally reserved when Frost raised the matter of the increased intensity of Tobias' drinking in the years before his death.

"He drank a lot, there's no denying that," Kearney said.

"Maybe he was drinking more, I'm not sure. I never thought it was any of my concern."

"You never thought of trying to get him into treatment?"

"Never. He was a grown man, and what he did was his own affair. He wasn't abusing any children and Great Kill went along very well without him." Kearney's unstated suggestion was that Great Kill in fact was better off being run by Kearney.

"Did Robyn ever talk to you about it?"

"Not really. A couple of times he forgot to tell me about something he'd told her she could have, something she could spend money on. She'd get mad and say he was too drunk to remember."

"Didn't you find his drinking was making him moodier? More suspicious?"

"Could be. But I let it roll right off my back."

Kearney was not going to speak ill of the dead, so Frost changed the subject. "You had a contract with Great Kill, didn't you?"

"Yes."

"I seem to remember the original one that Hendrik had drawn up."

"You should. You drafted it."

"So I did," Frost said, embarrassed at being caught out in his own disingenuousness. "It was for ten years, as I recall."

"That's right. Then the board, at Tobias' instigation, renewed it for another five."

"Which would run out when?"

Kearney was silent. Silent and nervous. "Roughly two months from now," he finally said.

"Had you talked with Tobias about another renewal?"

"We both knew it was coming up. There wasn't any need to."

"A totally unrelated question. Have you ever heard of a woman named Grace Alice Rourke?"

"No, sir," Kearney shot back at once. "Never heard the name."

"Tobias didn't ever mention her?"

"Never."

Despite Kearney's strong and negative response, Frost couldn't help noticing his continued nervousness, his slight ankle-jiggling and thigh-patting. Perhaps it was time to make the Great Kill bureaucrat even more nervous.

"Bill, let me go back to something you said earlier. You told me that you and Tobias had a business meeting every week. When did that take place?"

Kearney set his mouth, evidently determined not to show any emotion. "Sunday afternoon."

"Including last Sunday?"

"Yes, including last Sunday."

"What time?"

"We always met at two o'clock."

"And last Sunday? You saw Tobias at two?"

"Yes."

"At home?"

"Yes."

"And when did you leave him?"

"Just before four."

"Did you notice anything unusual about him?"

"No."

"Was he drinking?"

"He always did."

"A lot?"

"I think he had two whiskeys while I was there. Maybe three."

"Who else did you see at the Vandermeers? Who else was there?"

"Only Robyn. And that maid of theirs."

"That's it?"

"Let me see. When I was leaving they were getting ready for the party where he was killed. There was a waiter type there."

"Could you recognize him if you saw him again?"

"I'm not sure."

"Anyone else?"

"Nope."

"Anything else you saw, or want to tell me about?"

"Nope."

"Any bright ideas as to who the killer might be?"

"Nope."

"How about Sherman Deybold? Did Tobias have any kind of ongoing fight with him?" Frost asked, thinking of the dead man's thundered question, "What do you want this time?"

"Not that I'm aware of. Tobias was his best customer, judging by the checks that we made out to him."

"Would Tobias have ever called him a prick?"

"He called lots of people a prick, and worse."

"My questions are finished."

"I'm glad to be of help," Kearney replied without a trace of irony. "I'll show you out."

"I can find my way."

"Very well," Kearney said, then, hesitating, "Do you think the police will have to know I was at the Vandermeer's last Sunday?"

"I'm sure they will."

"You mean you're going to tell them?"

"I didn't say that. At least five people know you were there—Miss Boyle, the hired waiter, Robyn, my wife and me. The police probably already know about you."

"But I have nothing to tell them."

"Then there's no need to be worried."

"I don't want to get tied up in something that's none of my business."

"I stand by what I said. And I thank you for your time."

Frost shook hands very formally, and went toward the door. Then he turned around and asked Kearney another question.

"Oh, by the way, Bill—did anyone besides you know about that deed to Robyn?"

"Tobias told me never to tell anyone. So I didn't. She may have, but I doubt it."

"So the people at the Bloemendael weren't aware of it? They don't know the Trust will have to be kept in place for her lifetime, and that they won't get either the corpus or the income until she dies?"

Kearney, standing behind his desk, still looked edgy and nervous.

"They didn't know about it," he said in a tense voice.

"Thank you."

Back on the street, Frost muttered to himself that if the police didn't know about Bill Kearney already, he was certainly going to tell them. Stonewalling Detective Springer, under the baleful eye of Detective Mattocks, might not be so easy a performance as the one Kearney had put on for the last hour.

Frost walked hastily in the direction of the Gotham Club. Only a Gotham martini could improve the foul mood the bureaucratic Kearney had induced.

REVIEW AND REUNION

13

RETURNING FROM WORK THAT EVENING, CYNTHIA FROST heard monumental curses emanating from the library.

"Reuben! What's the matter?" she said with concern, entering the room.

"My goddam printer needs a goddam new ribbon!" he barked, hunched in helpless fury over his printer and wrestling with a new ribbon cassette.

"What language! Here, Thomas Edison, let me see," Cynthia said, nudging her husband out of the way. Studying the problem, and tentatively easing the cassette around, she soon had it snapped in place.

"All set to go," she said.

"Hmn," said Reuben.

"What were you going to print, anyway?"

"The upstairs/downstairs list. With Bill Kearney's name added."

Frost recounted the substance of his morning interview to his wife, telling her that "Kearney stonewalled me on everything except what might be damaging to Robyn. He was a cold fish, though he seemed mighty nervous about talking to me. And really nervous when he realized the police would probably question him about his whereabouts on Sunday afternoon."

"You think he could have killed Tobias?"

"Well, he was there at the right time."

"But why would he?"

"To be rid of Tobias? and Robyn?"

"Maybe," Cynthia said doubtfully.

"Also, there's the matter of his contract," Reuben said. "Old Hendrik Vandermeer gave him a very cushy employment contract. Great Kill renewed it once and—get this—it was going to expire in another two months."

"But renewing the contract wasn't up to Tobias, was it?"

"Not technically, no. It would be up to the directors of Great Kill, of which Tobias was only one. But if Tobias had a mind to, he could make renewing the contract difficult, or at least prevent improving its terms very much."

"Do you think the police know about Kearney?"

"If they don't, I'm going to tell them. Or at least I'm going to tell Luis—I got hold of him this morning, by the way, and he's going to stop by at six-thirty."

"Good. I'll feel better having him around."

"That makes two of us."

Detective First Class Luis Bautista, nattily dressed in a blue blazer, gray flannel slacks and a Bengal-striped shirt, rang the front bell at the Frost townhouse precisely on time. Reuben went downstairs to let him in.

"Luis! Come in. I can't tell you how glad I am to see you!" he said.

Once upstairs, Cynthia added her own welcome, including an enthusiastic kiss.

"You look marvelous!" she said to the well-tanned detective; there was none of Sherman Deybold's fashionable paleness here.

"It must be wonderful to work for the NYPD," Reuben said. "What was this, about your third vacation since Christmas?"

"No, Reuben, not exactly. Just a long weekend in Florida."

"With Francisca, I hope," Cynthia said, wishing as she

said it that one of these long weekends away would be a honeymoon.

"Sure thing. You think she'd let me go to Florida alone?" Bautista said, laughing. "Leaving me to be attacked by all those neat Hispanic broads down there? No way."

"Where were you, Miami?"

"Not this time. Going to Miami, for a New York cop, is like a busman's holiday. There's crime enough right here in the Big Apple for me. We went to Tampa."

"Tampa?"

"Yeah. Nice hotel there, and Ybor City—lots of Hispanics, even if they are Cubans. They thought our Puerto Rican Spanish was funny, but who cares? The food was great, the sun was great, the . . ."

"I can imagine the rest," Frost said, laughing, and steered Bautista into the living room. "Anyway, we're glad to have you back. You've heard about our mess?"

Bautista's face turned serious. "Yes, I have. I know what you told me earlier on the phone. And I spent an hour with Tom Springer this afternoon."

"What about the medical examiner?" Reuben asked.

"Springer and Mattocks just got the report. It was definitely cyanide."

"Could they tell how Tobias had taken it? Whether it was a poisoned capsule or in his drink? I told you about the capsules."

"Yes, they had been laced with cyanide. But the ME claims you can't tell whether the poison that killed Vandermeer was from a capsule or was in his drink."

"Do you believe that?"

"All I know about pathology is what I learned at the police academy and what I've seen since. With the fancy equipment they have these days I would have thought they could trace the means of ingestion. But they say not."

"Can't we get the FBI or somebody else in here to have a look?"

"Yeah, you probably could. But I'm afraid it's too late to run some supersophisticated test that might give the answer."

"Damn," Frost said. "Did your Medical Examiner know what he was supposed to be looking for? That there were two possible ways Tobias might have been killed?"

"Oh, yeah. He knew all right. Springer made sure of that as soon as they learned about the medicine bottle."

"What about Tobias' drink glass? Or rather drink glasses?" Cynthia asked. "If the poison had been in one of them, wouldn't that show up in a test?"

"You'd think so, wouldn't you?" Bautista said. "Springer said everybody agrees there were two glasses Vandermeer was drinking from. One of them got broken in the confusion when he conked out. The other one was clean. No sign of poison."

"What about the broken one?" Cynthia persisted.

"I'm almost too embarrassed to tell you."

"What do you mean?" Cynthia said.

"They can't find it," Bautista replied glumly.

"They can't find it?" Reuben exclaimed. "What kind of nonsense is that?"

Bautista explained how the fragments of the broken glass had been gathered up, bagged and labeled by the CSU technicians. "They're reasonably sure the plastic bag was with the other stuff they took away and turned over to the lab. But the lab can't locate it."

"That's incredible," Reuben said angrily. His whole life as a lawyer had been based on keeping things in proper order; he could not believe that police technicians operated any differently. He was sure in his own mind that the broken glass had been the one he had handed to Tobias; now he might never be exonerated. "What kind of dunderheads are in the police department anyway?" he demanded.

"Most of them aren't dunderheads, Reuben. But there are a lot of guys who go through the motions of their jobs or aren't very experienced, and they get careless. I can't excuse it, but that's the way it is."

"That really leaves us in the soup," Frost said in a very sour voice. "I was hoping the lab tests would tell us that I could tear up either my upstairs list or the downstairs list."

"Upstairs, downstairs?"

Frost produced his sheet of computer paper and explained the two lists to Bautista, filling in what he didn't already know about those on it, including Bill Kearney, the late-starting addition.

"I take it there were no fingerprints on the bottle?"

"None they could read."

"Damn and double damn. So we're left with three possibilities. Tobias took the poison in his bathroom, thinking he was taking his medicine. Or Tobias' drink was poisoned. Or—this is Cynthia's idea—his drink was poisoned and the killer left the open bottle upstairs as a diversion. Right?"

Both Cynthia and Bautista agreed.

"And with that broken drinking glass gone, we may never have the answer."

Again Reuben's listeners agreed.

"Now, Luis, you have all the information we have, and all the information your colleagues have. Who did it?"

"Let's make sure I *do* know everything. Let's see if I understand the setup in the living room."

Bautista opened his notebook and started making a sketch of the death scene. Reuben and Cynthia offered comments as he did so.

"This is correct?" he finally asked, tearing out the sheet and handing it to the Frosts.

"Yes," they both agreed.

"One or two more questions. I've heard conflicting things about the widow. I know her public reputation, like everybody else—one of our great benefactors. Happy and benign. But maybe not so happy, and maybe not that benign. Is that fair?"

"Yes, it is," Reuben said. "We thought we knew her pretty well, but there's a lot we don't know. Hell, we're not even sure who all her husbands were."

"Okay, to go back to your question: Who did it? I haven't seen any of the suspects. I think, though, I'd put her at the top of the list. A real motive and of course every chance to plant the poisoned capsules. I wouldn't rule out Deybold, either. He's on both your upstairs and downstairs lists. And the waiter."

"What about him?"

"They're still looking for him. The address he gave the caterers he worked for was a fake."

"Then there's this Kearney," Bautista went on. "I'd like to have a better line on him."

"That raises a question, Luis. Are you going to be involved in this case, I hope?" Reuben said.

"That's not possible," Bautista answered. "Springer and Mattocks caught the case, and it wouldn't be copacetic for me to try and horn in on it."

"Surely you can help in the background—at least help *me* in the background."

Bautista did not respond for a moment, as if collecting his thoughts. "Reuben, I've got to be frank with you," he said finally. "I know that you had nothing to do with Vandermeer's murder. It's inconceivable to me, and I'm one of the most suspicious guys around—cynical enough not to be shocked at almost anything. But let's face it. You're still a suspect. Until the dust settles, it's best for all of us that we don't talk together. For old times' sake, I checked out what Springer and Mattocks were doing and came here today. But for your good and mine, we've got to operate at arm's length in this thing."

"Luis, I'm sorry," Reuben said, shocked at the turn of events. "The last thing in the world we want to do is get you into trouble. But if you're convinced I'm innocent, where's the harm?"

"It would look bad, Reuben," Bautista said, himself upset by the drift of the conversation. "I regard you both as real good friends. So does Francisca. It's just that for the moment we shouldn't be doing things out of friendship. You don't want anybody saying you've unduly influenced the police's investigation. And I don't want anybody saying I was meddling to cover up for a pal of mine."

"There's nothing to cover up!" Reuben said sternly.

"Sorry, that wasn't a very good choice of words. I meant—"

"No, Luis, I understand."

"Look, if you get in a real jam, I'll be there. But I can't

be second-guessing my buddies behind their backs. I've told them, and I'll tell Joe Munson when I see him, that there isn't a chance in hell you had anything to do with the murder. You had the bad luck to be in the wrong place at the wrong time. I'm damn sorry, but I'm convinced that's the way we should leave it."

Bautista got up and buttoned his blazer across his barrel chest.

"Does this prevent you from having a drink before you go?" Cynthia asked.

"Can I take a rain check? I'm still on duty."

"Of course you can have a rain check. Just tell us when you want to redeem it," Reuben said.

"And give our love to Francisca," Cynthia added.

"Okay," Bautista said. "I'll certainly do that."

"I only hope this is over soon," Reuben said.

"Me, too," Bautista answered. "Take it easy."

"You know the way out, Luis," Reuben said.

"Sure thing."

Bautista made an awkward exit, leaving a devastated Reuben and Cynthia behind.

"Well, he learned something in that night law school of his," Reuben said quietly.

"What's that?"

"How to protect himself. Or, not to put a fine point on it, how to cover his ass."

"I'm not sure that's fair, Reuben."

"He washed his hands of us, that's what he did!"

"You mustn't get excited, dear. Luis is doing what he thinks is best."

"Oh, I know. He's absolutely correct. Even if it leaves me right up a tree."

"Well, you'll have to try and climb down," Cynthia said.

"Without falling. Well, we'll show him, and Springer and Mattocks and everybody else. It'll be easy. All we have to do is figure out who killed Tobias. Simple, heh?"

"We'll do it, Reuben. We *have* to do it!"

A SURPRISE FOR SOME

TOBIAS VANDERMEER'S FUNERAL WAS CONDUCTED WITH-
out incident late Wednesday morning at "the Marble," the
Marble Collegiate Church, home of the Collegiate Reformed
Protestant Dutch Church of the City of New York, to which
the Vandermeers had belonged for generations. Television
and still photographers clogged the narrow sidewalk in front
of the Gothic Revival entrance on Fifth Avenue, but inside
all was calm and decorous.

Reuben and Cynthia arrived early and were seated in a
pew (at Reuben's choice) toward the back. No churchgoer,
Reuben winced inwardly as the small door at the end of the
pew was shut behind him, heightening the feeling of claus-
trophobia he usually felt in holy places.

Frost observed that most of the assembled crowd were
friends of Robyn's, fellow veterans of the society-benefit
wars, interspersed with small multiracial groups that Reuben
took to be teachers from, or perhaps even beneficiaries of,
READ. Also Norman, the Mayor, who sat all by himself in
the front pew on the left-hand side.

Reuben did spot several directors of the Bloemendael
Foundation. But, aside from a few men he guessed were jazz
musicians, there were very few present who could be said to
be Tobias' friends.

118

Robyn, clad in the obligatory black, was ushered from a side door to a front pew just before the service began. To Frost's initial surprise, she was accompanied by Bill Kearney, to whose arm she held tightly. Then he realized that the widow had no known relatives, other than former husbands, so Kearney had probably been pressed into service out of necessity. In any event, the Great Kill executive's austere appearance was totally in keeping with the morning's solemnity.

As the service proceeded, Reuben's mind wandered as he glanced from the green palm trees at the altarless front of the church to the red-and-gold fleur-de-lis panels along the side walls. He could not decide whether the minister reminded him more of Jimmy Carter or Richard Nixon; he overused the word "superb" like the former, but had the slightly false gravity of the latter.

The minister eulogized the deceased elaborately; there was no hint that the man who had "crossed to the other side" had in many respects not been very attractive. Instead he was depicted as a caring man who had "gone the last mile" more than once, most probably a reference to Tobias' financial contributions to "the Marble."

Reuben was relieved when the minister asked the congregation to rise and sing the "Old Hundreth," followed by a prayer of dismissal and seemingly endless choruses of "Faith of Our Fathers." Then the dark mahogany casket was wheeled out, and Robyn, her face sheathed in a black veil, went down the aisle on Bill Kearney's arm.

Reuben broke away from Cynthia as they left the church to talk to Bob Millard.

"Didn't you say Monday that the Bloemendael Foundation was meeting tomorrow?"

"Yes, I did."

"And you're going?"

"Oh, yes. A command performance, as I told you."

As they talked, a television camera crew swept by and almost knocked the two men over. They had been photographing the Mayor's exit from the church and were now hurrying to focus in on Robyn as she entered her black limousine. Millard put out his hand to steady Reuben and they continued their conversation.

"I'd like to go to that meeting," Frost said. "Do you think it's possible?"

Millard looked surprised. "Why on earth do you want to do that?"

"Bob, there's precious little in the way of clues to Tobias' murder. We've got to search everywhere we can, look for every angle we can. A meeting of the Bloemendael directors probably won't produce a single lead. It will most likely be a total waste of my time. But I'd still like to go. I'd like to get the *feel* of how that board operates. What do you think?"

"Well . . . you're too old and distinguished to be my bag carrier, Reuben. But what the hell, why not? I'll just bring you. If anybody asks why, I'll simply say you're the senior lawyer in charge of Vandermeer family matters."

"That's stretching things a little, Bob. After all, I am retired."

"Don't worry about it. I doubt that the directors will know the difference, or would care if they did."

"It won't embarrass you?"

"Lord, no. In fact, I'll be glad for the moral support."

"Okay, then. What time?"

"Two-thirty at the Foundation's offices."

"Shall I meet you in the lobby at two-twenty?"

"Good."

"You talked to Robyn yesterday?"

"Yes. She's in good shape."

"That deed of appointment does the trick?"

"Absolutely."

"Bill Kearney knew all about it, by the way. Tobias had given him a copy of the deed."

"I'm not surprised," Millard said.

"Have you talked to Mark Small?"

"Not yet. I put in a call to him this morning."

"Duck him," Frost replied cryptically. "It'll be time enough for him to find out about it tomorrow."

* * *

The next afternoon Reuben met Bob Millard in the marble lobby of the office tower where the Bloemendael offices were located, on First Avenue in the not-for-profit enclave surrounding the United Nations. Millard had been caught in traffic downtown, so they were already two minutes late by the time they went up to the thirty-third floor and were shown by one of the two attractive receptionists to the boardroom, an impressive space with a panoramic view of the UN buildings, the East River and Queens on the other side.

As they approached the double doors leading to the boardroom, Wayne Givens, followed by two women, came up behind them. He greeted Frost amiably but managed at the same time to convey his surprise at seeing him.

"Reuben! Nice to see you. I hope this is a calmer occasion than the last time we met," he said, then added, "I didn't know you were still in harness."

Givens didn't wait for a reply and introduced his colleagues, Dr. Marguerite Baxter, the executive vice-president for research at the Bloemendael, and Lois Jordan, Givens' own secretary and an assistant secretary of the Foundation, who would keep the day's board minutes.

It was hard to tell which woman was prettier. Dr. Baxter was older and taller, but she had a distinctly unscholarly, outdoorsy blond look and a glittering smile. Frost was sure he had seen her before, but could not recall where. Her colleague was a petite black woman who was, to Reuben's eye at least, very comely. He wondered if it had been an accident that these two women, and the two receptionists seen earlier, had all been what he in his old-fashioned way would term "knockouts." Were they all handpicked by Givens? Did the notoriously lecherous Dr. Wayne have a harem within the Bloemendael Foundation?

"Do you want us to wait out here?" Bob Millard asked.

"No, no, no, come on in," Givens said. "We don't have any state secrets here." He took them inside the boardroom, where the other directors were scattered around in groups, all talking animatedly. Since the talk ceased when he and Millard entered the room, Frost assumed (correctly) that at least part of it was speculation over Tobias' death—and quite possibly the disposition of the Vandermeer fortune.

"You two can sit there," Givens directed, pointing to the single chair against the wall. "Oh, we need another chair. Here, Pete Gonzalez isn't coming today, after all. Take this one." He moved a chair from the table and put it against the wall, next to Reuben.

"You can take Pete's agenda, too, so you can follow our momentous deliberations," he went on, handing the green folder at one of the places to Reuben.

Frost and Millard looked at the agenda at the front of the folder while Givens made his way to the head of the table, shaking hands as he did so. They noted that "Robert Millard, Esq., Chase & Ward," was to address the meeting on the "Legal Status of the Vandermeer Trust."

The room was dominated by a large, impressive marble table at which fourteen places had been set, each marked by a green agenda folder. With the afternoon sun coming in the window and lighting the neatly arranged table, the effect was one of tasteful prosperity. The room and its furnishings were not quite opulent—the watchful eyes of Hendrik Vandermeer, looking down from the oil painting on the wall, would never have countenanced that—but they were certainly grander than the utilitarian, humdrum offices of Great Kill Holdings.

(Frost knew that Wayne Givens, aware of the plush spaces occupied by many other foundations, notably the Ford a few blocks downtown, had several years earlier toyed with the idea of erecting a headquarters building for the Bloemendael Foundation. Being the good politician that he was, he hastily backed off when there were rumblings on his board. The directors, normally docile and responsive to his wishes, insisted that all its available resources be dedicated to the Foundation's addiction programs, and not to expensive bricks and mortar.)

Frost had done his homework and gone over a list of the fourteen surviving Bloemendael directors (Tobias having been the fifteenth), sent up to him from Chase & Ward the day before. The list included Givens, Kearney and Dr. Baxter. Of the others, he had found that he had come across virtually all of them, one way or another, and now recognized most of them as he looked around. He realized the shrewdness with which they had been picked, presumably by Wayne Givens. He was sure there had been a special reason for selecting each one, and could guess what it was in most cases.

Take Jerry Halpern, for example. One of New York's most successful real estate developers, and one of the few in the good graces of what Cynthia had once called the "preservationist mafia," he had most likely been useful in easing the way for the drug-addiction centers the Foundation sponsored throughout the New York area. The exact opposite of the Vandermeers, with their quiet, passive investments in valuable real estate, Halpern was a flamboyant developer, with an exceedingly clever and shrewd public-relations operation behind him. Surely this PR apparatus had been put at the services of the Foundation as it confronted often vehement community opposition to the opening of new treatment facilities.

Or Dr. Jonathan Persky, a Nobel prizewinner for his discoveries in pharmacology. A prestigious authority for Givens to have on his side—yet one not really expert enough in addiction prevention and rehabilitation to challenge Wayne Givens' methods and theories.

A touch of celebrity, if not actual glitz, was added by Gregory Bonner, the new head of television programming at one of the networks. "I'm no artist," he was fond of saying, and most who saw the shows produced under his aegis would agree. Nonetheless, for three years in succession he had assembled a schedule of programs that put his network first in the ratings, moving from "brash whiz kid" to "genius" by the time the third season's triumph was announced.

And there was Mark Small, the recently elected head partner of Rudenstine, Fried & D'Arms, who had invited Millard to the meeting, and now came across the room to shake hands with Frost and Millard. And the almost obligatory investment banker and accountant: Blair McKenzie, the sixtyish head of the comfortably old-line firm of Hester & Company, and Emory Bacon of Sprouse & Walker, a small accounting firm specializing in not-for-profit organizations.

Then there were the "balancers," those who gave the board at least an outwardly democratic cast, without at all disturbing the elitist hegemony that Givens imposed. Eliza Russell, for example, an aging aristocrat from a New York family as old as the Vandermeers—kind, and no trouble. And Glenda Warren, a former administrative assistant (a secretary, really) at the Henderson Institute, who, on the wave of the women's movement, had emerged as head of the Institute, making her to secondary-education reform what Wayne Givens was to addiction. Her directorships in both the corporate and nonprofit sectors were legion, and if she was sometimes unkindly called a "house woman," she either did not know, or did not mind, the reference.

Another master of board service was Alvin Michaelson, head of an office workers' union in the metropolitan area. When he saw his name, Reuben had wondered cynically if Michaelson could any longer remember how to sit on the labor side of a collective-bargaining table, having so long been a "labor" spokesman in the halls of capitalism.

Finally, Frost had spotted the names of two minority representatives, the Reverend Henry N. Price, the pastor of a major black church in Harlem and a man of impeccable reputation, and Dr. Pedro Gonzalez, a former National Institutes of Health researcher now working for a commercial drug company.

"Ah, here's Bill Kearney," Givens said as Kearney entered the room, slightly out of breath and apologizing for being late. "That means we can begin. Everyone's here except Pete Gonzalez, who had an emergency come up, and Jerry Halpern. He just called from his car and said he's stuck in traffic. He shouldn't be long."

"The car! Calling from the car! Imagine!" Eliza Russell exclaimed, raising her white-gloved hands in mock horror. "I'm so old, I remember when you had to turn a *crank* to talk on the telephone!"

"The wonders of modern science, Eliza," Givens said, and immediately called the meeting to order, cutting off further small talk.

After the preliminary formalities, including a treasurer's

report confirming that the Foundation's total income for the previous year had been $7.4 million, Dr. Baxter reviewed the research proposals that the Bloemendael staff was asking the board to approve. The agenda booklet contained a summary of each, but she gave a brief description anyway, pausing for comment afterward.

If there had been any fear that the directors' comments would be critical, it was groundless. After a description of the largest grant, $1.6 million to an experimental addiction program at a midwestern university, Dr. Persky commended "Dr. Givens or Dr. Baxter, whoever is responsible." He praised the program as innovative and as being one that held out great promise. And also as one being run by a former student of his.

"Thank you," Dr. Baxter replied pleasantly. "As a fellow pharmacologist, I agree with you."

While another grant, to a research team in Indiana, was being described, Blair McKenzie interrupted to ask if one of the recipients wasn't "Meredith Owen's son." Told "yes" by Dr. Baxter, he nodded approvingly, as did others around the table who knew Meredith Owen, the beloved president emeritus of a local university.

When Dr. Baxter had finished, Alvin Michaelson asked, "How much did we give away today?" and was told $4 million. "Not bad for a little family foundation," Michaelson said.

Not to be outdone in the praise department, Gregory Bonner called the staff's efforts "dynamite" and "phenomenal." He screwed up his face and closed his eyes as he spoke, his customary signal that he was saying something important.

"There's an awful lot of talk out there concerning drugs. We saw it in the last election campaign. And, believe me, we hear it all the time at the network—from our listeners, from our producers, from everyone. But mostly that's what it is— talk. It's a great thing to sit here and learn that something is being *done*. I think you're right on track, Wayne, and I want you to know we're all behind you."

There was polite applause in the room as Dr. Givens modestly accepted the praise running his way.

Reuben couldn't help but notice the congenial atmosphere that prevailed. What a contrast to the meetings of the National Ballet board at which he presided, with its prima ballerinas (and those with the temperaments of prima ballerinas), its factions and its general disorganization! What accounted for the difference? he wondered. Was a foundation dedicated to science necessarily more sedate than a nationally recognized ballet company? Then the reason struck him: his ballet board had to raise money—this one had only to spend it.

Those who picked the NatBallet directors were on the prowl for separate and independent checkbooks, which meant an assemblage of separate and independent egos, all vying for attention and stroking. The Foundation's Great Kill dividends gave Wayne Givens the luxury of picking directors who were not buying their seats. They might, as Reuben had concluded, earn their places in other ways, but they did not have to provide or raise funds.

Givens could pick and choose as he saw fit. Frost saw it all while the new grants were being described. Tobias Vandermeer may have been an accomplished needlepointist, but Givens was an accomplished weaver who had wrought a harmonious tapestry in which the individual strands did not clash.

And look at the interconnections of those strands, Frost reflected, extending the metaphor in his own mind. Several directors were otherwise beholden to Wayne Givens. Dr. Wayne's highly successful television show appeared on Gregory Bonner's network. Emory Bacon and Mark Small were presumably grateful for the accounting and legal work the Foundation provided. Glenda Warren and Alvin Michaelson, who practically made a profession of being outside directors, must have been happy to add the Bloemendael to their list. And Marguerite Baxter, of course, owed her job to Givens.

Some members of the board had forged close bonds elsewhere. Reuben knew of a few instances and was sure there were even more. Blair McKenzie and Michaelson, quintessential icons of capital and labor, were close advisers to Nor-

man, the Mayor, and had formed a symbolic united front at
City Hall on several difficult occasions. Dr. Persky and the
Reverend Price had served at the same time on the house
committee of the Gotham Club, which Reuben knew from
his own experience bonded the committee members together
in dealing with the often petty and oddball complaints of the
Club's members.

And, if he was not mistaken, the present Mrs. Michaelson
had been the first wife of the still-absent Jerry Halpern. That
might have created a lifelong rift between Michaelson and
Halpern in the hinterland, but not among members of New
York's civilized ruling elite.

It was ironic, Frost thought, that the only "outsiders" on
the Bloemendael board, the only strands that didn't mesh,
were Bill Kearney and the late Tobias.

Frost's musings were brought to an end when Givens introduced the next item of business, a resolution memorial-
izing Tobias. He described to an attentive audience the events
of Sunday night—"one of the most horrible occasions of my
life"—and was peppered with questions from his fellow directors."

"Wayne, I can't believe that Tobias was *poisoned*," Eliza
Russell said. "It must have been something else. A heart
attack or, or . . . alcohol, or *anything* except poison."

"I'm afraid not, Eliza," Givens replied. "I was there when
he died. There's no question that it was poison. He died of
cyanosis. From cyanide, that is."

One or two shocked asides were heard around the room,
and Givens quickly brought the meeting back to order, fo-
cusing attention back to the draft resolution in the directors'
green folders. Dressed up with many "whereases" and "re-
solveds," the text was not unlike the eulogy at Tobias' funeral, as interesting for what it didn't say as what it did.

"I think this is super," Gregory Bonner said, once again
screwing up his face. "A great tribute to a wonderful man.
I commend the draftsman."

"Mark Small can take credit for that," Givens said. "Do
I hear a motion?"

The resolution, needless to say, was passed unanimously.

"All right, that completes our business, except for one small item," Givens said, his voice smug, his remark causing laughter in the room. "We have with us this afternoon Robert Millard, and Reuben Frost, of course, from the law firm of Chase & Ward. That fine firm has represented the Vandermeer family over the years, and we've asked Mr. Millard to join us and explain how Tobias' tragic death affects us here at the Bloemendael. Mr. Millard? Why don't you come over here?" Givens made room at the table and Millard moved his chair to the open space.

"Thank you, Dr. Givens," Millard said, adjusting both his horn-rimmed glasses and the two sheets of notes on legal foolscap he had placed in front of him. "As Dr. Givens told you, my firm is counsel to the Vandermeer family. I have been in charge of its affairs for the last four years, since the death of my partner, Arthur Tyson.

"The story I have to tell you today is very short. Most of you will recall that the Foundation was started in 1963, with an initial gift of two million dollars from Hendrik Vandermeer—the gentleman in the portrait up there. When Hendrik died eleven years later, his will, which had been executed in 1964, provided that half the stock in Great Kill Holdings Corporation would come to the Foundation. Great Kill is, as you know, the corporate entity that owns the Vandermeer real estate interests and, as your treasurer's report said earlier, the Bloemendael's income to this day derives largely from the Great Kill stock.

"The rest of Hendrik Vandermeer's estate was placed in a trust, called the Vandermeer Trust, administered by Bill Kearney here and the First Fiduciary Trust Company, as cotrustees. Pursuant to the will, the ultimate beneficiaries of the Trust were the children of Tobias or, if there were none, the Bloemendael Foundation, subject to a life estate in the income to Tobias and, after Tobias' death, a further life estate in such income that Tobias appointed to Robyn.

"What life estate to Robyn?" Mark Small interrupted. "Tobias didn't appoint a life estate to her. I read the copy of his will you sent over, Bob, and there's not a word in there regarding a life estate for his widow or anybody else."

"Mark, I agree with you, there's nothing in Tobias' will. But you will recall that there was a codicil to his father's will that allowed Tobias to appoint a life estate to Robyn. He appears to have done that in an irrevocable deed he executed back in 1974."

"What are you talking about—a deed?" Small asked, in a not especially pleasant voice. "I would have thought any appointment would be in his will."

"Mark, I agree with you. That would have been the normal procedure. But Hendrik Vandermeer's will seems clearly to permit an appointment either by will or by deed, and Tobias chose to do it by deed."

"Damned unusual, I'd say," Small replied. "Have you got a copy with you?"

"Of Hendrik's will, or the deed?"

"Both."

Millard pulled copies of the will, together with the later codicil, and the deed Tobias had given to Robyn, from his attaché case and handed them across the table to Small. The latter put on a pair of half-glasses and flipped through the documents.

"I see your firm didn't draw up this deed," Small said accusingly.

"That is correct. Tobias apparently wanted to keep this private between himself and his wife."

"He delivered this thing to Mrs. Vandermeer?"

"That's correct. He gave it to her on an anniversary trip to Paris."

"Is that good delivery—in Paris?"

"I believe it is. But for good measure, he gave a second copy to Bill Kearney."

Eyes turned to Kearney, who looked decidedly uncomfortable.

"When did you find out about this?" Small asked Millard.

"Tuesday afternoon. I tried to reach you yesterday, but we missed each other," Millard said, not explaining that he had been avoiding Small's return call on Frost's instructions.

"Does this mean what I think it does? That the Foundation

won't get the Vandermeer Trust income, or the corpus for that matter, until Robyn dies?'' Wayne Givens interrupted.

"That appears to be the case," Small said.

"That isn't what you told me when we talked three months ago," Givens said, clearly angry, as he gave Small an exasperated look.

"Wayne, this is the first I've heard of this thing," Small replied defensively.

"No one has ever told anyone here about this life estate," Givens said. "Are we sure this, whatever you call it, is genuine? It seems very strange to me that it comes to light only after Tobias' murder.''

"Now, Wayne, the instrument appears to be valid on its face, though of course we'll have to satisfy ourselves that it is," Small temporized. "Meanwhile, let's not be hasty."

Givens was not mollified. He turned on Kearney and asked why he had never revealed Tobias' action.

"The subject never came up. It never occurred to me."

"Never occurred to you that it might help us to plan how this Foundation operates?'' Givens shot back, raising his voice.

"I was under orders from Tobias not to mention to anyone what he had done. And besides, Wayne, the subject only became relevant four days ago, when Tobias died unexpectedly," Kearney said icily. "As long as Tobias was alive, it didn't matter what Hendrik's will or that codicil or Tobias' deed of appointment said. It was totally irrelevant to the Foundation.''

Givens, evidently realizing that his outbursts were subject to an unpleasant interpretation, calmed down and apologized. "I'm sorry, ladies and gentlemen. It's just that this comes as a great shock to me."

Mrs. Russell said she was confused and asked Millard to review the legal situation once again, which he did, to the discomfort of the others.

"I should have thought Tobias would have taken care of Robyn from his own estate," she said in exasperation when he had finished.

"Well, he chose not to, Mrs. Russell," Millard said.

"All I can say is, it looks like there'll be a lot more fighting of illiteracy than dope addiction," she replied with asperity.

Givens, still shaken but by now aware that further recriminations might tear a hole in his tapestry, asked for a motion to adjourn the meeting.

"I don't understand why we didn't know this," he said to Millard, as the group broke up.

"I'm sorry, Wayne. It was a surprise to Reuben and me, too."

"You knew this on Tuesday. You at least could have told our counsel."

"I apologize," Millard said. "I did try." But not very hard, he might have added.

Millard and Frost, as the bearers of bad news, thought it politic to leave as unobtrusively as they could.

"Bob, they should have put you through a security gate before that meeting," Frost said to his former partner, once they had reached the lobby.

"What do you mean?"

"That was a pretty big hand grenade you lobbed onto the table," Frost answered.

"Yes, I guess it was. You know, Reuben, I'm not so sure it was right for me to avoid Mark Small's calls. . . ."

"I'm sorry I put you on the spot, Bob, but thanks for doing as I asked," he told his puzzled colleague.

Frost was smiling broadly. It was not every day that he could both embarrass Mark Small—through no fault of Small's own—and perhaps, just perhaps, get closer to solving Tobias' murder.

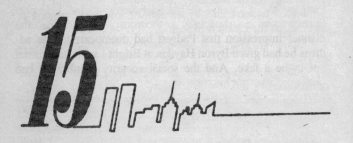

IT WAS AN ELATED REUBEN FROST WHO RECOUNTED THE tale of the stormy Bloemendael meeting to his wife that evening.

"So what have we got here?" he asked his wife, when he had finished his description. "It's absolutely certain that Wayne Givens thought the Foundation would get everything in the Vandermeer Trust right away if Tobias died. And— *and*—as I told you, he was so mad he blurted out that he and Mark Small, Esquire, had had a powwow not too long ago on the subject. Well, maybe not a powwow, but they'd certainly discussed it."

"I agree that what you say is very interesting, dear. There are two problems. If Tobias was poisoned in one of his drinks, Wayne wasn't anywhere near him. And we have no idea whether he went upstairs to Tobias' bathroom."

"We know he didn't while we were there, but he could have before we arrived."

"Yes, he could have. Are you going to tell Mattocks and Springer about this?"

"What is there to tell them? They already know Givens was there on Sunday. It would look like I was trying to shift the blame from me. If it were Luis, I'd tell him in a minute.

132

But I don't see the point with the other two, or their friend in the DA's office.''

There continued to be silence from the police, though Springer did come by the Frost townhouse one afternoon a few days later to ask some follow-up questions about Pace Padgett, the waiter at the Vandermeers' ill-fated dinner. Springer was not especially forthcoming, but Frost had the distinct impression that Padgett had disappeared. The address he had given Byron Hayden at Bright Lights had turned out to be a fake. And the social security number he had furnished was not his own.

Padgett's telephone number was in reality the number for a commercial answering service, which had no forwarding information for him and was in touch with him only when he called in. He came by in person each month to pay the subscription charge—in cash. The service's receptionist recognized the ''identi-kit'' picture the police had prepared from the descriptions of Padgett they had been given, but no one else there, nor Hayden, could offer the police any other help.

After this latest intelligence from Springer, Frost decided to pay another call on Robyn Vandermeer to question her about a number of things, including Padgett.

As he had already done with others, he asked the widow if she had any theories about Tobias' strange behavior before he died, shouting at Sherman Deybold and energetically stitching ''prick'' into his needlepoint. And if either of the Givenses had gone upstairs at the beginning of the evening.

Robyn was no help with either of these questions, though she did say she'd left the Givenses alone for a few minutes when they arrived, so that, conceivably, one of them could have sneaked upstairs. Nor did she provide new information about the elusive Padgett. Robyn told Frost that he had first been assigned to the Vandermeers by Bright Lights early the previous autumn, to serve at a luncheon Robyn had given for the vice-chairman of the benefit committee for the READ ball.

He had seemed pleasant enough, Robyn said, and when she wanted a waiter for the reading club meeting at the Vandermeers' in November (Miss Boyle having made her demand for extra help by then) Byron Hayden had asked if he should send Padgett, and Robyn had readily agreed. He had returned several times since.

"He was a totally unexceptionable young man," Robyn said. "You saw him—quiet, competent, unobtrusive. He got to know his way around the kitchen and the dining room and was really very efficient. Miss Boyle got along with him, too. Which was important as far as I was concerned."

"Did he have any quirks? Anything odd about him?"

"No more than any out-of-work actor. Actually he was a good deal less flamboyant than most of them. I was always glad when Byron sent him over. He reminded me of a servant I had when I lived in Chicago."

"Chicago? I didn't know you ever lived in Chicago," Frost said.

"You didn't know about my Chicago period, Reuben? That's hard to believe."

"I don't think you've ever mentioned it before."

"It was a part of my checkered past, dear Reuben," Robyn said, in her best *grande dame* manner. "I was married to a dull but very decent auto-parts maker."

"Do I know him, or know of him?"

"His name was Bernard Weldin. You see ads for Weldin Parts on television all the time. Mufflers, exhaust pipes, glamorous things like that."

"This was before the Principe, obviously."

"Obviously. I was a Chicago matron from 1951 to 1958."

"My, my. You never cease to surprise, Robyn."

"Honey, you don't know the half of it," she said, changing to a mock Mae West tone. "And I'm not about to tell you."

Frost stood up to leave when Robyn called him back.

"Reuben, while you're here, there's something I'd like to ask you about."

"Of course."

"As you probably know, I've never had anything to do with the Bloemendael Foundation. Now that Tobias is gone, there's no representative of the family on the board, unless you count Bill Kearney, which I don't. For that matter there isn't any family left except me. Do you think I'd be crazy to ask for a seat on the board?''

''Not at all, if that's what you want to do. It would be perfectly appropriate.''

''Specifically, I'd like to be Chairman of the Board. Wayne Givens is now the Chairman as well as the President. One job is enough for him, and I want the other one. He could still run the show and sound off to the world about drugs, but there'd be a little more control over him than there is now.''

''You think he needs that—to be controlled?'' Frost asked.

''The answer is yes. When Hendrik Vandermeer set up the Bloemendael, it was supposed to concern itself with drugs, alcohol and black education. Wayne got the directors to concentrate solely on drugs—including Tobias, who was always uneasy about the alcoholism part, for obvious reasons.''

''So you want to become Chairman of the Bloemendael and steer it into things other than drugs?''

''Things in addition to drugs, Reuben.''

''What do you have in mind?''

''You asked me and I'll tell you—illiteracy among blacks.''

Frost was momentarily surprised at Robyn's determined answer, then realized that of course he should not have been, given Robyn's almost fanatical interest in literacy.

''Well, Robyn, the Foundation should hear what the family's wishes are. And, as you say, you're the family. Just don't be surprised if Wayne Givens and his captive board try to give you a hard time.''

''I've thought about that. I'll be prepared for him and them.''

Frost hurried home and called Cynthia at her office to tell her the tidbits he had unearthed, knowing that she would be intrigued.

''Three down, one to go,'' Frost said to his wife.

''What do you mean?''

''We've identified three of Robyn's four husbands.''

''That's very titillating, my dear, but what does it mean?''

''I don't know.''

''And how about Wayne Givens? Poor fellow! First he doesn't get his hands on the rest of Great Kill, and now he's going to have Robyn poking around in his backyard!''

"I wouldn't worry about him if I were you," Reuben said. "He can take care of himself."

That night, Frost told his wife that he had an idea. Why didn't she go to see Byron Hayden, the owner of Bright Lights? Perhaps, unlike Robyn Vandermeer and Miss Boyle, he could supply some useful—or at least tangible—information about the elusive Pace Padgett.

"I have a sneaking feeling our gumshoe friends didn't get as much out of Hayden as a social butterfly like you might— a charming social butterfly, I mean. The police have probably scared him to death and made him tongue-tied."

"I'll call him tomorrow morning. We haven't had a dinner party in ages. There's no time like the present to plan one."

"Just what I was thinking."

Byron Hayden's ever growing catering business operated out of a basement kitchen-office on East Fifty-fourth Street. The Frosts had used the Bright Lights agency several times with success ever since it had first been recommended to them by Robyn Vandermeer. It was not cheap to hire Bright Lights, but the food it prepared was always good, and less trendily aberrant than that of many of its showy competitors, and the service was impeccable.

After lunch the next day the caterer was waiting in response to Cynthia's call; he sat down with her at a butcher-block table amid an array of large-size cooking pots and pans. Hayden was now in his forties and slowly losing the battle to keep the button-faced cuteness that had won him his fame as a juvenile actor. With wrinkles and jowls threatening, his manner had become less grown-up and more adolescent, as if to compensate for what was happening physically.

Cynthia and Byron compared calendars and decided that Bright Lights could do a dinner for twenty on May first. "A May Day dinner is a fabulous idea, Cynthia. It reminds me of the old rhyme . . . Oh, it's too dirty to tell you," he said, giggling.

"I'm a grown woman, Byron."

"Oh, all right. It's very silly. 'Hey, hey the first of May! Outdoor, um, screwing begins today.'"

"Sorry to disappoint you, Byron. Our guests will be charming, but I'm afraid they're a little too sedate—or a little too old—for fun in the grass."

"Oh, Cynthia, you're a sketch. You really are."

Hayden was prepared to discuss the menu for the May Day fete at length; Cynthia made her decisions quickly in order to get to her real business, which she casually introduced, once the food was picked.

"Byron, what do you know about Pace Padgett, the waiter you sent the night Tobias Vandermeer died?"

"I forgot. You were there, weren't you? I read that. It must have been *gruesome*."

"It was."

"Poor Cynthia! As for Pace Padgett, I'm sorry I ever heard the name."

"I gather he's disappeared. What happened, exactly?"

"Well, he came in here about, oh, a year ago, looking for work. He said he was an actor—my dear, who isn't?—not having too much luck, and wanted something to tide him over. He said he'd had experience with Marvelous Meals, my biggest competitor—all that icky California food. Naturally, I didn't want to call them to check up—they're *appalling* people, Cynthia—so I tried him out on a couple of big charity jobs. Mrs. Fastner's birthday dance at the Met was one of them. Were you there?"

"No, Byron. We don't travel in those circles."

"Too bad. It was *fabulous*. The flowers! I've never seen such flowers! Baskets and baskets—"

"Byron, what about Padgett?" Cynthia interrupted, eager to keep Hayden on the subject.

"Oh, okay. He worked the Fastner dance and two other parties and was just fine. I was glad to have another reliable name for my list.

"He was different from the other boys, Cynthia. Most of them want you to believe they're so busy in show business that you have to call and call and call to get them. And then they act as if they're doing me a big favor by working, when *I* know the only money most of them earn is right here. Padgett wasn't like that. He used to come in and ask what was available. You didn't have to chase him."

"Did he ever ask to work for the Vandermeers?"

'You know, Cynthia, I can't honestly say. He might have. I'm sure he knew we did her work, with all the delicious publicity we always got for the READ ball. I do remember that he was here one day when we were trying to get some-one—just a server—for Robyn. She'd requested Raymond, one of our best—and absolutely dreamy-looking, Cynthia, *dreamy*—but he said he couldn't do it. I remember being upset—Raymond was so ungrateful—and Padgett said he'd take the job. So I said to myself, why not?

"Anyway, he got along *famously* with Robyn. She always asked for him after that. He did her reading club dinners . . ."

"That I know."

"And last fall, for the ball, Robyn had a real house party for about three days. It was wild for us—we did the whole thing. She had a houseful of Eurotrash, if you'll excuse the expression. All those contessas and principessas and barons that she'd known in Europe and brought over to dress up the ball. Padgett worked the whole thing, for which I was very grateful."

"How about his disappearance, Byron?"

"He vanished into thin air. A ghost. Everything about him turned out to be phony. The social security number he gave me was somebody else's. He must have pulled it out of a hat. The police told me the number he used turned out to belong to a schoolteacher on an Indian reservation in New Mexico. Can you imagine? He had a post-office box for his mail—not that he ever lived at the real address he gave us—and if you called him on the phone you got an answering service—not the answering machine most actors have.

"Now he's gone," Hayden concluded. "And good riddance."

"That's quite a story."

"Cynthia, do you think he—he killed Tobias? I'd never forgive myself if he did."

"Anything's possible, Byron. All I can say is, if he turns up, call the police. And please don't send him around on May Day. I don't want Reuben falling over the way Tobias did."

Byron Hayden laughed nervously all the way to the door as he showed Cynthia out.

SHERMAN DEYBOLD

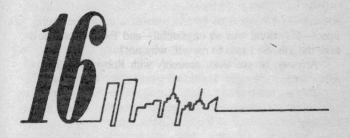

IT WAS THE IDES OF MARCH, AND TEN DAYS HAD GONE BY since Tobias' death. Sitting at home in the late afternoon, Frost turned on the local television news. The day's lead stories were two murders: the rape-slaying of a young Wall Street secretary in her Lower East Side apartment the night before and a predawn rubout of a "major" crack dealer in Harlem.

Depressing enough in themselves, these murders meant, Frost was certain, that the police would have still less time for the Vandermeer case. This realization left him immobilized. What could he do? How could he unravel that Sunday night's events? He stared at the books that lined the walls of his library, then idly watched the passers-by on the street below his window. Finally he fixed his gaze on his new computer. Could it help?

He knew from past experience that seemingly unrelated facts and impressions had a way of coming together in revealing ways. He knew, too, that his own memory was not what it once had been—pretty damn good, yes, but there were notable lapses, like the failure to tell Springer and Mattocks about the drink he had poured for Tobias.

What if he put everything he had learned on the machine? And added in his own perceptions and opinions? Might not a solution burst forth, if not now, then at a later time when there was more information in hand (though Frost, for the life of him, couldn't imagine what this new information might be)?

It was a worth a try, he concluded, and booted up his PC.

An hour later, Cynthia found him typing away earnestly at his Compac.

"What are you up to now?" she asked.

"I'm making an index of everything we know concerning Tobias' death—and about Tobias, and Robyn, and Wayne Givens, and Pace Padgett and everyone else connected with this mess. And a chronology of events, past and present."

Reuben seemed so enthusiastic about his new project that Cynthia left him to go and prepare supper. Later, at the dining-room table, he seemed discouraged.

"So far it's a jumble. Nothing connects up to anything else."

"I think it's a fine idea, Reuben."

"We'll see," he said dubiously.

Reuben worked at his "index" off and on for the next few days, feeding into his computer a miscellany of facts as they occurred to him. He was not pleased with the result; as far as he could tell, all he had done was assemble a hodgepodge that simply did not fall into any clear pattern. "Garbage in, garbage out," he told Cynthia, who urged him not to give up.

As he read over the electronic file he had created, Frost realized that a significant gap existed concerning his knowledge of Sherman Deybold, who was on both his "upstairs" and "downstairs" lists. He had put down such details as Deybold's cheating at the reading club meetings and Tobias' shouting at him before he died, but they didn't add up to very much. How could he fill in the gap? He searched his mental index of names and decided that Wilkes Mobeley, the auctioneer, might be able to help. He called him and made an appointment to see him first thing Monday morning.

Wilkes Mobeley had made a recent splash around Manhattan as the very visible head of Hawkins & Co., an art auction house that had begun in its small way to challenge the giants, Sotheby's and Christie's. Through an energetic public relations apparatus, glossy ads and a subtly xenophobic appeal to American collectors, it had attracted attention, and the quality of the works it offered for sale at auction was steadily improving.

Hawkins' chief executive was a cheerful, outgoing forty-year-old who had bounced around the New York art scene from the time he received his Master of Fine Arts degree from Yale, writing for little magazines, dealing privately in contemporary art and then taking over at Hawkins. He was a member of the Gotham (a "youth" movement a few years earlier had produced a dozen or so members under forty, including Mobeley), where Frost had met him over lunch at the common table.

Mobeley had responded willingly when Frost called him, and now Frost, in mid-morning, was sitting across from the younger man in Hawkins' antique-filled quarters on Seventy-ninth Street.

"So what's this hush-hush matter?" Mobeley asked, running his hand through his poorly cut hair. (Frost was convinced Mobeley went to a cheap barber, not out of stinginess, but to get an unstyled haircut that looked distinctly boyish.)

"I didn't mean to overdramatize it, Wilkes. I'm trying, on a more-or-less confidential basis, to get a line on Sherman Deybold. I'm going to impose on our friendship and not tell you why, unless you insist."

"Maybe someday you'll be able to tell me?"

"Perhaps."

"I'm intrigued, but I won't press you. What do you want to know about him?"

"Anything regarding his character, his business dealings, that sort of thing."

"Well, he's queer, for starters. You knew that already."

"Yes, I'm even acquainted with his friend."

"Michael?"

"Yes."

"Anyway, being queer's no obstacle in the world Sherman

travels in. May even be a help. But you didn't come here to find out that he's gay.''

''No.''

''You also know, I'm sure, the kind of work he deals in. Dutch genre painting. The kind of art you used to be able to buy for twenty-five dollars a square yard and now pay six figures for. With the prices for Impressionist and modern works out of sight, it's coming into vogue with people who have an itch to collect but not enough money to compete with the South American drug dealers and the Japanese. Sherman's very adept at his business. He's got branch galleries in London and Amsterdam, where a lot of the stuff comes on the market. He's very smart, very knowledgeable. He's written a lot on Pieter de Hooch.

''You've got to hand it to him. He did the right thing at the right time. Started his gallery—the big one, I mean, not that trendy outpost downtown—oh, fifteen years ago. Started on a shoestring, I think, though he became friendly with a lot of rich collectors.''

''Like Tobias Vandermeer?''

''Yes. His biggest customer, I'm willing to bet. You've seen the collection. Some of it Tobias got at auction, but most of it was assembled by Sherman.''

''Is there any, um, scandal involving Deybold? Involving his art dealings, I mean.''

''That's a delicate question. He's not a member of the Art Dealers Association. They've a funny, exclusive bunch, and they do have standards. Not just anybody can get in. I have a feeling that they think he's just a little bit . . .''

''Untrustworthy?''

Mobeley considered Frost's characterization. ''Yes, I guess that's it.''

''I see he's been put up for the Gotham.''

''Not through any of my doing,'' Mobeley shot back.

''In other words, Wilkes, you find him slightly untrustworthy, too?''

''Reuben, you've trapped me. Look, I deal with Deybold all the time. He's started to give us business, so I don't want to knock a good customer.''

"I understand what you're saying. Let me add two things. There is an important reason why I'm asking, and I'll never reveal the source of anything you tell me."

"You're a gentleman, Reuben. So, okay. Besides, this is only the rawest suspicion. A guess on my part, really."

"I'm all ears."

"You may or may not be aware that one of the biggest, if not the biggest, gold mines for the sort of Dutch pictures Sherman deals in is the U.K. Lots and lots of them were bought generations ago for next to nothing. There are treasures in country houses all over England.

"You also probably know about British taxes. Even with Mrs. Thatcher's reforms, they're damn high. Death duties of forty percent, a capital gains rate of thirty-some. And you know about the Waverly Rules?"

"You've got me there."

"Those are the rules governing the export of U.K. art treasures. If a work is important artistically, worth more than thirty thousand pounds and imported into England more than fifty years ago, you have to apply for an export permit to take it back out. If the powers that be then find that the work is important enough, they can delay its export up to six months to give British museums a chance to match the purchase price. At best, it's a pain in the neck, and even if your application is granted you can be damned sure Inland Revenue will be around to collect the taxes you owe on the sale.

"With all these complications there's a temptation for Lord Hardup to do things differently," Mobeley went on. "Once he's decided to fiddle, this is what I think happens. He sells the work to our friend Deybold, taking in return a promissory note for the purchase price.

"Deybold, or his operative, then spirits the object out of the U.K. and parks it—not at the Deybold Gallery—that would be too dangerous in case the authorities ever started nosing around. He's got a legitimate business of his own in London to protect, after all. No, what he does is 'consign' the work to an obscure gallery somewhere, Switzerland maybe, and lets it sit for, say, three years. Then he 'buys' the work from the foreign dealer and has that dealer pay off the note Lord Hardup's holding, let's say to an account in Zurich.

"It's all very neat. Lord Hardup gets his money tax-free in Switzerland, his only risk being that Deybold might default on his note. And Deybold has the risk that what he's got parked will decline in value. But that's almost never happened, at least not yet.

"Then, to finish up, Sherman brings the painting to New York and puts in on the market, or puts it up for auction. If any questions are asked, he produces his bill of sale from the foreign gallery and an affidavit from them that they owned it for three years. Lord Hardup's name never gets revealed."

"You mentioned Switzerland. Could this fiddle, as you call it, be done in other countries as well?"

"Certainly. Anywhere. The further away the better, to make it tougher to ask questions. Australia would be perfect."

"I thought everybody was obsessed with 'provenance,' " Frost said, "wanting to be sure there's a chain of title going back to the original artist."

"Not really. For example, if somebody comes in here with a painting and says he owns it, that satisfies me, assuming there isn't anything fishy, and assuming I think the guy who brings it in is good for the sale price if it turns out to be a fake or he doesn't own it. Obviously I wouldn't touch it if there were anything suspicious. As for provenance, Reuben, you have to remember these works were painted in the sixteen-hundreds. A clear chain of title is difficult to put together and verify in the best of circumstances."

"I see. Very interesting. So we're not talking about stolen works, or fakes. Just 'hot' ones where taxes and import restrictions are avoided."

"That's right."

"Is this sort of thing common?"

"No, but it goes on more than you'd think. Deybold isn't unique," Mobeley said, no longer "supposing," Frost noticed, but speaking definitely.

"My impression is the rich everywhere are less willing to pay taxes than they used to be," he continued. "This can slip people over the line from what you lawyers call 'tax avoidance' into tax evasion. Let's say Sherman Deybold is profiting from a trend."

"This has been most instructive," Frost said as he prepared to leave Hawkins & Co. "And don't worry, I'll keep everything you told me in confidence."

"Good. I don't need either a slander suit or a lost customer."

Maybe Sherman Deybold *is* a prick, Reuben thought to himself when he was back on the street.

GRACIE

FROST ENTERED THE INFORMATION HE HAD GLEANED FROM
Mobeley in his "index," fighting off as he did so a feeling
that he was engaged in a pointless exercise. What he had
learned about Deybold was interesting, but he did not think
it advanced the cause much. What he really wanted to do
was talk to Bautista; the silence of the police was both puzzling and annoying. And Reuben could not suppress a mild
feeling of anxiety since, as far as he knew, he had not been
eliminated from the list of suspects.

For the first time in his life, he felt some compassion for
those waiting to be indicted or tried or sentenced. If he,
totally innocent, felt anxiety at a criminal process over which
he had no control, what must it be like for someone who was
guilty? He recalled having seen Ivan Boesky in a restaurant
shortly before his sentencing hearing and had found his os-
tentatious bonhomie unattractive, like so much else about
the man. But now he understood perhaps a little better why
the Boesky party had been a trifle too boisterous that evening.

As far as Reuben was concerned, one welcome side effect
of the inactivity had been a sharp drop in the interest in
Tobias' poisoning on the part of the newspapers and television. Even the murder of one of the city's richest men had a

news life, it seemed, only slightly longer than the supermarket shelf life for a quart of milk or perhaps a dozen eggs. There were too many new crimes of violence to warrant continued attention to Tobias by the press and, Frost was bitterly certain, by the police.

This sense of relief came to an abrupt end when his wife called him at lunchtime that Monday.

"Bad news," Cynthia told him. "You'd better go out and get *New York* magazine. There's a story on Tobias."

"Oh, God."

"Couldn't be worse. It's the cover story. 'Who Closed the Book on Tobias Vandermeer?' "

"What do they say?"

"You'll have to look at it. There are pictures of all the guests, including the two of us. And they had the *nerve* to use an old publicity still of me from my dancing days!"

Frost rushed to the newsstand, muttering to himself that this was not the ideal way to start the week. He tried to start reading the story on the street, but decided that he'd better wait until he was safe within his own library.

As Cynthia had told him, the story was illustrated with photographs: a drunken Tobias at a nightclub piano, taken years earlier; a staid Bachrach portrait of Robyn; and a motley assortment of pictures, arranged like a series of mug shots, of the members of the reading club, his own cropped from a *Women's Wear* shot taken at a black-tie benefit. "Is One of These a Killer?" the headline over the photographs read.

The article, by one Anita Fiddler, was a purple one, starting with its breathless lead:

"An unanswered question at the end of *Vanity Fair*, William Makepeace Thackeray's masterful comic novel about mid-19th century English society, is whether the book's amoral heroine, Becky Sharp, murdered her old friend, Joseph Sedley, to collect his insurance.

"Last March 5, the socially prominent members of society matron Robyn Vandermeer's reading club, gathered to discuss *Vanity Fair*, found themselves the unwelcome subjects of another unanswered question. . . ."

Frost had to steel himself before reading on. At least Ms. Fiddler seemed to be literate, he consoled himself. The consolation did not last long, as he found an "anonymous police source" quoted as saying, "It's hard to believe, but the victim may have been poisoned by a respectable member of the city's upper crust." Springer, Frost thought. Damn Springer.

Ordinarily Reuben might have enjoyed the reference to him as a "powerful Wall Street superlawyer" or (for different reasons) the description of Cynthia as the "formidable arts czarina." But in this context he did not.

Hastily finishing the article, which had nothing new to say, he tossed the offending magazine aside and sat with his head in his hands. "This bad dream has got to end," he muttered. He felt very isolated and lonely as he realized there was no one to whom he could direct his *sotto voce* command except himself.

Robyn Vandermeer was on the telephone to Reuben within hours of the appearance of the *New York* piece, panicked at the thought of appearing at Gracie Mansion the next day to receive her award for READ from the Mayor.

"I don't know what to do, Reuben," she said. "That dreadful girl and those sly references to Becky Sharp! The most manipulative woman in all of fiction, and she compared her to me!"

Frost tried to calm her down, saying—quite correctly—that there had been no one-to-one comparison between Thackeray's heroine and Robyn.

"I agree that the article's appalling," Frost told her. "But Ms. Fiddler pointed the finger at each of us, not just you. It was a silly piece of work and I'd ignore it."

"Oh, that's easy for you to say, when *I'm* the one that has to go on public view at Gracie Mansion tomorrow afternoon."

"Robyn, we discussed that last week. It would be a great mistake to cancel out now. How many people have been invited? Two hundred?"

"Around that."

"It would look terrible, as if you had something to conceal. You've got to be brave and go ahead with it. Summon up all your dignity—which is considerable, my dear—and brazen it out.''

"But you know Norman. He always wants to milk every event for the maximum publicity.''

"Yes, yes, the Prince of Photo-Ops,'' Reuben said, repeating the derisive nickname that he had heard recently from some journalist friends.

"It will be a circus. Every sensational reporter in the City will be there.''

"Let me talk to Norman. He certainly has to understand the circumstances. If it's a circus, let me at least see if we can't confine it to one ring.''

"Reuben, you're wonderful. I only agreed to accept this stupid award to get some publicity for READ—not to give the tabloids a field day with a new Becky Sharp.''

"I'll do my best.''

"Bless you, Reuben. *Please* make Norman understand.''

Frost had always gotten on with the Mayor. He had taken on a number of tricky, unpublicized assignments for him over the years, some involving hard dog work, others simply consisting of frank and objective (if not necessarily welcome) advice. And he had never asked for anything in return, his reward always having been the totally intangible one of doing something of possible use for the City that he so much loved.

He had never been certain whether Norman, in fact, remembered his name, though others assured him that there was nothing personal in this; the Mayor didn't remember anyone's name. (There was even the apocryphal story, told to him by another reporter, of the time that Norman, in his early campaigning days, shook his own mother's hand on a street corner without recognizing her.)

Frost made a late-morning call to City Hall, leaving his name and number in the hope the Mayor would call back during one of the ''phone breaks'' Frost knew he took between appointments. He was gratified when Norman was on the line within the hour.

"Reuben, how's by you?" the Mayor said, employing the ungrammatically distinctive greeting that had become his trademark.

"I'm fine, Mr. Mayor."

"What can I do for my old friend?"

Frost explained Robyn Vandermeer's fears concerning the next day's ceremony.

"That's easy. I'll talk to Bob Twitt, my press secretary. We'll limit the press to the City Hall crowd. Most of them are too lazy to make it uptown to Gracie anyway."

"You're sure that's right when Robyn is the featured attraction?"

"Yeah, you've probably got something there. Okay, we'll let everybody in for the ceremony, but that will be it. No questions, no press conference. Just photographs of the presentation." The Prince of Photo-Ops seemed pleased with his solution.

"Robyn will be grateful. She's under a great deal of strain, as you can imagine. The uncertainty of not knowing who killed her husband is pretty terrible."

"I'm sure it is. The police doing okay?"

Frost leaped at his unexpected opportunity. "I can't honestly say, Mr. Mayor. Those of us involved—of which I'm unfortunately one—haven't heard from them in the last few days. The officers assigned seem conscientious enough, but I don't know how many other things they've got on their plates."

"Well, if there's anything I can do, just call me."

"Fine."

"I'll see you tomorrow. Bye-bye."

It was ironic that Norman, that most urban of mayors, lived in what had once been a farm mansion, built by Archibald Gracie at the end of the eighteenth century on land that may well have belonged originally to the Vandermeers.

"If they can't get photographed at the White House, they want to do it at Gracie," Norman had once told Reuben, speaking of his fellow members in the National Mayors' Conference.

The residence, newly and tastefully restored through the generosity of private donors, was an attractive oasis, preserving the feeling of a country estate amid a dense urban environment. Only implacable adversaries of the Mayor refused invitations to it (a circumstance that did not occur often; Norman, the tough but highly sensitive Mayor, knew who his enemies were, and they were simply never asked there).

Reuben and Cynthia arrived separately for the Vander-meer ceremony, he from home, she from her office. He was delighted that it was a fine spring day, and the reception preceding the six o'clock ceremony was outside on the splen-did lawn, looking out toward the East River. The inside rooms were somewhat small and confining; the outdoor expanse was much more inviting.

Being the veteran of many of these receptions, Reuben commanded up a martini from the bartender, knowing that the liquor bar was reserved for the select guests at the pre-ceremony party; the unlucky hordes at the reception after-ward would be limited to soda water and, most likely, a truly lamentable New York State white wine.

Strolling the lawn, Frost was stopped by Wayne and Bar-bara Givens.

"Liked your picture in *New York*," Givens said.

"Thanks. Yours was pretty flattering, too," Frost said.

"Reuben, when is this going to end? It's very embarrass-ing. And Barbara's a nervous wreck."

Mrs. Givens gave every evidence of living up to her hus-band's description, looking pale and smoking nervously.

"I wish I knew. Heard from the police lately?"

"Not since last week, when they wanted to know about the waiter at Robyn's party. Were they after you on that?"

"Oh, yes. Did you have anything to tell them?"

"Nothing. Except that I think he did it," Givens said. "Why don't they have an all-points alarm out for him?"

"They probably do. But why do you think he was the murderer?"

"Who else could it have been?" Givens demanded.

"How about the lady on the porch steps?" Reuben asked, as he directed his listeners' attention to Robyn's arrival. Again

on the arm of Bill Kearney, she came down to the lawn with
almost a regal sweep. She was dressed in black, but high-
fashion black, not grim widow's weeds. She was wearing an
elegant black knit suit—Chanel or Missoni? Frost wondered—
and black stockings and shoes, the dark effect relieved only by
her pearls and the small gold buckles on her shoes.

"That's rather a nervy question," Givens countered.

"Wayne, anything anyone says at this point is going to be
considered 'nervy' or worse. I asked the question to show
how hopeless the case is." Except for my lingering suspicion
about you, he could have added.

"There's the Mayor!" Barbara said, almost with excite-
ment, as Norman made his entrance and kissed Robyn. He
was handed a glass of white wine (an adequate Macon Village, unlike the swill that would be available later), which he
carried with him, but did not drink, as he "did" the lawn.

"The fix is in," he said, as he came up beside Reuben, in
a low voice the Givenses could not hear. "Photos when I
present the award to the honoree, and that's it."

"Excellent, Mr. Mayor," Frost replied. "Robyn will be
pleased."

Moments later, completing his circle of the guests, Norman cupped his hands around his mouth and shouted out,
"Okay, everybody inside! Time to go inside!"

Undignified though it was, his barked-out order had its
effect, and those on the lawn dutifully went up the porch
steps, through the main entrance to the mansion, and on
down the narrow corridor that led to the area where public
functions were held.

The Susan Wagner wing, the mansion's meeting hall
named for the late and well-liked wife of a former mayor,
was now arranged for the ceremony, with rows of chairs
facing a podium in front of the handsome antique fireplace.
As those from the garden entered, they found the room half
filled with others not privileged enough to be invited to the
preliminary lawn party.

As Reuben looked around, he was startled to find that the
audience seemed to resemble very closely the one that had
attended Tobias' funeral, with a sprinkling of political fig-

ures and their wives whom the Mayor was most likely culti-
vating at the moment.

Reuben and Cynthia sat on folding chairs midway back in
the room. They had deliberately taken places off to the side
to avoid what was sure to be a crush of cameramen rushing
down the center aisle, once they were admitted through the
wide doors at the back.

A string quartet of students, recruited from one of the
City's music schools, played on the other side as the guests
took their seats in the airy, yellow-walled room. The Mayor
and Robyn, arm in arm, came in last, to warm applause.

The program began with testimonials to READ from three
diverse pupils who had learned to read under its auspices: a
young Hispanic teenager; a black woman, not much older than
the boy, who identified herself as a former welfare mother now
employed by the city's Human Services Administration; and a
thin, rugged white man in his sixties, a building superintendent
who told the crowd of his decision to reveal his lifelong secret
of illiteracy in order to enlist in the READ program that
"changed my life." A cynic might have found the parading of
these speakers exploitative, but the three seemed both proud
and eager to tell their stories and seemed startled, but pleased,
at the enthusiastic applause they received.

The Chancellor of the City's secondary schools spoke next,
praising Robyn for her efforts "in giving hope to young people
where we, with our slashed budgets, could not." He looked
pointedly at the Mayor as he referred to. "slashed budgets,"
but got a fixed, perhaps even frozen, smile in return.

Then the Mayor spoke, in a manner that came as close to
approaching eloquence as he ever did. Robyn's "pioneering"
and "determination" in advancing the "unglamorous" cause
of literacy were lauded, consolation for her "recent tragic be-
reavement" was given and the Certificate of Appreciation—no
Steuben apple, after all—was produced and presented.

Robyn, who had been facing the audience and staring into
the middle distance, a sad smile on her face, rose and accepted the certificate and a kiss from the Mayor amid tumult.
The spectators gave her a standing ovation, almost drowned
out by the click and whirr of cameras and the cries of "just

one more!'' Mercifully no one attempted to shout questions at her, and the photographers, duty done, retreated behind the rear doors from whence they had come.

Her remarks were brief, stylish and moving. Her chin thrust elegantly forward, she thanked ''my old friend Norman'' not for honoring her but for the implied recognition of READ and its work.

''It has been a struggle, raising the public's consciousness about the terrible curse of illiteracy,'' she said. ''I salute my colleagues who have made READ what I immodestly say is a force for good in this City. And I salute each and every volunteer who has given time, and energy, and love, to the cause of lifting that scourge for adults and children everywhere, to the cause of bringing the gift of literacy to them.

''Those of us who founded READ were determined to make better this City that we so much love. Our gift was made joyously and gratefully. And now this afternoon you have given me something back—something that at this moment I badly need. The gift of sustaining love and affection that I know will strengthen my resolve to forget the horror of recent days and go forward with you to making this a better, more civilized New York.''

Robyn sat down as everyone else in the room rose, giving her another standing round of applause. As the only one seated, she looked vulnerable and alone as she wiped a tear from her eye.

Reuben and Cynthia looked at each other sympathetically as they stood and applauded. Whatever suspicions they may have harbored about the new widow were forgotten for the moment in the wave of sentiment that swept over the audience.

When the applause died, the Mayor invited the assemblage for ''refreshments'' in the main part of the mansion and, if they chose, to take tours of ''the house where your Mayor lives.'' Then he led the guest of honor out the side door, the other spectators following in their wake, screened by a watchful aide from the City Hall press office to keep out any reporters.

An informal receiving line had started in the living room by the time the Frosts got there. They both waited their turn to greet and embrace Robyn, Reuben whispering a ''well done'' in her ear after kissing her cheek, and a second "well done'' into the Mayor's ear as they shook hands.

Frost noticed, as predicted, that the liquor bottles had disappeared, replaced by the Empire State plonk. He was ready to leave and go to dinner.

"You want to take the tour?'' he asked Cynthia.

"Reuben, for heaven's sake. The only thing to see upstairs, as you well know, is Norman's exercise bicycle, and I can do without that.''

"Then let's go eat.''

As he nudged Cynthia toward the door, he met the Givenses again.

"What are you doing for dinner? Want to join us?'' Wayne asked.

"Sure,'' Reuben said, looking at Cynthia for confirmation. "Nothing fancy, and not too late.''

"Should we see if Robyn wants to go, too?'' Cynthia asked.

"She's going to be stuck here for a good while,'' Givens said. "And I'm sure the Mayor must be taking her out.''

"Let's make sure. Okay?'' Reuben asked.

"Of course, of course,'' Givens answered.

The Mayor, Bill Kearney and Robyn were standing together in a corner of the living room. Reuben went back and took Robyn aside. They had a brief whispered conversation, ending with Robyn's poking Reuben with her elbow and laughing.

"The Mayor is entertaining Robyn and Bill here for dinner,'' Frost reported when he returned.

"What was the big joke?'' Givens asked.

"Oh, I warned Robyn that I'd just read that Norman has a new cook, some stray Hungarian, and I said I hoped she liked goulash. She said she'd be grateful for food of any kind since both her Mr. Obuchi and that Miss Boyle have Tuesday afternoon off.''

"She may get the Chinese dinner we were joking about, ah, that night, after all,'' Givens said.

"Ycch. A Chinese dinner prepared by a Hungarian chef,'' Cynthia said.

"If Robyn's taken care of, let's go,'' Givens said.

No harm in looking over a suspect, Reuben thought, as the foursome went out the front door of Gracie.

THE FROSTS AND THE GIVENSES PAUSED BY THE POLICE CU-
pola outside Gracie Mansion to consider the early-evening
question asked daily by thousands of Manhattanites: Where
should we eat?

"There's always Elaine's," Reuben offered. "It's the
neighborhood restaurant up here."

"Can we get in?" Barbara Givens asked.

"That's no problem," Reuben said, having been a customer of Ms. Kaufman's bistro for almost twenty-five years.

"How about . . . No, Elaine's is fine," Wayne Givens
said.

"If you have another suggestion, speak up," Reuben said.

"No, no. I'll go for Elaine's. Haven't been there in a
while."

"I've only been there twice in my life," Barbara added.

"Let's go," Frost said, bringing the inconclusive debate
to an end. He led the group down the Gracie Mansion driveway and across toward Second Avenue.

As they walked, he realized that he had perhaps made a
gaffe. The Frosts had seen Dr. Givens at the restaurant several times but, Reuben now realized, always with a female
companion other than Barbara. In fact, now he knew where
he had seen the Bloemendael's Dr. Baxter before—at Elaine's

with her boss. (Givens, Reuben guessed, was undoubtedly a subscriber to the New York rake's old rule: Never take a woman not your wife to a romantic, dimly lit restaurant; always opt for one that is open, notorious and in the public eye.)

"I hope you can smoke at Elaine's," Barbara said as they walked toward their destination.

"Ha," Cynthia replied. "Elaine herself is a smoker and the only nonsmoking tables are somewhere down by the furnace."

"I thought the security guards were going to arrest me back there when I lit a cigarette on the Mayor's lawn. I practically had to swallow the butt when I finished."

"Poor Norman," Cynthia said. "He smoked like a chimney when we first knew him. Now he's one of the fanatical converted."

Once seated at the restaurant with drinks in front of them (neither Elaine nor her headwaiter, Jack, having blinked with shock when Givens appeared with his wife), they dissected the Gracie Mansion ceremony.

"Norman was downright eloquent," Cynthia said. "That business about 'Mrs. Literacy' made poor Robyn sound a little like Miss Liberty. Otherwise it was very gracious and generous. The man *can* be gracious and generous if he wants to be."

"I agree," Wayne said. "So was Robyn."

"I felt so sorry for her," Barbara said.

"Sorry? She loved it," her husband answered. "That woman's had some trip, from being a bartender at the Blue Heaven to an award from the Mayor at Gracie."

"Wayne, what are you talking about?" Cynthia asked.

The Frosts had both come to life, startled by his statement. Givens enjoyed the reaction he had gotten.

"Let's order and I'll tell you."

"What's good to eat?" Barbara asked.

"The squid salad and the veal chop are unassailable," Reuben said.

Frost spoke with such authority that all the others followed his advice, though he himself ordered a shrimp cocktail and a steak.

"Surely you know all about Robyn's past," Wayne said, once the ordering was completed.

"I don't believe we do," Reuben answered. "We'd never met her till she became involved with Tobias, back in sixty-three or sixty-four. She was the Principessa Montefiore del'Udine then. I just found out the other day there'd been a Chicago period before the Principe, when she was married to someone named Bernie Weldin. She also admitted to me that she had been married in her 'youth,' presumably before Weldin, but we don't know anything more. Or even where she's from."

"You've come to the right place," Givens said. "I happen to know everything about her early life."

"Tell all," Cynthia said.

"I don't see any reason why not to. It's quite a story. I'm just amazed you don't know it."

"Robyn's never dwelt very much on her past."

"Well, that's true. Maybe you'll see why when I tell you about it."

"Will a bottle of wine help the flow?" Reuben asked. Without waiting for an answer, he ordered a bottle of "Riserva," the house shorthand for a passable Chianti.

"Okay," Givens said, sipping from a glass of the wine. "You know, I'm sure, that I'm a Hoosier. Lafayette, Indiana. I lived there until I went down the road to Bloomington to college at I.U. What you obviously don't know is that Robyn—she was then Robyn Mayes—grew up in Lafayette, too. I didn't know her then—she's a good ten years older than I am—but my sister did, and most of what I'm going to tell you I learned from her. They were in high school together, back in the late forties. My sister was a couple of years older, but she and Robyn were good friends. Basketball was the big thing out there—still is—and both my sister and Robyn were cheerleaders, traveling around the state in the winter in one of those orange-colored school buses, first to the regular games, then to the playoffs.

"Robyn and her family were as poor as anybody in Lafayette. Not as bad off as the kind of crack families we see these days, but pretty poor. Robyn's father was a garage mechanic who was unemployed most of the time. An itinerant French Canadian with some Indian blood, my sister says. Damn good-looking—I did meet him a couple of times. Robyn got her looks from him, her complexion from her mother. Her mother was a waitress around the local restaurants—blond, brassy and blowsy, not at all like the Principessa Montefiore or 'Mrs. Literacy.' "

"Who gets the shrimps cocktail?" interrupted the latest addition to Elaine's polyglot staff of waiters. The "shrimps cocktail" and the squid salads were quickly distributed once Reuben owned up to ordering the shrimp.

"Anyway," Givens went on, "I don't think Robyn was much of a scholar. Most who followed the basketball team weren't—there wasn't time. My sister always said there were two kinds of cheerleader, though today there's probably only one. Type One was the sweet young virgin. Sweet and full of enthusiasm, but not ready to go 'all the way,' as they used to put it so elegantly. That's what my sister was—at least I think she was. Then there were the Type Two girls who cheered the players both on and off the court. Robyn definitely was of the latter persuasion, letting the boys probe around in the back rows of the team bus or 'giving it away' in the backseats of secondhand Chevrolets.

"She ended up 'going steady' with the captain of the basketball team, apparently a nice guy but not the smartest one God ever created. I don't know what it was like where you grew up, but 'going steady,' for a Type Two girl, usually meant a prodigious amount of screwing. She and her gallant captain probably knew, or cared, as much about birth control as they did about nuclear physics. They were among the unlucky ones and Robyn got pregnant her senior year in high school. This being 1949 in Lafayette, there was no question of an abortion, and Robyn and her boyfriend were forced by two indignant sets of parents to get married. My sister says the marriage was completely loveless. The only attraction between the two had been sex, and after Robyn's pregnancy even that was gone.

"The irony was that Robyn didn't have the baby after all. She had some kind of infection and had a miscarriage. Rumor had it that it was a complication from venereal disease, but that may have been just gossip. As a high school dropout, she didn't have much of a future—waitressing like her mother, or maybe hairdressing if she could scrape up the money to go to a school of cosmetology, I believe they call it, in Indianapolis.

"This is where Denise, my sister, got into the act," Givens went on. "She was an exception, a Type One girl who always did well in school, had a lot of ambition, and was quite a talented artist. She packed her bags as soon as she finished high school and took the next Greyhound to New York. She was lucky and landed a part-time job at an advertising agency that supported her through a night course at Parsons. She did real well and was soon working full time at the old Benton and Bowles agency."

"Wayne, you have to eat," Barbara Givens admonished, pointing to her husband's untouched veal chop.

"Sorry, I got carried away," he said.

"Please go on," Reuben said. "I'm fascinated. But, yes, do eat as well."

Dr. Givens continued between bites. "Anyway, Denise came home for the holidays, Thanksgiving or Christmas, I forget which, and ran into Robyn. Robyn Schenk then, though she was about to leave her husband and discard the 'Schenk.' Robyn told my sister her tale of woe, and my sister, not realizing how lucky she had been to get the job in New York without any experience or training, urged Robyn to come to the City and invited her to share her apartment.

"Robyn jumped at the idea and came here about two weeks later. She was all of twenty, I would guess, and had no talent or experience—just her wholesome Hoosier good looks, which turned out not to be enough to get a 'clean' job in an office. Somehow she ended up as a bartender—not a waitress, a girl bartender—at the Blue Heaven, on Fifty-second Street.

"I don't know whether you remember it. The Blue Heaven was quite a well-known jazz club, even though it was a bit

sleazy. Maybe not like the B-girl joints that lined Fifty-second
Street then, but I gather it wasn't all jazz music either—a
little hooking and some of the B-girl stuff. It was Tobias
Vandermeer's hangout. He was there all the time and was a
good enough customer that they couldn't turn him down when
he wanted to sit in at the piano.''

"Now wait a minute," Reuben interrupted. "What year
is this?''

"Oh, I'd say 1951, 1952.''

"And are you going to tell me that Tobias met Robyn
then?''

"Let me finish. The answer is yes. Tobias met the new
girl bartender and went utterly gaga, or so my sister says. It
didn't take much for Robyn to figure out that Tobias had a
lot of money to spend, and she went after him. My sister was
very put out. She didn't like waking up and finding Tobias
and Robyn shacked up in the living room. And she liked the
prospect of losing half the rent even less. She was sure they
were going to get married. Robyn couldn't talk about anything or anyone else.

"Then the ax fell. Tobias took Robyn home to Papa. Hendrik was polite enough to Robyn at their one meeting, but
afterward he exploded, informing Tobias in no uncertain
terms that if he chose to marry a bartender from the Blue
Heaven, he would be completely and irrevocably cut off—
both his allowance and his inheritance.

"That didn't leave Tobias much choice. He threw Robyn
over and never went back to the Blue Heaven again.''

"Are you sure about this?" Reuben pressed. "I know
something about their relationship and had always assumed
Robyn and Tobias had met in the early sixties for the first
time.''

"Wrong. They met at least ten years before that.''

"So what did Robyn do?" Cynthia asked.

"She bounced back, as you might expect. Picked up Bernie Weldin on a night out in New York and was married to
him within six weeks of being dumped by Tobias.''

"Did your sister keep up with her?''

"No, I don't believe Denise ever saw Robyn after she left

for Chicago. As my sister tells it, the only communication she ever had from her after that was a letter, just before the marriage to Tobias. My sister'd gone back to Lafayette by then. Robyn's letter said she knew Denise would be interested to hear that she'd landed Tobias at last.''

"I'll be damned. She's even more relentless than even *I* thought,'' Reuben said.

"She sure as hell is that. No trace of the innkeep in that lofty lady we saw an hour or so ago.''

"What about Tobias? How did he react after giving in to his father?''

"He called Denise a couple of times, to cry on her shoulder. Always drunk—more so than he had been when Robyn was around. Then my sister lost track of him, though she says she heard that not only had his drinking gotten worse but that he was wenching as if it were going out of style. Then he went off to Paris, and she went back home, and as they say on TV, that's it for tonight.''

"Quite a news broadcast,'' Reuben said.

"I had a hunch you'd like it. That's really why we asked you to dinner.''

"There's one thing I don't understand,'' Cynthia said. "If Hendrik was opposed to the marriage in the fifties, why wasn't he equally violent when she reappeared a decade later?''

"I've wondered about that,'' Givens said. "All I can guess is he never made the connection between the bartender and the Principessa. She'd undergone quite a transformation— look at her today—and, as I was told the story, he'd only met her once when she was in the bartender phase. And he would've been really ancient by the time she appeared a second time.''

"Amazing,'' Cynthia said.

Givens reached for the check, which had arrived, no one having ordered either dessert or coffee.

"No, no, I should pay this,'' Frost said. "With an entertainment charge for you thrown in. At least let's split it.''

This finally was the arrangement, and each of the two men sorted out bills to pay his share. While they were doing so, a couple from the "Siberia" (or bridge-and-tunnel) section of the restaurant approached the Frost table, unaware of Elaine's strict house rule that strangers do not go up to those (especially celebrities) not known to them.

"Dr. Wayne?" the middle-aged man said, holding his wife's hand for moral support.

Givens responded to his television moniker with an expectant smile.

"I just wanted to tell you how great your show is. We've got a teenage boy and a twelve-year-old girl and your advice about drugs has been a big help to us."

"So practical," the woman chimed in. "The kids really relate to you!"

"Why, thank you very much," Wayne responded, beaming.

"Could we . . ."

". . . have your autograph for the kids?" the woman said, finishing her husband's sentence.

Seeing what was going on, a flying squad of waiters appeared to enforce the house rule. Givens magnanimously waved them away.

"What should I write on?" he asked. The autograph seekers had not considered this problem. Givens asked for a menu, upsetting the waiter patrol further, signed it and handed it to the couple.

"Thanks, Dr. Wayne. We're much obliged," the man said as he steered his wife toward the door.

"My public," Wayne said wryly, though unquestionably he was pleased. "Unfortunately, I still have to pay half the check."

Outside the restaurant, the two couples briefly discussed logistics and decided it would be most convenient to take separate taxis home.

"Thanks again for the entertainment," Reuben said. "We ended up talking about the Vandermeers, but not the murder. That was a blessed relief. I'm afraid nothing you said got us closer to a solution, though."

"Did you expect that it would?" Dr. Givens answered.

* * *

"Did you really mean that?" Cynthia asked her husband, once they were in a taxi.

"Mean what?"

"That the things Wayne told us didn't get us any nearer to solving the . . . problem?" Cynthia said, refraining from using the word "murder" in the presence of the driver.

"I think we'd better wait till we get home."

"Why did you try to shut me up back there?" Cynthia demanded, once they were inside their front door.

"Look, my dear, our pictures are all over *New York* Magazine. I have no idea whether taxi drivers read it. They probably don't. Half of them can't read anyway. But I didn't think it was such a hot idea to talk in front of him, and have him running to Springer and Mattocks."

"I'm sorry, dear. What's the answer? Do you think Wayne's extraordinary story helps us any?"

"I don't know," Reuben answered, slumping wearily into a chair in the living room. "I'm of two minds about what he said."

"Yes?"

"We've known right along that Robyn is a determined lady. But the more we hear, her determination seems almost genetic, to the point where I'm about ready to believe she was steely enough to poison her husband. You agree?"

"Reluctantly, but yes."

"The other theory is pretty obvious."

"And it is?"

"That Wayne told us that tale so we *would* be more suspicious of Robyn. He admitted he'd sought us out for dinner so he could tell it."

"In other words, the more suspicious we are of Robyn the less likely we are to be suspicious of him?"

"Precisely."

DETETAILS

19

THE NEXT FRIDAY, CYNTHIA REMINDED HER HUSBAND THAT they were scheduled to leave for Rio de Janeiro in one week. For years their friends Alfredo and Luiza Herculano had been urging them to visit.

Alfredo was an entrepreneur in a country where it was not unusual for individuals, or at least individual families, to own their own banks. In Alfredo's case it was the large, prosperous and successful Banco Abrantes, S.A. Eager to hedge his bets against Brazilian inflation and potential upheaval, he had years earlier retained a group of American advisers to assist him in investing some of his massive wealth in the United States. On Citibank's recommendation, these advisers included Chase & Ward, and Reuben Frost in particular.

Frost had always treasured the relationship. Herculano was a generation younger than he was, but this was an asset rather than a detriment. Unlike the go-go financiers in the United States, who increasingly preferred to take advice from Yuppies like themselves, rather than venerable figures like Frost, Herculano was delighted to have access to the wisdom and astute counsel of an older lawyer.

As so often happened, what had begun as a narrow professional engagement—to help Herculano buy a significant minority interest in a medium-sized New York bank—broad-

165

ened into a rapport in which the younger man consulted the wise lawyer on many matters, ranging well beyond technical points of American law.

Their personal friendship blossomed as well, and Reuben and Cynthia became avuncular confidants of the younger Alfredo and Luiza. The Frosts always socialized with the Brazilians when they came to New York, and over the years had also met up with them in places as diverse as Hong Kong and Portofino.

Where Reuben had never been was Rio—Cynthia had stopped there briefly back in her ballerina days—despite endless importunings. Somehow the scheduling never worked out, though both of the Frosts very much wanted to see their friends in their home territory.

Finally Alfredo Herculano, on a visit to New York the previous January, had invited the Frosts once again.

"After so many, many years, it is ridiculous you have not come," he had said to them both. "I put it to you, you'd better come while you can."

It was uncertain whether Alfredo's admonition was directed at the Frosts' age or deteriorating political conditions in Brazil. It had its effect, however, and Reuben and Cynthia had agreed to come for a week at the end of March.

"You remember, there's a little problem about leaving the City. That young Perry Mason in the DA's office said we couldn't leave without his permission."

"That's why I'm reminding you," Cynthia replied. "Everything else is in order, so it would be a shame to be held up by your officious friend."

"I hate the idea of even talking to him," Reuben said, groaning. "He's do damnably naive that if I even mention Brazil he'll go crazy. He'll have us in preventive detention. I'm sure Brazil to him is just a likely getaway spot without an extradition treaty, and that he's incapable of understanding that someone might actually have friends there. Why couldn't we be traveling to Russia or China, or some less sensitive place like that?"

"What happens if we just go?"

"I honestly don't know. I can't believe we're on any sort

of watch list so that we'd be stopped at Kennedy Airport. That isn't the point. I gave him my word that I'd notify him if we left town, so I have to do it.''

"Why don't you go to the top and call Larry Vickers?" Cynthia asked, referring to New York County District Attorney.

Reuben groaned again. "If I were just an ordinary citizen, I could. But I was on Larry's finance committee in all three of his campaigns. Normally that's supposed to give you 'access,' as the euphemism goes. But Larry's so straight, he's apt to treat a phone call from me like a bribe offer.''

"Oh, come, Reuben, don't exaggerate. You're not really asking a favor. All you'd be doing is keeping your promise and telling them you're going away for a week."

"You're right, as always. But I will call Vickers. At least he's a grown-up.''

Someone had once said that Lawrence Vickers, the veteran District Attorney, was so zealously incorruptible that if the necessity arose he would prosecute his own mother. Or, more exactly, would stand aside because of the conflict of interest and let another lawyer prosecute her. Reuben Frost did not look forward to confronting this rectitude, even on the telephone.

Eventually he braced himself and made the call. "Hello, Larry, this is Reuben Frost.''

"Hello, Reuben. Nice to talk to you. What can I do for you?''

"How's Jeannette?" Frost inquired, either not hearing or at least not answering the District Attorney's question.

"She's fine, thanks. And Cynthia?''

"Very well. She sends her regards.''

"Thank you. Now, what can I do for you?''

Frost realized he had clumsily delayed as long as he could. "Larry, you know about Tobias Vandeemer's murder?" he said, perceiving too late that this was a particularly dumb question.

"Of course, Reuben. It is after all, the most important unsolved murder case in the City.''

"And you may know that I was, ah, present when Tobias died."

"Yes. I've been fully briefed on the case."

"When I talked to your Mr. Munson the night of the murder he requested me to notify him if I had any plans to leave town."

"Yes?"

"Well, Cynthia and I want to go to Brazil."

"Really?"

"We have friends there and we'll be gone a week."

"I see. Have you told Joe Munson this?"

"No. I guess I wanted to check with you to make sure there was no problem."

"Reuben, I can't imagine there is. You're obviously, uh, important to the Vandermeer investigation, but I don't see it as a problem. You should call Munson, though. He's the ADA in charge."

Was this a reprimand or advice? Frost could not tell. It was clear he had failed in his effort to avoid talking to Munson.

"Many thanks, Larry, I appreciate it." Frost said, though he was not sure what it was he appreciated.

"Any time, Reuben. Nice to talk to you."

Bowing to the inevitable, Frost called Munson, only to find that he was in court. He returned Reuben's call later in the day.

"Mr. Munson, when we talked the night of Tobias Vandermeer's death . . ."

"I remember it. I questioned you in the Vandermeer kitchen." "Questioned," not "talked with," Reuben noted.

"Yes, that's right. At any rate, you said that I should notify you if I had plans to leave the City."

"That's correct."

"Thus the purpose of my call. My wife and I have had plans for some time to visit old friends in Rio de Janeiro, starting a week from today."

"You're going to Brazil?"

"We are planning to. I wanted to notify you in accordance with our understanding."

"When did you make these plans?"

"Oh, in early February, I would say."

"Not since Mr. Vandermeer's death?"

"No, indeed."

"You didn't mention this when I brought up the subject of travel at the Vandermeers'."

(You young hotshot, Reuben thought to himself.)

"No, that is quite accurate. Can I say in my defense that I had other things on my mind at the time?" Frost said coolly, reining in his temper.

"I understand. As I recall, you were a bit confused that night."

(You little bastard! Frost shouted inwardly.)

"How long will you be gone?" Munson asked.

"One week. Seven days."

"Where are you staying?"

Frost hesitated. "I'm not sure."

"You're traveling to Brazil, but you're not sure where?"

"We're going to Rio. Rio de Janeiro. To visit some old friends named Herculano. People I've known for twenty years," Frost said, wanting to say "People I've know since before you were born." "I only hesitate because I'm not certain if we'll be staying at their home or if we'll be put up in a hotel."

"I see, I see," Munson said, slowly and deliberately. "When will you find out?"

"I'll call them tonight."

"Would you let me know?"

"Of course."

"And you're coming back at the end of the week, the end of the seven days?"

"Yes."

"Do you have a flight booked for your return?"

"Yes, I do."

"What is it?"

"I'm sorry, I don't have the information in front of me. A Varig flight, I believe."

"Can you get me that information as well?"

"Of course."

"This is quite unorthodox, you understand, allowing a key figure in an investigation to leave the country. I remember we did it a couple of years ago. Let a guy go to Palermo to visit his sick mother. He never returned and we couldn't indict him."

"Am I about to be indicted, Mr. Munson?" Frost demanded, seething.

"I can't comment on an ongoing investigation, Mr. Frost. But I agree your circumstances are somewhat different than the party I mentioned."

"Thank you. And I do point out that you have a statement from me covering everything I know about the case."

"So you tell me. Everything that you remember."

"So where do we leave this?" Frost asked, eager to wind the conversation up before giving young Munson a lecture on manners. "If I tell you where we'll be staying, and our return-flight information, may I assume there will be no difficulty concerning our trip? No obstacles?"

"Based on the facts I have now, your assumption is correct. However, facts could change in the next week, so I can't give you an unqualified okay."

"But if there's no change, if there are no surprises, we can go?"

"Yes."

"Thank you."

Frost had to restrain himself from slamming down the telephone. That myopic little twerp! he thought, as he drummed on his desk to calm himself. Oh, well, he reflected, as equilibrium returned, he probably doesn't deal with nice fellows like me all the time.

Douglas Gilmore, Reuben's elderly computer guru at the Gotham Club, was an expert on other subjects as well, particularly those involving bargains or, as Gilmore put it, "good value."

One of Gilmore's tips, when Frost mentioned that he had

to buy some "summer gear" for his jaunt to Brazil, was Banana Republic, a clothing store featuring tropical wear.

"The one I go to is down in the Village, on Bleecker Street. Don't be put off, it's mostly for young people, but they have good things."

Late the next morning Reuben set out on the Lexington Avenue bus for Gilmore's bargain store. The bus was unusually crowded, and when he boarded, a young woman sitting at the front got up and offered him her seat.

"No, no, miss, please sit down," he said.

She smiled and pointed to the printed message to the effect that the seat was to be given up "for the elderly and the handicapped." Frost was appalled, but saw no alternative except to sit down.

Did he look that old and feeble? he asked himself. If so, why was he headed to a youth-oriented clothing store?

He carefully inspected the windows of Banana Republic before entering, concluding that he might be able to find something. Once inside, he was taken in tow by another attractive young woman, this time a smartly dressed black. He started off by asking her about a bathing suit.

"Is it for your granddaughter or your grandson?" the girl asked innocently.

Is every young person in New York trying to persecute me? he wondered.

"Actually, miss, it's for me."

The girl gave him a dubious look, which Reuben understood when he saw the selection being offered. Surfer's trunks were not what he had in mind; perhaps his new swimsuit should come from Brooks Brothers.

He did find, with careful looking, two cotton sport shirts, a pair of khaki walking shorts and a lightweight bush jacket. He was tempted by a billowing and good-looking pair of tan trousers but, thinking of the Michelin-man clothes Sherman Deybold and Michael Costas had worn to the fateful reading club meeting, he decided against them.

"How about one of these?" his guide asked him.

"What is it?"

"A genuine Italian waiter's jacket. It's great for the summer."

"I don't think so, thank you." He paid for his purchases and thanked his young helper; she probably thought he was senile and crazy, yet had the decency not to show it.

Out on Bleecker Street, Frost realized that his shopping had gone with such dispatch that he had time to kill before the lunch he planned to have at the Gotham Club. His memory so recently jogged about Deybold and Costas, he decided to visit their downtown gallery. He had never been there; he knew only that it was located in nearby Soho. He went back inside and found the address in Banana Republic's telephone book, then headed east to Broadway.

Deybold/Costas, as it was called, was one of a number of galleries in a loft factory building in the heart of Soho, handsomely refurbished inside in post-modern style. Located on the second floor, it was a large, light space with a polished wooden floor and white walls. There appeared to be no one else in the gallery except a woman sitting behind a counter at the far end. She paid no attention to his entrance, so he took a leisurely stroll around, looking at the works of Vitalia Ashley, the artist on exhibition at the moment.

The ten works of Ms. Ashley on display were all enormous. Frost estimated that the very smallest was ten feet by eight feet. Why do so many young artists paint to museum scale? he wondered. Wouldn't smaller paintings, appealing to the buyer interested in works for a home or apartment, be more appropriate?

All Ms. Ashley's paintings were similar except for variations in the colors used. Each consisted of a painted background in pastels, with what appeared to be melted wax dripped across this surface. Jackson Pollock's drip-painting it was not, Frost concluded; in fact, his impression was that it wasn't much of anything. The canvases were pleasant enough as decorative color patterns, but to his eye they seemed boring as works of art. The muddled printed description of the artist's work did not help, either:

The vibrant surfaces of Vitalia Ashley's wax paintings are distinctive with this artist. The melted wax superimposed on a pastel background forms a tactile pictorial plane that is resonantly beautiful to the viewer, and also suggests the oxymoron "receding surface." The use of wax also recalls an earlier, less complicated time before the advent of electricity and our technological society, as well as the mystery of ancient religious rituals.

Frost was trying to decipher this masterpiece of commentary when Michael Costas appeared from a rear room. No Michelin man today, his clothes were skin tight—a red T-shirt and white Levi's, both accentuating a neatly sculpted body. The Greeks must be given credit for Adonis and Costas, Reuben thought; certainly the young gallery owner was more attractive than anything on his walls.

"Mr Frost! What brings you here?" Costas asked warmly.

"Hello, Michael. I was in the neighborhood doing some shopping, so I thought I'd have a look at your gallery. I've never been here before."

Costas either did not notice or ignored Frost's Banana Republic shopping bag. "How do you like Vitalia's work?"

"It's very colorful," Frost replied, latching on to the only compliment he could make. "How's the show doing?" he asked.

"Pretty well. Around half the things are sold, I guess. Vitalia doesn't like us to put up those colored dots showing what's been sold. She says it detracts from the pictures."

"Interesting." Frost said, not certain that he believed the young man's explanation. "What do they go for?"

"They're all fifteen thousand. She was in the last Whitney biennial."

In Frost's opinion Ms. Ashley's output was overpriced. And he knew enough about the Whitney credential to know that it and five dollars would buy a tube of paint at Pearl Paint, a few blocks down on Canal Street. And, for that matter, so would five dollars.

"How does Sherman feel about these paintings?" Frost asked.

"I think he likes them okay. He's a traditionalist, but

he's very open. We pretty much divide things up. He lets me do what I want down here. He's very good about it.''

''I see.''

''Anything new about Mr. Vandermeer?'' Costas asked.

''Nothing that I know of. How about you?''

''No. Those cops keep coming around every few days, asking the same old questions. Sometimes one, then the other, then both of them, like they're trying to trick me. They seem disappointed when they get the same answers every time.''

Frost wanted to ask if any of the questions concerned him, then thought better of it. No sense in giving the young man ideas. ''It's a puzzle. Do you have any theories?'' he asked instead.

''Me? Wish I did. The uncertainty isn't too cool.''

''I agree with that.''

The two men shook hands and Frost left the gallery. Taking the bus to the Gotham Club, he could not help thinking that Michael Costas was a costly toy for Sherman Deybold. The Deybold/Costas gallery space must be expensive and, unless it represented artists more promising than Vitalia Ashley, was unlikely to be paying its way, let alone Michael's upkeep.

Maybe the whole thing was a tax dodge, offsetting Sherman's profits from sales of old masters. Or perhaps Deybold/ Costas was a large cash drain. If so, could that relate somehow to Tobias and his murder? The bus took forever to get uptown, but it wasn't long enough for Reuben to figure out any connection.

FLYING DOWN TO RIO

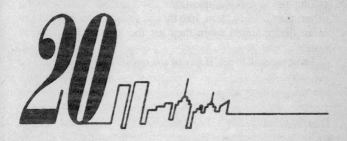

FRIDAY NIGHT, REUBEN AND CYNTHIA SETTLED THEM-
selves into first-class seats aboard the Varig 747 bound for
Rio. Reuben had had a slight frisson of fear at the check-in
desk, half expecting ADA Munson to loom up and block
their passage. Now that he was on the plane, he felt liberated.

This feeling intensified after the aircraft took off, temporarily leaving behind everything that had to do with Tobias'
murder.

"Reuben, what on earth are you humming?" Cynthia
asked as her husband started his first cocktail of the flight.

"Why, 'The Carioca,' of course. From *Flying Down to
Rio*. Didn't you recognize it?"

"No, truthfully, I didn't. You're so exuberant you'll be out
dancing on the wings, like Fred Astaire in the movie."

"Who wouldn't be exuberant? Getting away to visit old
friends, in a place that's supposed to be beautiful. Why not?"

"Oh, my dear, I quite agree. We've had an awful month.
We deserve a celebration. And, in fact, I've got some things
here to celebrate with." She pulled out a canvas tote bag
from under the seat in front of her and produced a can opener,
a knife, a box of water biscuits and a six-ounce jar of Beluga
caviar.

"Good Lord, Cynthia. They have caviar here on the plane, you know."

"They never have enough anymore. And these days they try to stretch it by mixing it with dreadful other things."

Reuben attacked the canapés Cynthia prepared with enthusiasm, trading his martini for a glass of cold vodka as an appropriate accompaniment.

"Cynthia, you never cease to amaze me."

"Good. It gets harder to surprise you after all these years, but I try. Which reminds me, I have another surprise." She reached back into her bag and produced a letter, which she handed to Reuben.

"What's this?"

"It came this morning from my new friend in Chicago, Diane Schrader. She's the woman who's trying to start a new ballet company there. I'd met her before, but I spent a lot of time with her on that flying trip to Chicago a month ago. She's a real dynamo and I liked her a lot."

"I don't get it."

"Read it and you will. You remember when we were trying to reconstruct Robyn Vandermeer's life, the Chicago piece was missing. I wrote Diane and asked if she could help. I think you'll agree she has."

Reuben looked at Cynthia incredulously as he took the letter from its envelope and began reading the bold, cursive handwriting:

DEAREST CYNTHIA,

What a pleasant surprise to hear from you! When I received your letter, I hoped it brought word of an *increase* in the promised grant for New Chicago Dance, but after getting over my disappointment I set to work immediately on finding out everything I could about Robyn Vandermeer (or Robyn Weldin, as she was known in her Chicago phase). It turns out that Mummy and some of her friends knew her then, and I also got Ardis Sutherland, the dance critic you met out here, on the case. She came up with several nuggets from her newspaper's files.

Even our Chicago papers were full of accounts of Tobias

Vandermeer's death. When most murders are related to narcotics these days, an old-fashioned poisoning of a wealthy man can still attract attention, I guess.

Even so, I had no idea Mrs. Vandermeer used to be Robyn Weldin until I read your letter. Her husband was Bernie Weldin, a very rich heir to the Weldin Parts Company fortune (your friend Robyn seems to know how to pick them). His family had been on the fringes of Chicago society for many years—let's be brutally frank, the segments of Chicago society that money can buy. (Meatpacking has always been okay as the basis for a Chicago fortune; auto parts not so much so.) Mummy knew Bernie, though not very well, and tells me that he was quite the playboy, both here and in New York, where he didn't have to be as discreet as he was around home. I've met him several times. He's all right, but not very interesting. Just rich. He's been married to the same woman now for years and has a large family of kids, half of whom seem to have gone to Harvard or Yale and the other half to two-year colleges in Illinois. (His wife is on my New Chicago Dance committee, but I don't think you met her.)

According to the newspaper files, Robyn Mayes and Bernie were married at City Hall here on September 22, 1951. She was described in the story as an actress from New York and there wasn't anything about parents or college or things like that. Mummy says there always was a rumor that Bernie had picked her up in a bar in New York. Nobody claims to know the particulars.

A friend of Mummy's, who did know her pretty well, says that she and Bernie's mother got on famously. The mother, Doris, was trying every which way to make it big in Chicago and she took her new daughter-in-law under her wing. This friend remembers her as being shy and a little clumsy at first, with a hairdo that looked like a cheerleader's (or a waitress's maybe?).

That changed in a hurry. Robyn was really good-looking and pretty soon the hairstyling and the clothes were the best money could buy. The Weldins were at all the charity benefits, and Robyn fit right in. The news photographers loved her, if the old clippings are any indication.

As best I can find out, Doris and Robyn were very active in one of the ten thousand attempts to have serious dance in Chicago. It failed, of course, like all the others (except, dear Cynthia, the effort your Foundation is going to back!!) but it brought Doris (and with her, Robyn) a step closer to the important social circles here. (Robyn herself spent a lot of money helping an early American music group here that still exists today, resurrecting both classical and jazz music. Robyn apparently was quite the expert on jazz and ragtime, though nobody knows where she came by her knowledge.)

Robyn and Bernie split up very quietly around 1958. There was no one else involved, at least that anyone knows about. The rumor was that Bernie wanted children and Robyn either wouldn't or couldn't have any. (Given the comfortable life she was leading, I'd guess the former.) At any rate she disappeared and, according to the gossip, took a big block of stock in Weldin Parts with her. (My husband says that Weldin Parts went public around this time, so she probably received stock that could be sold on the market.)

As near as I can tell, Robyn closed the Chicago door forever when she took off. Everybody seems to have heard of her marriage to that Italian count, or whatever he was, but I don't know anyone who's been in touch with her, and I've really asked around.

You wanted to know if anybody had strong impressions of the Mrs. Weldin that was. Mummy's friend who knew her from the beginning says the transformation was amazing and fast—from actress to very cultivated lady. People liked her, but I'm told that those who worked closely with her on committees, etc., found her very single-minded and stubborn when she put her mind to something. Usually it was for a worthy cause, not that that made it any easier for those coming up against her. I don't think she was much missed after she disappeared.

That's really all I can tell you, Cynthia. If you want me

to keep digging, I'll be glad to, but I thought you'd be interested in this preliminary report.

Best to you—and I'll say it unashamedly—to the Brigham Foundation.

Love,
DIANE

"I'll be damned," Reuben said, when he had finished. "This is very intriguing. Why didn't you show it to me before?"

"It just came this afternoon. I wanted it to be a surprise. And I didn't want to take the very slim chance that somehow you'd want to cancel the trip."

"Why would I do that?"

"Well, this letter *does* add to the impression that Robyn is a very, very determined woman."

"Determined enough to kill Tobias, you mean?"

"You said it, Reuben. Now that we're forty thousand feet up and over international waters, is there any point in denying it any longer?"

"No," Reuben answered deliberately, "no, there isn't. We've had our suspicions about Robyn all along, and they've hardened in the last few days. That cool performance at Gracie Mansion, for example. The way she was treated, the fortune she stood to get, her easy access to Tobias' pill bottle—and her determination—all add up as far as I'm concerned."

"It's not easy, is it? Realizing that a person one's been a friend to is a murderess?"

"No, it certainly's not."

"What an embarrassment for NatBallet—having one of its major contributors a criminal!"

"I'm glad to see you're putting first things first, my dear. What about all those newly literate little children, now able to read about their benefactor in the *Daily News*?"

The flight's dinner service afforded a welcome (and comparatively tasty) respite to the Frosts' dark thoughts. They ate in near-silence, commenting tersely on the food, each knowing that it would be hopeless to try to start a real conversation on any subject other than the Vandermeers.

Finally, over coffee and brandy, Reuben said that he had concluded "that NatBallet and the little literates are safe."

"What do you mean?"

"They're never going to pin the murder on Robyn. She planned it too well. Unless, of course, they can prove she bought some weed killer containing cyanide in Nutley, New Jersey, or something like that."

"She did have to get the poison from someplace."

"Anyone who can start out as a pregnant cheerleader and end up as the venerated Robyn Vandermeer is probably pretty good at covering her tracks," Reuben said.

"These things have a way of coming unwound, my dear."

"They're going to have to come unwound without me. I'm becoming a beach bum for a week. And right now I'm going to rest up for it."

Both Frosts reclined their luxurious stretch seats, put on eye masks and slept until awakened for the enormous breakfast their first-class passage entitled them to.

"I can't eat all this," Reuben complained.

"Then don't. Besides, if you're going to be a beach bum, you should watch out for your figure."

CIDADE MARAVILHOSA

21

THE FROSTS' ARRIVAL AMID THE NEVER-ENDING CONFUSION of Galeao International Airport was made easier through the deft help of Delfim, the Herculanos' driver. Through some magic (the payment of a few *novo cruzados*, in fact), he met them at the arrival gate, carrying a cardboard sign saying FROST, and shepherded them with comparative ease through customs and the baggage-claim area.

It had been established by telephone—Reuben had needed the information for his friend, ADA Munson—that the Frosts would be staying at the Copacabana Palace Hotel, rather than the Herculanos' residence.

Delfim guided them to a waiting Mercedes. "We go to Dr. Herculano at two o'clock for lunch," he said. "Now we go to the hotel so you can rest."

The driver, a dark, mustachioed man who appeared to be in his late forties, was full of smiles, and the Frosts were grateful for his aid. They were slightly disconcerted, however, when he placed a menacing-looking revolver on the leather seat beside him and locked the doors before starting out. He neither apologized for nor explained his precautions.

"Is very old hotel you go to," he said, as they drove into Rio proper. "I think is better than the new ones. Very sympathetic."

He also told them they would be staying not in the main hotel building but in an adjoining building of *apartamentos*. "Is better," he told them.

The Herculanos' driver stayed with Reuben and Cynthia until the luggage arrived in their spacious two-room suite. He opened the door to the balcony overlooking the hotel's huge swimming pool and pointed out Avenida Atlantica, Copacabana Beach and the invitingly blue Atlantic beyond.

"Is very beautiful," he commented.

"Yes, indeed," Reuben said. "Is it always this busy?" he asked, gesturing toward the colorful horde of bodies on the beach, beyond the distinctive wavy black-and-white mosaic sidewalk.

"Many people come every day," Delfim said. "Saturday and Sunday, everybody comes."

"I can see why," Cynthia said. "It's absolutely gorgeous."

Delfim thanked her for the compliment and said he would meet them in the lobby at one forty-five. "Now you can rest or take a swim, whatever you want," he said.

"Rest for me," Reuben said.

"Me, too. Maybe we should wait until Monday for the beach, when not everybody comes."

Promptly at the appointed hour the Frosts were on their way to the home of their friends.

"Cosme Vehlo," Delfim explained, as he drove up a hill below Corcovado Mountain. "That is Corcovado. The hunchback. It's a clear day. You can see the Christ at the top."

Indeed one could. The massive statue of Christ the Redeemer was silhouetted in the cloudless sunshine at the top of the peak.

The Mercedes stopped at a closed gate well up the hillside. An armed security guard opened it, admitting the car to a long driveway surrounded by lush green foliage and brightly colored tropical flowers. Delfim drove to the front of an inviting colonial house, its cool pink color a relief from the day's bright sunshine. A houseboy in a white jacket admitted them and in mixed Portuguese and English, accompanied by interpretative gestures, indicated that they were to wait in the living room.

"Welcome to *Cidade Maravilhosa!*" Alfredo Herculano boomed out, as he entered the room moments later. Luiza came in behind him, and the foursome was soon locked in a melange of *abraços*, kisses and laughter.

Alfredo, casually dressed in a sport shirt and slacks (in contrast to Reuben's jacket and tie), was a lighter-skinned version of Delfim, with slicked-back hair and a thin mustache. His wife looked glamorous in a simple cotton dress, her trim figure and smooth, unlined face giving no hint that she was the mother of six, let alone already a grandmother several times over.

"We finally got you here!" Luiza said. "I almost don't believe it."

"You were here before, Cynthia, yes?" Alfredo asked.

"For four days, back before the invention of the wheel," Cynthia said. "I've seen more on this trip already than I did then. Copacabana Beach and the ocean, for example. Back then I saw my hotel room, my dressing room and the stage of the Teatro Municipal."

"We'll fix that," Luiza said, laughing. "We're not going to give you a minute's peace."

"How about a drink?" Alfredo asked, as the butler reappeared. "The usual martini, Reuben?"

"Not today. I'm still a little rocky from the flight. Can I have a gin and tonic?"

"Good. And Cynthia?"

"Campari?"

"Sure."

The houseboy returned with a tray containing bottles and ice, deftly mixing three gin and tonics and a Campari and soda to individual specifications.

"Let's go outside," Luiza directed. "It's not too hot."

She led the way out to a stone terrace, with a breathtaking view of the ocean in the distance.

"Is that Sugarloaf?" Reuben asked.

"Yes indeed. You've been reading your guidebook," Alfredo said.

"Not really, Alfredo. Even I have heard of Sugarloaf."

"You New Yorkers should feel right at home here," Alfredo said. "Our murder rate is around five hundred a month, even higher than yours. We have cocaine and all kinds of drugs. Just to keep up-to-date, we now have crack. And AIDS."

"I noticed the . . . guards," Reuben said, tactfully not mentioning Delfim's revolver.

"A necessary evil, my friend. We have to keep alive so that the inflation can kill us."

"How is your hotel?" Luiza asked.

"It's fine," Cynthia replied.

"We decided it was better to have you there," Alfredo said. "It will be more restful. We still have two children at home, and there are grandchildren running around all the time. This place is more like a railway station than a home. You are better off at the Copacabana, believe me."

"It's very old-fashioned, but we thought you'd prefer it to the modern horrors that have gone up here, which are very luxe, but very cold," Luiza said. "The Copa's now a national landmark."

"We have no complaints," Reuben said. "You did very well by us."

The small talk among old friends continued as lunch was served in the dining room by the houseboy and a woman in a starched white uniform.

"We haven't planned your whole stay," Luiza explained, as they ate delicious small steaks and delicate French-fried potatoes. "Tomorrow we thought we would take a sail around Guanabara Bay. Alfredo has his little boat moored down at the Yacht Club, so we'll go out for a sail, have lunch and come back."

As she talked, two young teenagers, a girl and a boy, came into the room. Both had black hair, still wet from a recent swim, and deep, dark eyes; it was impossible to say, Reuben thought, which was the more attractive. Following them were two very small boys in bathing suits.

"Ah, my babies!" Luiza said, greeting all four with enthusiasm, smothering the little ones with kisses. "Come and say hello to our old friends,'' she said to the adolescents. Joaquim and Teresa dutifully and politely shook hands and then stood awkwardly by the dining-room table, in their jeans and polo shirts looking like teenagers anywhere.

''And these are my grandchildren, Eduardo and Manoel. Jorge's children,'' Luiza said, and to the teenagers, ''What are you up to?''

''We're going to take these two home. Then Joaquim and I are going over to see Roberto Dias,'' Teresa said. ''His sister, Maria Angelica, just got back from New York with a whole suitcase of new CDs.''

''All right, my dears. Don't make yourselves deaf.''

The children, relieved at their dismissal, left the room, but not before kissing each of their parents good-bye. The grandchildren did likewise.

''What splendid creatures, Luiza,'' Cynthia said.

''Yes, they are, aren't they?'' Luiza said with a sigh. ''They're good, too. Sometimes I think mine would rather listen to music than study, but we are lucky. They are nice.''

''Most of the time,'' Alfredo added.

''Now, let me go on with the plans,'' Luiza said. ''Tonight, if your stomachs are okay, we will go out. A nice restaurant with the very authentic food of Bahia. Does that sound all right?''

''By this evening I'll be ready for anything,'' Reuben declared.

''That's my Reuben,'' Luiza said. ''Monday, we can sightsee, and Monday night we are having a little dinner party for you. Just a few friends we would like you to meet. After Monday? We'll see. Maybe we will go up to Petropolis. See our house there.''

''Whatever you say, Luiza,'' Reuben said.

''But what do you want to do?''

''We'll leave everything in your good hands.''

''No suggestions?''

''There is one thing. Do you know a woman named Ines Amarante? I believe she runs an art gallery here,'' Frost said.

''Ines Amarante de Sousa. Yes, we know her some. She

used to be married to a guy in New York. Did you know her there?"

"No. We've never met."

"She's quite the bohemian," Luiza said. "She has a very artistic coterie around her all the time. I would ask her to our dinner, but, as I say, she travels everywhere with a crowd."

"No, no. I didn't mean you should invite her. But she does have a gallery?"

"Yes, not too far. Alfredo, where is Ines Amarante's gallery?"

"Downtown. Avenida President Wilson, I think."

"You want to visit there?" Luiza asked.

"Yes, I'm curious," Reuben said, without explanation.

"It is closed Sunday and probably Monday," Luiza said. "We will go Tuesday morning."

Cynthia, with the perception that comes from a long marriage, noticed that Reuben was flagging slightly and signaled him that it was time to leave. Delfim was summoned and took the Frosts back to the hotel.

"Isn't it nice to see *happy* rich people," Cynthia said, once in the privacy of their suite.

"You have any comparisons in mind?"

"You know very well who I mean."

"Yes, it is. But how long can it last, Cynthia? I recall reading somewhere that one percent of all Brazilians control fifty percent of the wealth. That's like keeping a can of gasoline next to the stove."

"Well, at least they're enjoying it while they can. And we should, too, even if it's only for a week."

Cynthia and Reuben tried hard to follow her admonition about making the most of their stay. That night they joined their friends at the Chalé Restaurant for a delicious Bahian dinner of seafood, notably a delectable fish stew called by their hosts *moqueca*. It was well past midnight when the Frosts returned to the hotel, this time driven by Alfredo himself.

"Is it true it's unsafe to walk along the beachfront at night?" Reuben asked him.

"It's an exaggeration, like everything else in Rio. The worst that's likely to happen is that one of the night ladies will come up and proposition you. But, as they warn you, don't go out with your wallet or your handbag or your pearls. It is not good."

Thus warned, the Frosts went directly to their room.

The next day turned out to be beautiful, and the sail around the bay, on Alfredo's 108-foot ketch, was spectacular. The only casualties were a slight sunburn in Reuben's case—he had forgotten to pack a hat—and a mild stomach upset in Cynthia's.

Monday, still feeling some distress, she asked the concierge where she could buy some paragoric, her old-reliable remedy.

"There's a drugstore on the other side of the hotel," she was told.

"Don't I need a doctor's prescription?"

"No, no, senhora," came the reply. "You can buy almost anything there without."

While Cynthia was buying her medicine, Reuben decided that the time had come to explore the beach. He put on his sedate Brooks Brothers swim trunks under his khaki shorts and striped shirt from Banana Republic and set out for the beach, stopping to buy a cotton hat from a street vendor on the way.

Spreading out his towel beyond the reach of the ocean surf, he sat down and took in the scene. His pink-white skin, reddened only in spots from the previous day's sun, made him conspicuous amid the sea of evenly tanned bodies around him. He stared unabashedly at sexy girls in the briefest bikinis he had ever seen (except, of course, the bikinis the local boys were wearing).

His memories of wartime Navy days in the South Pacific notwithstanding, he was sure that the setting, both natural and human, was the most voluptuous and sensual he had ever seen. He bought a Coca-Cola from a passing vendor and felt downright randy as he drank it in relaxed contentment amid the tanning flesh on all sides of him. Then, reluctantly, he realized that he had absorbed his day's quota of sunshine and returned to the Copacabana's swimming pool for a cooling swim.

"I wonder if the Herculanos' 'little' dinner party will be like their 'little' boat," Cynthia said to her husband as they dressed for dinner.

"You can rest assured it will be," he answered.

Reuben was right. A touch of grandeur was suggested as soon as they entered the Herculano grounds that evening, lighted torches lining the passage to the front door. There, Saturday's houseboy was now in full livery as he met the guests.

The 'little' dinner was a sit-down affair for forty, seated at five tables for eight in the rearranged dining room. Everything about the meal was impeccable—the floral decorations, the chicken basquaise, the Puligny-Montrachet, the service by a vast and discreet staff.

All the guests spoke English, some better than others, though this did not prevent some of them from occasional bursts into excited Portuguese even when one of the Frosts was listening. Reuben sat between Luiza and the spirited and witty wife of a local newspaper publisher. Cynthia fared less well. Alfredo, on her left, was good company, of course, but her other partner, the chargé d'affaires at the American embassy in Brasilia, she found exceedingly dull.

"If that man has one single opinion about Brazil he concealed it from me," she told Reuben, as they relaxed later over a nightcap at the hotel. "I've never seen anyone so careful. And not very knowledgeable, either. I asked him if there were any cultural-exchange programs with Brazil at the moment, and he simply didn't know. Where do they find these bland people?"

"The field and the farm," Reuben answered. "Now, let's go to bed. Don't forget we have to look Ines Amarante over tomorrow."

The Galeria Amarante was sleek and modern, with a glass front that allowed the sunlight to flood in on its walls. Luiza had come to the hotel with Delfim to pick up the Frosts and take them there. The trip to the city's center was filled with Cynthia's compliments over the previous night's dinner.

"Luiza, may I ask you a personal question?" Cynthia said to her hostess on the way. "How many servants do you have? Is that too vulgar a thing to ask?"

"No, no. When I'm in New York, I'm very curious how you live. You can do the same. Let me see. . . . " She paused and did some mental calculating. "Twenty-two."

"Twenty-two?"

"Yes. That includes the couple that takes care of the apartment in New York and the couple and the gardener in Petropolis. And the schoolmaster."

"Schoolmaster?"

"Yes. We have a schoolmaster to teach the others— English, or a little bit anyway, how to set the table, things like that."

"I'm amazed."

"It's a big job. A big responsibility. Some of them have been with the family for years. Some are children of servants Alfredo's parents had. We are very lucky, Cynthia. They, most of them, anyway, are very good to us and we try to do what's right for them."

Cynthia could not help comparing Luiza's situation with the Vandermeers' and was still stunned by what her hostess had told her when the Mercedes pulled up in front of the gallery. The three got out and went inside, where a fifty-ish good-looking woman greeted them. She was Ines Amarante herself, and Luiza introduced the Frosts as "friends from New York."

"Please come in," the owner said. "We are showing two local artists now, Nina Barata and Aristides Moreira. This is Nina's work here. She is a young woman who lives here in Rio and this is her first show."

The works on display were pleasant abstracts, saved from mediocrity by bold, almost brazen, swirls of color.

"Nina is only twenty-two and very promising," Senhora Amarantes explained. "Would you like some coffee?"

The owner took her visitors to her office at the back of the gallery, a disorganized, comfortable room with paintings stacked around the walls. A white-coated houseboy—does everyone in Rio have one? Reuben wondered—was summoned and appeared with small cups of *cafezinho*, to each of which he added a large quantity of sugar.

"Mrs. Frost, you look very familiar to me," Senhora Amarante said after they were all seated. "Weren't you a dancer at one time?"

"Yes, many years ago. I danced with the National Ballet."

"Yes, I thought so. I used to live in New York and had many friends who went to the ballet all the time. I used to go with my friend Jasper Johns, the painter. A true ballet-omane. Do you know him?"

"We've met," Reuben said. "But no, I can't say that we know him."

"He's doing very well, no?"

"That's something of an understatement," Frost replied.

"He's too expensive now, even for the rich Brazilians. Only the Japanese can afford him."

"It's clear that someone can," Reuben said. "His auction prices are phenomenal."

"Oh, I miss New York. So vital! So exciting! Always something new and interesting. I came back here in 1964. I left behind many wonderful memories—and a drunken husband. Perhaps you knew him? Poor wretched man was murdered last month. Poisoned, they tell me. Tobias Vandermeer?"

Senhora Amarante looked directly at Reuben as she spoke. Did she, he wondered, know that he had been Tobias' lawyer? Or even more?

"Yes, we knew him," Frost replied noncommittally. He saw no need to add that he and Cynthia had been present when he died.

"Have they found the murderer? I have not heard."

"They hadn't before we left."

"Tobias was a dreadful man who caused me much unhappiness. But I was sorry to hear of his nasty death. No one deserves that." She shook her head vigorously, as if to erase memories of both the living and the dead Tobias. "Come, let me show you the other room. Aristides is also a young artist, who lives in Minas Gerais, in Belo Horizonte.''

His works were smaller in scale than Senhorina Barata's and were quite pleasing oils showing colonial facades and doorways, all rendered in the bold yellows, pinks and greens the Frosts had observed in the older houses they had seen around Rio.

"I like these very much," Cynthia said to her guide.

"He is very good," Senhora Amarante acknowledged.

"Do you show mostly Brazilian artists?" Cynthia asked.

"Oh, no. We have many North Americans, and have done very well with them. Last year we had a marvelous show of Nabil Nahas. Do you know him?''

"I know his work," Cynthia said.

"Very strong, very forceful. And Mark Innerst? What about him?''

"Again, I know his work."

"Very clever. Very clever. We could sell everything he paints right here in Brazil."

Reuben, browsing, picked up a small leaflet that listed, as best he could read the Portuguese, artists who had been exhibited at the Galeria Amarante recently, or were about to be shown. Nahas and Innerst were listed—and so was Vitalia Ashley, the artist of the wax drippings at the Deybold/Costas Gallery.

"I see that you are going to have a show of Vitalia Ashley's work," he said.

"You know her things?"

"Yes," Reuben said, with authority. "She uses melted wax a lot."

"That's right. I saw her work on my last trip to New York and liked it. Do you?"

"Frankly, no."

"Ah, too bad. I think she is very good, but, as always, opinions can differ. She is having a show in New York now and we will have one here in three months."

"I saw the show," Frost said. "At the Deybold/Costas Gallery. In Soho."

"Yes."

''Do you know them?''

''Who?''

''Sherman Deybold and Michael Costas.''

''Of course,'' Senhora Amarante said. ''I know them all. Castelli, Angela Westwater, Holly Solomon. Everybody. I even know the ones in jail,'' she said, laughing.

''I fear we must go. It's time for lunch,'' Luiza said. Thus prodded, the Frosts exchanged ''nice-to-meet-you's'' with Senhora Amarante and departed.

Cynthia was bursting to talk to Reuben privately, but had to wait for the briefest of opportunities when Luiza excused herself in the restaurant where they ate.

''Reuben, I've got to tell you! Nosy me, I happened to see the mail on that woman's desk. *Two* letters addressed to her from the Deybold Gallery.''

''She did say she knew the boys.''

''Yes, but she said she knew everyone else, too.''

''And, as you heard, she's going to show the wax lady from Deybold/Costas. *And*—and—how about that still life in her office?''

''Which one do you mean?''

''There was a still life of a fish that to my untutored eye looked old and Dutch. Just the sort of thing Sherman deals in. Very odd, in a gallery that sells contemporary art.''

''I missed it completely.''

''Well, I didn't,'' Reuben said with satisfaction. ''It looks to me like Senhora Amarante, Deybold and Costas are pretty good friends.''

''And?''

''And I wish I knew if that meant anything. Do you suppose . . . ?''

''That she put one of them up to killing Tobias? Sweet revenge after all these years? God knows, my dear, anything is possible, though I thought we'd agreed that the second Mrs. Vandermeer was responsible, not the first.''

''I know. But isn't this an interesting new alleyway? We'll have to talk about it later. Here comes Luiza back,'' Cynthia said, resigning herself to postponing a good, speculative chat with her husband until later in the day.

ANOTHER COUNTRY
· HEARD FROM

22

THE FROSTS DID NOT GET BACK TO THE COPACABANA PAL-ace until late afternoon. Both looked forward to discussing their odd encounter with Ines Amarante, and Reuben, at least, was hoping to take a nap.

Neither the discussion nor the nap took place. Picking up their room key, Reuben was handed a phone message from Bob Millard in New York, marked *urgente*, and a brown envelope that contained a fax from Millard:

FOR RUSH DELIVERY TO REUBEN FROST FROM ROBERT MILLARD.

    Reuben: I've been trying to reach you for several hours. Please call me as soon as possible. I was visited this morn-ing by a lawyer named Drew Hammil, who represents one Stephen Rourke. Hammil claims Rourke is the illegitimate son of Tobias Vandermeer and the proof he presented ap-pears to bear this out. Sorry to interrupt your holiday, but want to speak to you most urgently. Millard.

"Cynthia!" Reuben called out to his wife, waiting for him at the elevator. "Read this!"

She took the sheet of shiny fax paper and read the mes-sage. "Well, there goes your computer," she said.

"What on earth do you mean?"

"My dear, you feed this little morsel into that electronic file of yours and the thing will explode."

"That's not funny."

"*This* isn't funny," she countered, waving Millard's fax.

"I've got to call him right away."

"Can I listen on the other phone?" she asked.

"Why not?"

Frost dialed Millard's direct number at Chase & Ward, only to find that he was still at lunch.

"What the hell time is it in New York?" he sputtered. Millard's secretary told him it was shortly after two. "If and when he comes back tell him I'm waiting for his call," he said sharply.

"What do you think this means?" Cynthia asked.

"How do I know?" he snapped back at her.

"Can we talk about Mrs. Amarante while we're waiting?"

"I'd rather not. This fax has thrown me for a loop and I want to be as clearheaded as I can be when Millard calls. There's the phone now." Reuben picked it up and began talking with a very agitated Bob Millard.

"What the hell's going on, Bob?" Reuben asked.

"Plenty. Tobias Vandermeer apparently had a son, for God's sake."

"By who?"

"Someone named Grace Alice Rourke. Remember that name?"

"The woman mentioned in Tobias' old will."

"That's right. They had this kid back in 1952."

"Bob, why don't you start at the beginning."

"Okay. I'll try. I got a call yesterday morning from a lawyer named Drew Hammil. Never heard of him before so I checked him out. He seems to be a pretty-well-known show-business lawyer. He said he'd found out that I represented the Tobias Vandermeer estate and he wanted to talk to me regarding a matter involving the estate. I asked him what it was and he refused to tell me on the telephone. I asked him if he could at least tell me who his client was, and he said Stephen Rourke. He wouldn't identify Rourke any further.

Said he preferred to discuss the matter in person. So we made an appointment for the first thing this morning.

"I didn't know what to expect. Hammil turns out to be a perfectly gentlemanly fellow who started out by asking about the terms of Tobias' will. I asked him why he wanted to know, and he dropped the bomb. Said his client, Rourke, was Tobias' illegitimate son and he was wondering what rights he might have under the will."

"Can a bastard inherit in New York?" Reuben interrupted.

"This is the twentieth century, Reuben. The law is clear and the answer's yes. As long as he was recognized by the father, he can inherit just like a legitimate heir."

"So if this Rourke is on the level, he will get what's in the Vandermeer Trust when Robyn dies, and not the Bloemendael Foundation?"

"Precisely."

"Has anybody told Wayne Givens this cheery news?"

"I haven't talked to anybody except you, Reuben."

"Good. Cynthia's on the line, by the way. You don't mind, do you?"

"Hello, Cynthia. Of course not."

"Sorry to sidetrack you, Bob. Keep going."

"Hammil says that Grace Alice Rourke was a struggling singer in New York back in the early fifties. Somehow she met Tobias, and one thing led to another and . . ."

"Yes, yes, you don't need to draw me a picture. When was the kid born?"

"Hammil had a birth certificate. He was born in Saint Vincent's hospital on September 22, 1952."

"Who does it say his father was?"

"Tobias."

"Hmn. I don't know how these things work, but couldn't this Grace Alice have *said* Tobias was the father?"

"That's right. But Hammil has a handwritten letter from Tobias to the mother, acknowledging that the kid is his."

"What does it say?"

"I've got a copy here," Millard said. He read from the document, which said "how sorry" Tobias was over what had happened, how he regretted that marriage was out of the question—citing the objections he knew old Hendrick would have—and saying that he would "always take care" of Grace Alice.

"That's all there was, this letter?"

"Apparently so. But if it's real, I think it's enough. Hammil left me a Xerox, and I must say it looks like the stuff in Tobias' handwriting we've got in the file."

"Where's the mother now?"

"Hammil said she died in December 1984."

"And Tobias was supporting her till the end?"

"So Hammil said."

"Have you talked to Kearney? He might know."

"No, I haven't."

"How did the conversation go once Mr. Hammil dropped his bomb?" Frost asked.

"It turned out he knew quite a bit about the Vandermeer setup. He said he'd represented Rourke for several years and was very frank that he'd searched Hendrik's will in the probate records."

"Can you do that?"

"Sure. Once a will is admitted to probate it's a public document."

"What about Robyn's life estate? Did he know about that?"

"Not surprisingly, it turned out that was what he was most interested in—whether Tobias had exercised his power of appointment."

"And you told him?"

"Sure. There was no reason not to. I gave him a copy of Tobias' will and the deed of appointment."

"That damned deed's becoming a best-seller."

"You can say that again."

"How did he react when he found out that Tobias had exercised his power? Surprised? Shocked? What?"

"No reaction, really. He was very calm, very unemotional. Just interested in what the facts were."

"How about the police? Have you told them?" Reuben asked.

"That's one of the things I wanted your advice on."

"The two cops involved in the murder investigation are a pair of charmers named Springer and Mattocks. I've got their numbers here somewhere, if you hold on." Frost fished for his address book as he continued talking. "Call them up and have them come to see you. Or you go and see them. Tell them I said they should check up on this Rourke. Including where he was on March fifth."

"I don't understand."

"The day Tobias was killed," Frost snapped.

"Oh . . . I see . . . You don't think . . . ?"

"I don't think anything. Just do as I tell you."

"Of course, Reuben."

"One other thing. And this is the most important of all. Get hold of Robyn right away, tell her what's happened and *tell her to be careful*. She mustn't find herself in a dark alley with Mr. Rourke."

"Do you really think, Reuben . . . ?"

"Bob, as I said, I have no thoughts at this point," Reuben said impatiently. "But we've had one murder, and I'd as soon not have our problem multiplied by two. What does this Rourke character do, by the way?"

"Hammil says he's an actor."

"I should have known. Where does he live?"

"In Chelsea, he told me."

"Do you have an address?"

"No."

"Well, get one from your Mr. Hammil. The police will need that. And of course you don't have any idea what he looks like?"

"Nope."

The line was quiet while Reuben considered the situation. Cynthia was in the living room of their suite, so he could not consult her about the next step he'd decided on. "If it's possible, Bob, we'll try to get out of here tonight, on the overnight flight. If we can't, I'll let you know. Otherwise, have a car meet us at Kennedy. It'll be the Varig flight from Rio. Got it?"

"Yes."

"So unless you hear from me, I'll see you tomorrow morning. Before then, I'll expect you to call the police and Robyn. And I wouldn't say anything to anyone else—like Kearney or Wayne Givens—until I get back."

"Okay, Reuben. Thanks for your help."

"Sorry about that, Cynthia," he apologized to his wife after hanging up.

"You did the right thing, dear. It's important that you be back there."

"What do you make of this one?"

"An actor, was he? I wonder if he ever played a waiter?"

"Funny you should suggest it. I was thinking the same thing."

"Maybe Pace Padgett has been found."

The next few hours were a tumult of confusion. A lengthy explanation was required for the Herculanos, and Alfredo had to exert his influence to get the Frosts booked on the Varig eleven o'clock nonstop to New York. First class was impossible to arrange, even for him, but he managed to get two business class seats.

The faithful Delfim was not available to take them to the airport, so the Frosts endured a hair-raising, lane-shifting, tailgating taxi ride through the evening Rio traffic. Then there was the matter of changing their tickets, a shortage of *novo cruzados* for the exit tax and a painfully slow and methodical security check.

The pre-takeoff champagne offered to the couple, once they had dragged themselves aboard their plane, was satisfyingly welcome. Relaxing for the first time since getting Bob Millard's fax, they tried to make some sense of the confusion they felt.

"Is Mr. Stephen Rourke our man?" Cynthia asked.

"We'll have to see what he looks like. It's probably far-fetched. But who can say?"

"There's one thing I don't understand, dear. Even if Rourke, or Padgett, killed Tobias, what good would it do him? He wouldn't see a dime of the Vandermeer money until Robyn dies."

"He didn't know that until after his lawyer saw Bob Millard. He almost certainly knows now, and that's why I insisted Bob Millard warn Robyn. If Stephen Rourke is Pace Padgett, he's a very calculating fellow who planned to murder Tobias for a long time, going through all that monkey business with Byron Hayden you uncovered before we left. If he could be so cunning and cool about killing his father, I doubt that he'd have any qualms about murdering his stepmother.''

"It's funny, isn't it? We were so sure five days ago that Robyn was the guilty one, and now we're worried about her life.''

"Look, she may well be guilty. This Rourke may have had nothing to do with the murder. Or he may be an imposter—who knows?''

"And what about Sherman Deybold?''

"After what we learned today, there are at least three possible connections between Deybold—and Costas—and Senhora Amarante. Vitalia Ashley. Those letters you saw. And possibly that picture of a dead fish that I spotted.''

"So where do those three connections lead, dear?''

"It's probably too absurd. But listen to me for a minute. You remember I told you I thought Michael Costas and that elaborate modern gallery downtown might be expensive toys for Sherman. So expensive that a large sum of money from a rich Brazilian woman . . .''

"You mean, she might have *paid* Deybold to kill Tobias?''

"Possibly. Or remember what Wilkes Mobeley told me about the tax swindles he thinks Deybold is doing? Senhora Amarante may have been running his parking lot. And might have blackmailed him into killing Tobias. If Mobeley is right about what Sherman's doing, and Ines is in on it, she knows enough to ruin him.''

"Well, she certainly had a motive. She hated Tobias.''

"That's another thing. I had the distinct impression she knew who I was. She knew who you were. And back when she was mud-wrestling with Tobias over their divorce, I can't imagine Tobias didn't threaten her with the big, bad Chase & Ward juggernaut—including big, bad me.''

"So what?''

"I mean her pity for poor, poor Tobias may have been an

act. And she may have been pretending not to remember me, or who I was.''

''We're getting awfully suspicious of people, Reuben. It makes me dizzy just trying to sort things out. Let's try to sleep and nail the killer in the morning.''

''I'm going to have another brandy. I'm so keyed up there's no hope of sleeping. Especially in these seats. And with that party going on back there.'' He was referring to a large tour group, traveling together in economy class, who were joking and singing at full cry, their voices carrying up into the more sedate reaches of business class.

''You want to be clearheaded when we get to New York,'' Cynthia admonished.

''I will be,'' Reuben grumped.

Before Cynthia settled in and Reuben tackled a new brandy, they took turns going to the bathroom.

''I walked back to the rear to see where all the noise was coming from,'' Reuben explained, when Cynthia returned. ''A tour group from Rochester, New York. John Deere caps, and those funny hats they were selling on the beach, and about three hundred pounds of hand luggage apiece, stuffed all over the place.''

''They're harmless,'' Cynthia said.

''Harmless but noisy. You'd think they'd be samba'ed out.''

''They're determined to enjoy every minute. You can't blame them for that.''

''Just think, my dear,'' Reuben said, taking his wife's hand across the seat divider between them, ''if I hadn't gone to law school, and attracted Charlie Chase's attention, and married you, I might be back there with them. Upstate New York meeting Latin America.''

''I suppose you're right.''

''Instead, I'm a lucky fellow sitting up toward the front of the plane with not a care in the world. Except being smack in the middle of a murder investigation that gets more complicated by the day. Who could be luckier than that?''

NOT WHAT WAS EXPECTED

23

THE FROST'S PLANE LANDED PRECISELY ON TIME; THEIR suitcases were in the first batch on the luggage carrousel at Kennedy, and they had no trouble getting through customs. (Their premature departure from Rio had meant that they had no shopping items to declare, and ADA Munson did not have a dragnet ready to haul them off to Rikers Island.)

The car Bob Millard had arranged was waiting, and they were on their way home to Manhattan before eight-thirty. Their driver was from Communi-Car, presumably the dial-car service with which the Chase & Ward office manager was not currently feuding.

"You from New York?" he asked, giving early warning that the trip would not be a silent one. After a thorough interrogation about where they had been, the length and quality of their flight and other irrelevancies, Reuben was going to tell him to be quiet when he launched into a tirade about the "terrible things happening in New York these days."

"Were you here when that rich guy was killed?" he asked before Reuben could cut him off. "Vanderbilt, Vandermeer, one of those names."

"Yes."

"Awful thing, poisoned."

"Yes, we know about that." Reuben looked at Cynthia and raised his head in silent despair; he did not need this serendipitous distraction on their return home, yet he was intrigued that the driver was still interested in month-old news.

"And now the wife—imagine, strangled in her own home."

"What! What are you saying?" Both Frosts leaned forward, gripping the back of the front seat.

"Yeah. It just came on the radio while I was waiting for you. Strangled sometime yesterday in her dining room. Can you beat that?"

Reuben and Cynthia both assaulted the driver with a barrage of questions—who, what, where, when and why?—but he turned out to know only what his radio had told him: Robyn Vandermeer had been killed by an unknown assailant sometime on Tuesday.

"Probably one of those out-of-control kids from Harlem," the driver offered. At least he didn't say "nigger" or "black," Frost thought with relief, but taxi-driver racism was not what really interested him at the moment. He looked over at Cynthia, both of them bursting to talk over this startling development, yet knowing better than to do so in front of their voluble chauffeur; there was nothing to do but wait until they reached Seventieth Street. Then Reuben spotted the cellular telephone resting in the space between the two front seats.

"Does that contraption work?" he asked.

"Sure. Want to use it?"

"Yes, I do." He hesitated. Having always disdained car telephones as a particularly vulgar curse of the late 1980s, he hadn't the faintest idea of how to operate it.

"Just pick it up and dial," the driver told him helpfully. "It'll go on your bill for the car. We're still in Queens, so dial one, the area code and the number."

"Thanks," Frost said, grasping the portable instrument and poking out Luis Bautista's home number—the first time he had done so since their last face-to-face meeting a month earlier. A groggy voice answered, followed by an apologetic explanation that Bautista had been up all night.

"I'm on this damn drug-dealer case," Bautista said. "All the people I want to locate only surface in the middle of the night."

"Luis, I'm sorry. I had to talk to you. I assume, by the way, that since I was in Brazil when Robyn Vandermeer was killed I'm in the clear and that we can speak without getting anyone in hot water."

"What the hell you talking about, Reuben?"

"Tobias Vandermeer's widow, Robyn, was apparently strangled yesterday."

"News to me. As I said, I haven't exactly been traveling in Park Avenue circles the last thirty-six hours. But you're in the clear anyway, old friend."

"Oh?"

"Yeah, I saw Springer a couple of days ago. They've had no breaks in the case at all. But he did tell me that the Keystone Kops that lost those pieces of broken glass from the Vandermeers' found them. Under a shelf in the CSU's wagon, for Christ's sake. The lab says they're clean—no cyanide—so I guess you're going to walk."

"That's comforting." In any other circumstances, Frost would have been jubilant and reexamined his upstairs/downstairs list in the light of what he had been told. But he was now preoccupied with pressing his friend into service.

"So what about this Mrs. Vandermeer? I was out with the night creatures and didn't hear a thing. Hey, can you wait a minute while I get a cup of coffee? Francisca made some before she went to work."

While he waited, Reuben, in the lowest voice possible, told Cynthia of his exoneration. He would have added the new confirmation that their old friends Luis and Francisca were living together, but that could wait, too.

"Will Springer and Mattocks investigate her murder?" Frost asked, when Bautista came back on the line.

"That's the way it would usually work," Bautista replied. "I'm sure they think they're looking for the same guy."

"Luis, I've got to have your help on this. With this second

murder, the stakes have doubled. And, not to go into it—I'm not at home—there was another country heard from yesterday, if you take my meaning.''

"I don't get it.''

"There's a new party that may be of interest to you people. Springer and Mattocks were supposed to be told about it yesterday. With this new angle, and Robyn's death, you've *got* to jump into this. I know you say Springer and Mattocks are experienced and all that, yet so far the only positive things they've done have been to hound me and lose the evidence that would vindicate me.'' (The hell with it, Reuben decided, let the driver's ears get pink.) "These cases need Bautista and Frost. And right away, like this morning.''

"I can't do it, Reuben. I'm up to my eyes in three other kinds of crap. And it's not SOP. Good old Standard Operating Procedure is very big in the Department, and I can't buck it.''

"Why don't you leave that to me?'' Frost said, recalling the Mayor's offer to be helpful. "I don't want to discredit your colleagues—I have an idea we're going to need all the help we can get—but I want you right at my side. Will you do it?''

"Oh, Reuben, what can I say?'' Bautista groaned. "For old times' sake, yes, I'd do anything for you. But you'll have to straighten out the politics.''

"Consider it done. Can you round up Springer and Mattocks and be at my house at, let's see, it's eight-fifty now—how about ten o'clock?''

"Ten-thirty? I'm exhausted, and I don't even know where the hell they are.''

"Listen, I'm talking to you from the middle of the Triborough Bridge, for God's sake. There's no one you can't get in touch with if you try.''

"You're a hard man, Reuben. We'll be there as soon as we can.''

Frost put back the telephone with satisfaction. "We've got him!'' he said to Cynthia, clasping her hand.

The remainder of the trip was made without further interruption, the driver keeping a respectful silence. He probably thinks I'm either a murderer on the loose or a bigwig in the Police Department, Frost thought.

Frost hauled the bags up to the master bedroom and then called Bob Millard immediately. Millard was full of remorse, convinced that he could have saved Robyn's life if he had done things differently. He had called the widow the previous day right after his overseas conversation with Reuben, warning her, as instructed, to be careful. But with the sensitivity and discretion of the good trust and estates lawyer that he was, he had not told her the reasons, feeling that this should be done in person. He had arranged to meet her for drinks at home at six o'clock. That had been too late; he had arrived minutes after Miss Boyle, who had found the body, had called the police.

Frost assured him that he had acted perfectly correctly, and that no one could have foreseen that Robyn was in such imminent danger. Millard was not mollified, and Frost himself silently regretted the unfortunate chain of events.

"You talked to Springer and Mattocks?" Frost asked.

"Yes, before all this happened. I had a helluva time getting hold of them, but they came down here around four."

"What did they think?"

"Reuben, I can't say they were enthusiastic."

"Did you tell them that I said they should get on Mr. Rourke immediately?"

"Of course I did. But as I told you, they weren't very enthusiastic."

Millard's information made Frost ready for war when the three detectives arrived shortly before eleven. He herded them into the library and, with their permission, had Cynthia join them.

"Gentlemen, I don't mean to be imperious," he said, after they were seated and had started drinking the coffee Cynthia had prepared. "But I'm afraid I'm too tired to be polite. We're just off a long and very tedious flight from Rio. We're back early because of the weird new development—Tobias' purported son—that came to light yesterday. Plus—*plus*—the terrible news we got this morning. So right now, the first question is, are all three of you going to be able to concentrate on the Vandermeers? Are you available?''

"Reuben, as I told you—'' Bautista began.

"Yes, I know, Luis, I have to fix it up downtown. If I do that, what do you gentlemen say?'' he added, turning to Springer and Mattocks.

"Mr. Frost, if you've got any useful information, we're here to listen to it,'' Springer said. "But I'm not sure we can let you run the case.''

Frost gave him a look of cold fury and with some effort controlled himself. "I'm trying to get these murders solved, Mr. Springer. I have no interest in glory or credit or running anything. Though I'll have to be frank with you, I'm not certain who—if anyone—*is* running the show. I just want to get the job done, and the murderer found. Now, I'm going to make a telephone call, to which you are welcome to listen.''

Reuben called the Mayor and received the usual reply that he would get back to him. Not wanting to wait for the next ''phone break,'' he urged the person he was talking to to tell the Mayor as soon as possible that he was calling and that it was an emergency concerning the murder of Robyn Vandermeer.

"Now, while we're waiting, do I understand correctly, Mr. Springer and Mr. Mattocks, that Bob Millard told you about Stephen Rourke?'' Frost asked.

"Reuben, you'll have to fill me in,'' Bautista said.

"Fine, let me do it for the benefit of everyone,'' Reuben said, possibly implying that a second rendition might improve Springer and Mattocks' understanding as well.

"So what have we learned about Rourke?'' Frost asked, when he had finished. "Where was he on March fifth?''

Both Springer and Mattocks shifted in their chairs, plainly uncomfortable.

"I'm afraid we don't know anything yet, sir. We were going to start this morning, then we were called over here,'' Springer said.

"I realize you can't be in two places at once. But I don't believe there's any time to waste. Did it occur to you, when you found out about Mrs. Vandermeer, that he might be her killer?''

"We were told he was Vandermeer's illegitimate son," Mattocks replied.

"Well, put two and two together. He was Vandermeer's heir, but he wouldn't get the income from the family Trust as long as Mrs. Vandermeer was alive."

"Got it," Mattocks said.

Frost looked at Bautista with a stern expression. These boys were slow learners.

"But that's not the reason I wanted you to check him out yesterday. I didn't know about Robyn then. You've never been able to find the servant that was at the party the night Tobias Vandermeer died, have you? Pace Padgett?"

The two detectives shook their heads glumly.

"Did it not occur to you that Rourke might be the missing Pace Padgett?"

It clearly had not. As the possibility sank in, the phone rang. It was the Mayor, and Frost told him why he had been calling.

"Norman, I'm not trying to interfere with the Police Department, but they now have two Vandermeer murders on their hands. I'm trying to help solve them, give them the benefit of what I know about the Vandermeers and what happened the night Tobias died, but I'd quite honestly feel more comfortable if a particular detective I know named Luis Bautista got brought in, in addition to the detectives that are already assigned. I'm not criticizing, Norman, but this is a ticklish situation, and I think Bautista would be helpful. What can you do?"

"I always hesitate to interfere with the police," the Mayor told Reuben. "You're right, though, this is a hot one, and Robyn was a good friend and supporter of mine. Let me talk to the Commissioner. I'll get hold of him at once."

"As a matter of fact, I have Bautista and the two other detectives, named Springer and Mattocks, here with me now. Could the Commissioner call here?"

"I'll do my best."

"We'll have to wait for your boss to call," Frost explained. "In the meantime, can one of you tell me exactly what happened yesterday?"

"Sure thing," Mattocks said. "A call came to nine one one

around five forty-five. Five forty-six, to be precise. A Miss Boyle, Kathleen Boyle, the Vandermeers' maid, called to report that she had found Mrs. Vandermeer's body in the dining room when she returned from her afternoon off. The victim had strangle marks on her neck and had been pushed halfway under the dining-room table. The portables who answered the call gave us the word around six-thirty, and we found the body just as Boyle had described it, with the strangle marks on her neck. Except for an upended dining-room chair, there was no sign of violence other than the marks on the victim's neck. No struggle at all. We surmised that the perpetrator must be somebody she knew and had probably let in.''

''When did all this happen?'' Reuben asked.

''The ME figured she'd been dead at least two hours. The Boyle woman said she was 'stiff as a board' when she called, which probably means rigor mortis had begun. That takes at least two hours, which brings you back to around three forty-five. Then, Mr. Frost, your colleague, Millard, told us he'd talked to the deceased on the telephone at roughly two forty-five. So we've got a break, a good fix on the time. Somewhere between two forty-five and three forty-five.''

''There's one other thing,'' Springer interjected. ''The place was in good order, as Mattocks said, but there was a picture of some kind missing from the dining room. It had been ripped out of its frame and the frame was on the floor.''

''The Jasper Johns,'' Frost said, looking at Cynthia. The art world was intruding on the case again.

''Yeah, that's the name. That's what Boyle told us,'' Mattocks said. ''Do you know anything about it? She wasn't very good at describing it. Said it was a lot of blotches and scrawls that were meant to be numbers.''

''It was called, I believe, 'O through 9,' '' Frost said. He described the missing painting as best he could.

''I assume it was valuable,'' Springer said.

''I'm told ten million at least,'' Frost said, quoting Deybold's estimate.

''Jeez,'' Mattocks said.

''Sounds like somebody was after the picture,'' Springer added.

"Yes, except it's hard to believe anybody would think they could ever get rid of it," Frost said. "Johns is famous and still alive and the painting's surely known in art circles. Trying to sell it legitimately would be a little like peddling the Mona Lisa."

The call from the Police Commissioner interrupted their speculations. Reuben picked up the telephone and was told that the Commissioner wanted to speak to the three detectives jointly.

"We don't have a speakerphone here, Commissioner. I'll put them on separate extensions if you hold on," Reuben said. He directed Springer and Mattocks to the kitchen and the upstairs bedroom, and put Bautista on the phone he himself had been using.

The Frosts watched Bautista's face as a very one-sided conversation ensued. The grimaces he made, coupled with an occasional smile and an upraised arm and fist, indicated that Springer and Mattocks were getting their marching orders; Bautista's own participation was limited to an occasional "Yes, sir" and "No, sir."

"We're at your service, Mr. Frost," a chastened Springer said when he returned, coolly but without any remaining edge of hostility. "Where do you suggest we go from here?"

Frost decided not to inquire further about the Commissioner's call, but hastened to seize the initiative in answering the now compliant Springer's question.

"Gentlemen, here's the way I see it, though if you think I'm half-cocked, say so. The first priority is to find out everything we can about Stephen Rourke. Most especially where he was on March fifth and yesterday afternoon. Luis, you're new to all this, I think that's a job for you."

He also told him to contact Drew Hammil, after telling the group about the lawyer's visit to Millard. "It will be very interesting to know if and when Hammil reported the things he'd found out to his client."

"Now, let's turn to Robyn," Frost went on. "Unless we're dealing with a stranger after the Jasper Johns, I think our working assumption should be that whoever killed Tobias killed Robyn. Any disagreement there?"

Reuben's question was met with silence.

"In case Mr. Rourke doesn't pan out, it would be useful to find out where the other suspects in Tobias' death were yesterday. We're now down to five, as I make it. Robyn's obviously eliminated, and, I'm told, so am I," Frost said, glancing at Springer and Mattocks, without pausing to give them a chance to explain or apologize, or even to confirm what he had said. "That leaves Bill Kearney, Wayne Givens and his wife, Sherman Deybold and Kathleen Boyle, each one of whom could have planted the poisoned capsules. How are you dividing them up?"

"Before we do that, you can eliminate Boyle," Mattocks said. "We checked her out last night. Yesterday was her afternoon off and she took an old Dominican friar to the movies. Unless he lied to us, she was with him all afternoon."

"Okay," Reuben said. "How about the others?"

"I'll take Kearney and the two Givenses," Springer said. "Mattocks can take Deybold—and Pace Padgett, if he's not this guy Rourke."

"Thanks a lot," Mattocks said.

"And when do we meet again?" Frost asked. "How about same time, same place tomorrow?"

"That doesn't give us much time, sir," Springer said.

"There isn't much time, Detective Springer," Frost countered. Forty-plus years at Chase & Ward and a lifetime of crash legal projects had not prepared Frost for any counseling of delay. "All I can ask is that you do your best—and happy hunting."

"As Sir Thomas Beecham said, 'That ought to keep the buggers hopping,' " Reuben said, once the policemen were gone.

"Oh, Reuben, I hate that story," Cynthia said. "That tyrant Beecham, saying such a thing after conducting a performance of *Swan Lake* at double speed."

"That's because you're a dancer. But I'm sorry, dear."

AROUND EIGHT THE NEXT MORNING, FROST GOT UP AND began fiddling with his computer "index." After making a series of entries covering what had been learned the previous day about Robyn's death, he printed out the entire document. Was there information buried in his compilation that might be relevant? With this in mind, he began scrutinizing each scrap that he had stored away.

One item that caught his notice was the peculiar fact that Tobias Vandermeer had fairly recently been interested in adoption. What could that mean? Maybe he should have a look at the memorandum Chase & Ward had prepared on the subject for Tobias.

He looked up Bob Millard's direct number at the firm and dialed it. He was nonplused when a child answered the phone.

"I was trying to reach Robert Millard," he said.

"Daddy."

"Could I speak to him?" Reuben asked, slowly and deliberately. It was not at all clear that he was communicating, when Millard himself came on the line, apologizing for the child.

"You bringing your children to the office these days, Bob?" Frost asked.

"No, no," Millard said, laughing. "I'm polishing up a

bitch of a brief to be filed in Surrogate's Court next week, so I decided to hole up at home today.''

"But I called your office."

"Oh, Reuben, you don't know about the fancy new phone system at Chase & Ward."

"I know everything I care to know about," Frost said acidly, thinking of his own frustrations at coping with the "new" system on his occasional visits to the firm.

"Well, you can forward calls from the office. Since my secretary's decided that this beautiful sunny day would be a good one to get sick, I had no choice but to get my calls routed here."

"Hmn. Modern science, I guess. Let me tell you why I called. You remember that memo you described to me, the one written for Tobias Vandermeer about adoption?"

"Sure."

"How can I get a copy?"

"Easy. I'll get one of my associates to messenger it up to you."

"Excellent. Right away?"

"Right away."

Millard was true to his word, and a Xerox of the adoption memo was delivered by an office messenger just before eleven. Frost should have been meeting with his police colleagues, but they were late, so he read it. It was immediately clear that Millard, back on the day after Tobias was killed, had read it too hastily. It was true that it dealt with the rights of an adopted child—but the emphasis was very clearly on such a child's *lack* of rights, once legally adopted by another, against his natural parent, and not on his rights against an adoptive parent.

Frost was too pleased with his discovery to find fault with Millard's cursory reading, or the fact that the younger lawyer had missed a short, and perhaps meaningful, paragraph toward the end of the memorandum that informed the reader that not only a minor, but also an adult could be adopted.

Well, well, well, Frost muttered to himself. Wasn't it likely that Tobias was thinking of persuading Stephen Rourke to be adopted by another, thus cutting him off from his rights in the Vandermeer Trust? And wasn't it perhaps significant that the memo dated back roughly to the time Tobias had begun drinking more heavily?

Frost was going to consult with Cynthia, who was reading the morning paper at the breakfast table in the kitchen, when Bautista, Springer and Mattocks arrived together.

"What have we got?" he asked, as the five of them reconvened in the library. "Any good news? Any bad news?"

"How do you want to proceed?" Bautista asked.

"One by one," Reuben answered. "Starting with Stephen Rourke."

"Okay," Bautista said. "Here's what I have. Stephen Hendrik Rourke—"

"I like the Hendrik part," Frost interjected.

"Stephen Hendrik Rourke, born in Saint Vincent's Hospital September 22, 1952. He lives at 425 West 21st Street, way west in Chelsea. Lives alone, but has a girlfriend who's around a lot. I'll come back to her.

"I had a hard time finding the guy. No answer on the phone—he's listed in the book—or when I went to his apartment house. I called Hammil, his lawyer—"

"Had he talked with his client?" Frost asked.

"He said that was privileged information," Bautista answered.

"I think that means he had," Frost said. "Sorry, Luis, I didn't mean to interrupt."

"Anyway, Hammil suggested I try Rourke's agent, guy named Irwin Decker. I did, and Decker told me that Rourke's just started rehearsals for a play, something called *Marble Balls* . . ."

"Good God," Cynthia said, before she could stop herself.

"Yeah, great title, right?" Bautista said with a grin. "Anyway, the play's supposed to open at the beginning of May, off Broadway. Rehearsals began Monday, and they were rehearsing yesterday in a loft down on lower Broadway. I rushed down there and found him. I waited for a break and we had a good talk."

"What does he look like?" Cynthia asked.

"Medium height, five feet eight or nine. Brown hair, very blue eyes. He's getting bald, which makes him look older than he is."

"It doesn't sound like Pace Padgett to me," Cynthia said. "Remember those green eyes, Reuben? Not to mention the black hair and the mustache."

"Let's hear the rest of the story," Reuben said, slightly irritated at his wife's interruption, although Padgett's appearance had been the question foremost in his own mind.

"Rourke was friendly and polite. Very relaxed. I told him why I wanted to see him and he didn't seem surprised. 'I figured you guys would be around,' he said. I had one of our new detectives with me, by the way."

"Shillaber?" Mattocks said.

"Yeah," Bautista said. "When I told Rourke what I was interested in, he admitted right away that he was Tobias' son. He said he didn't know anything about the killing, only what he'd seen on TV and read in the papers. He claimed he hadn't heard about Mrs. Vandermeer's death. 'I've been concentrating full time on this play,' he said.

"He says he remembers reading about Tobias' death in the *Post* the Monday after it happened. The day before, he said he was home in his apartment all day, except for brunch with his girl, name of Terry Hartley, and dinner with her that night. He said he'd gotten the script of *Marble Balls*, and was busy studying it to get ready for a casting call a couple of days later."

"Any corroboration of his story?" Springer asked.

"I'll get to that. He says he and Hartley had brunch at the Chelsea Central, a restaurant near his apartment—I had the feeling Hartley had slept over Saturday night. She wanted to go to a movie uptown that he'd already seen, so he left her to go back home. Said this must have been around two-thirty, because he remembers that she was going to the three o'clock show. He says he told her to give him a call when she left the movie, and maybe they could go out to dinner. He also says that he talked on the phone that afternoon, or early in the evening, he couldn't remember exactly, with his agent, Decker, and his acting teacher, Guy Gunther."

"What about Tuesday?" Frost asked.

"He seems to be in the clear on that. They started rehearsals at one and went right through till seven, except for coffee breaks. I had Shillaber stay around and check that out. Everybody agreed Rourke had been there the whole afternoon."

"You said rehearsals began Monday, Luis?" Cynthia asked.

"Right."

"So yesterday was only the second day the actors had been together?"

"Right again."

"That means the cast wasn't yet a close and intimate family where everyone knew everybody else."

"I suppose that's true. But Shillaber was very diligent, and I don't see any reason to doubt what he found out. Anyway, after I left Rourke, I tracked down—"

"Just a minute," Reuben said. "I'm sorry to interrupt you again, but I have one question before I forget it. Did Rourke say he'd ever met his father?"

"I asked him that. He said he didn't know who his father was until just before his mother died, when she gave him a letter from Vandermeer in which he owned up to being his father. He said he'd gone to see Tobias once. It was apparently a brief meeting, and once his curiosity was satisfied, and it was clear his father had no interest in establishing a relationship, that was it."

"Even though Tobias was colossally rich? That didn't interest a struggling actor?"

"He was very calm about that. Said Tobias had his life and he had his own, and that was fine with him. He seemed sincere enough, though I grant you he's an actor. Now, let me go on. I got hold of Decker again, and Gunther. And first thing this morning, Hartley, the girlfriend. Just to prick up your ears, she works at a clinical lab downtown."

"Where they make cyanide?" Frost asked.

"We didn't go into that on our first date," Bautista said. "I was too busy trying to see if her story checked with Rourke's. And it did. Brunch, then the movie, then she called

Rourke at his apartment and they agreed to meet for dinner at nine o'clock.''

"Where?" Frost asked.

"Indochine, downtown across from the Public Theater on Lafayette Street. Going back, when I talked to Decker—on the telephone, I didn't have enough time to go see him—he at first didn't remember any phone conversation with Rourke that Sunday afternoon. He said his whole business consisted of telephone calls and he couldn't remember specifics, though he would try and get back to me if he could recall anything. He did call back, about a half hour later. Says he's pretty sure Rourke left a message on his machine that day, asking the agent to call him at home. Decker returned early from a winter weekend in the country—Southampton—and is certain he did call Rourke, though he can't remember the conversation exactly. He said Rourke was real anxious to get the part in *Marble Balls* and had been on the phone seeking reassurance in the days before he got it.''

"And he talked to him at home sometime late Sunday afternoon?" Reuben asked.

"Correct. So did Gunther. Rourke had been trying to get him all weekend, it looks like—same thing, he wanted reassurance from his old coach—and finally reached Gunther a little after three on Sunday. Then, Gunther remembered very clearly, Rourke had said he had another call waiting and could they talk later? Specifically, he asked if Gunther could call him back around four-thirty. Gunther did so and Rourke told him then that he wanted to meet with him in person, that he wanted to go over some things in the script with him. Rourke had said they could meet any time, but Gunther and his wife had a dinner party to go to that night, so they agreed on Monday morning.''

"And that meeting took place?" Frost asked.

"Yes, first thing Monday morning.''

"Anything else, Luis?''

"No, that's it. The bottom line is Rourke's clean as far as last Tuesday's concerned, and seems to be on March fifth as well.''

"Can we come back to that?" Frost said. "Let's hear

about the others. What about Sherman Deybold? Where was he Tuesday afternoon?''

"Open and shut," Mattocks said confidently. "There were three important buyers here Tuesday from the Cincinnati Museum: the director, a curator for modern art and a lawyer who's chairman of their acquisitions committee. They were interested in looking at the stuff the Deybold/Costas gallery's showing, a painter named, wait a minute, I've got it here . . .''

"Vitalia Ashley," Frost said.

"Yeah. Right," Mattocks replied, put off balance by Frost's omniscience. "The deal was important enough to get Deybold himself into the act, not just the young guy, Costas. They had lunch around one-thirty at the Manhattan Bistro on Spring Street in Soho, shot the breeze for a while and then went to the gallery. I contacted the Cincinnati crowd at the Regency this morning and confirmed this, and also found out that Deybold had brought the three of them uptown and had a drink with them at the hotel.''

"Which takes us beyond four o'clock?" Frost said.

"Right."

"What was the lawyer's name, by the way?''

"Daniel Babson."

"Oh, hell, I know him from way back," Frost said. "He's not the sort who's apt to lie to the police. Unfortunately, he is exactly the type to put his museum's funds into Vitalia Ashleys. But that's neither here nor there. What did you find out, Springer?''

"I have two easy ones and a hard one. Mrs. Givens and Kearney are the easy ones. She does volunteer work at New York Hospital and was there all Tuesday afternoon. As for Kearney, he had lunch at his desk that day and never left his office until six or six-thirty. Unless, of course, he got everybody there to lie for him. If the bookkeepers sitting in that bull pen outside his office are to be believed, he was there the whole afternoon.''

"I'm familiar with the setup," Frost said. "I don't believe there's any way he could've snuck out without being seen.''

"Now, for Wayne Givens," Springer said, "he's a little harder. For one thing, I didn't get to talk to him directly. He went to Washington to testify on some drug thing yesterday and won't be back until this afternoon. But his secretary said he went to lunch on Tuesday with his assistant, Dr. Marguerite Baxter. She said it was Baxter's birthday, and they went to celebrate at a place called the San Felice, over on East Forty-fifth.''

''Never heard of it,'' Frost said.

''Oh, Reuben, it's very hot,'' Cynthia said. ''It's been written up everywhere recently. Big and always crowded, is what I hear.''

''Anyway,'' Mattocks continued, ''they left the Bloemendael Foundation offices around one-fifteen, one-thirty and walked over to the San Felice. When I talked to her, Dr. Baxter said she can't remember exactly when they left—it sounded like quite a celebration—but probably around three-thirty. She wasn't feeling well, she said, and Givens took her home and stayed with her until she felt better, around six.''

''So he never left her?''

''That's what she said, yes.''

''What does the restaurant say?''

''The maître d' told me on the phone that he knew Dr. Givens and Dr. Baxter, and that three-thirty was probably about right.''

''So there was a window of fifteen minutes between when Givens left the restaurant and the outside time when Robyn was strangled. Could he get from Forty-fifth Street to Seventy-fourth and kill her in fifteen minutes?'' Frost asked. ''Not bloody likely. Agreed?''

There was no dissent, and now the group looked toward Reuben for a variety of reasons, from connubial affection and old friendship to orders from the Police Commissioner. In the discussion that followed, they agreed that Deybold, Kearney and Barbara Givens were out of contention, at least temporarily, though Reuben said the possible link between Deybold and the stolen Jasper Johns still intrigued him.

''He sounds like the best lead to me,'' Reuben said, when Rourke's name came up. ''Sure, he's bald and blue-eyed, but he is an actor, for Christ's sake. Pace Padgett's black hair and mustache would have been no problem for him. And can't you get colored contact lenses these days? I think so.''

Cynthia agreed that this was possible.

"So, can't we get a picture of Rourke?" Reuben asked.

"What about that agent, Decker?" Cynthia said. "He must have pictures and would probably be delighted to give them away, even to the police.''

"Good idea, Cynthia," Frost said. "Besides, Luis, when you see Decker you can recheck his recollection of his phone conversation with Rourke.''

"Good.''

"And while I've no doubt your new colleague, Officer Shillaber, did a thorough job with the cast of *Marble Balls*, that's worth rechecking. If Rourke was, in fact, clever enough to create Pace Padgett, he may have had a doppel-gänger covering for him while he went uptown to kill his stepmother. And he certainly was less than candid with you, Luis, about Tobias. He may have only seen him once, or so he says, but hiring that lawyer, Hammil, which he appears to have done some time ago, shows that he was interested in more than what his father looked like.''

"I agree," Bautista said.

"And I'd go back over the tracks with Gunther, the acting coach, and Ms. Hartley," Frost said.

"No problem.''

"Then there's Dr. Wayne. I'd certainly go over those tracks, too. In addition to talking to him, of course.''

"Can I make a suggestion?" Springer asked.

"Go ahead.''

"I didn't say it before, but I detected a slight fish smell when I talked to Givens' secretary. I had the gut feeling she wasn't telling me everything. No offense, Mattocks, she's a dynamite black girl. Maybe you with your obvious charm could do better than I did.''

Frost was nervous at the racial reference, though he need not have been; the partnership between Springer and Mattocks was thoroughly relaxed.

Mattocks grinned and affected a slight accent that had not

been detectable up until then. "Sure thing, man. If you honkies can't get to the chick, leave her to me!"

"I'm probably being obstinate," Frost told the others. "At this point Rourke looks promising, but I think it's too soon to give up on the rest, especially Deybold. Those folks from Cincinnati may have been so starry-eyed after seeing those dazzling Vitalia Ashleys that they weren't certain of the time sequence on Tuesday. If they're off by an hour, or even less, Deybold could have gotten free in time to kill Robyn. Why don't you have a go at it, Springer?"

"All right," the detective said doubtfully.

"And would you do one other thing for me? Ask Kearney to come in for questioning around, say, five o'clock this afternoon. Don't do anything unconstitutional, but if you could be a bit menacing, a bit threatening, it would serve my purpose."

"I don't understand. Don't we think he's in the clear?"

"Probably so. But I want to talk to him," Reuben said. "And I have an idea the more scared he is, the more productive our chat will be."

"It's kind of unusual," Springer said, hesitating.

"Hell, Tom," Bautista said, "you're entitled to question him again. And it would be voluntary."

"Well, okay."

"As a matter of fact," Frost added, "as far as I'm concerned you can call him up at four forty-five and cancel. If the trick works, I'll have my answers by then."

Slightly mystified, the detectives went away, promising to report back, using Reuben as a clearinghouse, as soon as there were developments. Only Cynthia, after they had left, probed to find out what Reuben had in mind.

"It's worth a try," she said, as he went to the telephone to call Bill Kearney.

GETTING CLOSER

A VERY NERVOUS BILL KEARNEY RECEIVED FROST IN HIS office Thursday afternoon.

"Do you know what's going on?" Kearney asked his visitor. "The police were here yesterday asking all kinds of questions. And now they want me to come down at five o'clock! What do they want with me?" His voice was pleading, and he was almost shaking, as if he had a vision of an interrogation with blinding lights and rubber hoses.

"Bill, as I told you the last time we talked, I've taken an interest in the Vandermeer case—cases, with Robyn's death. I'll be very frank with you. The police are scrutinizing everyone who had anything to do with the Vandermeers. That of course includes you. You were, after all, one of the last people to see Tobias alive."

"Do you think they suspect me?" Kearney asked in a quavering voice.

"They suspect everybody. But don't worry. Truth will prevail."

"I hope so. My anxiety level is pretty high right now."

Frost did not commiserate further, but got to the point.

"Bill, what can you tell me about a person named Stephen Hendrik Rourke?"

"Never heard of him," came the negative reply, just as it had before, when Frost had asked about his mother.

"You're sure?"

"Positive."

"I'm afraid I'm going to have to lay my cards on the table," Frost said. "As you rightly guessed, you are a suspect in Tobias' murder. And, until the police are satisfied with your alibi, Robyn's as well. I happen to believe you're innocent, but the police have to be convinced. The surest way, Bill, to avoid having them make a mistake is to do everything you can to put the blame where it belongs."

"What does this Stephen Rourke have to do with that?"

"Isn't it just possible that Rourke killed his father and stepmother?"

"So you know that Rourke was Tobias' illegitimate son?"

"Yes, I do."

"Well, since you've found out the truth elsewhere, I guess I'm free to talk."

Frost did not comment, waiting for Kearney to speak.

"Yes, Stephen Rourke was Tobias' son, born out of wedlock in 1952. His mother, Grace Alice Rourke, was an aspiring singer when she met Tobias and had an affair with him for several months."

"This was after the breakup with Robyn that Hendrik Vandermeer forced?"

"Exactly. And before he went to Paris and met Ines. Much against my will, I became his confidant after Grace Alice got pregnant. Should he present his father with a *fait accompli*? Should he force her to have an abortion? In the end he decided to do nothing, and she gave birth to Stephen.

"Tobias supported Grace Alice from then on. She never resumed her singing career after the baby was born and was totally dependent on Tobias for support. She had Tobias' problem, too. Drink. He paid for her to dry out a couple of times. It didn't work and she ultimately died of cirrhosis."

"When was that?"

"The end of 1984. December. I remember because Tobias was in Paris with Robyn, and I had to break the news to him by phone. Grace suffered a long time, and Tobias paid all her medical bills. Her deal was that she was never to tell Stephen who his father was. Believe it or not, she apparently kept her word until just before the end, when she told him everything.

"About two weeks after Grace Alice died, Stephen confronted Tobias. Said his acting career wasn't going too well and he wanted support. He didn't mention inheriting or anything like that. Just a monthly stipend, like his mother had received.

"It got dicey," Kearney went on. "Tobias was furious and said absolutely not. He felt he'd discharged whatever obligation he had by taking care of Grace Alice. As Tobias told it to me, Stephen said he'd go public with it and announce to the world who his father was. Said it would help his career and look great in *People* Magazine—son of multimillionaire struggles as starving actor.

"Tobias was beside himself, but he had second thoughts. I believe he consulted your firm about getting the kid adopted, which your colleagues said would cut him off from any rights to the Vandermeer Trust or Tobias' estate. When Tobias learned this, he made Stephen an offer—two million outright if he'd agree to be adopted."

"Who was going to adopt him?"

"Who do you think? Me. All Stephen had to do was consent and it could've been done. I was willing. It was purely a paper transaction. It wasn't as if I'd have to bring him up. He was a little old for fatherly advice."

"What happened?"

"The offer was a huge mistake. I really believe Stephen did just want a monthly allowance. But when he heard that two million figure, he must have realized there were bigger stakes to be had. He got that lawyer, Hammil, into the act and asked for four million—then changed his mind and upped it to eight.

"Tobias went crazy. He hated the idea of having Stephen go public, but he hated parting with eight million even more— this would have been *his* money, remember, not the Trust's. So he turned him down."

"What did young Rourke do then?"

"He told Tobias, fine, he'd wait him out. He said he was young and could afford to be patient. Tobias wouldn't live forever. And with Hammil's advice, he knew that there wasn't a thing Tobias could do to change the terms of the Vandermeer Trust, so that he would ultimately inherit the entire fortune.''

"Obviously he never did take his story to the press," Frost said.

"That's right. Tobias was so adamant, Rourke probably decided the publicity wouldn't do him any good.''

"Can I ask you one more question?''

"Sure."

"Why didn't you tell me this before? Or tell the police?''

"Why should I have? From what I knew of the situation, there was no way Stephen could have killed his father. So why desecrate Tobias' memory, or cause even more pain for Robyn? I'm only telling you now because things have changed. I don't see how, but you certainly suggested that Stephen might have killed his father and Robyn.''

And the police are breathing down your neck, Frost thought, but did not say. "Any other surprises that I should know about, Bill?" he did ask.

"Nope."

"Was this quarrel the reason for Tobias' increased drinking?''

"It was a combination of things, starting with Grace Alice's death. As I told you, the woman had a drink problem. Tobias was very sympathetic, even if he never would face his own difficulties with the bottle. I also suspected that he may still have been in love with her, at least a little. Tobias was a bit of a romantic, you know.''

"I've heard that before.''

"Anyway, Grace Alice's death set him off. He started drinking heavily after he got the news in Paris and never stopped after that. The son's escalating demands made things worse. Unlike what he felt toward Grace Alice, Tobias didn't have any romantic feelings toward the son. He had never had a chance to experience the joys of real fatherhood, and was not going to try with a stranger in his thirties—especially one who seemed to get more and more greedy for money.

"Robyn's increasing eminence didn't help. He thought everyone regarded her as a paragon of civic virtue, and him as a drunken bum. His perception was pretty much right, and it didn't help a whole lot in the self-esteem department.

"And he had lost the one weapon he might have had—control of the family money. His father, when he set up the Vandermeer Trust, denied Tobias the ability to decide how the family fortune would be disposed of. And he'd lost the only authority he had over the income when he'd given Robyn that deed ten years earlier.

"So there he was, a rich man with no power. And a son and a wife waiting for him to die. He tried to buy off the son and to coerce Robyn into surrendering her life estate. It didn't work. All he could do was cut Robyn out of his own will—even if that wouldn't have been effective—and torture her over her living expenses. And, of course, drink."

"It's a sad story," Frost said, thinking back to Tobias' last words at the reading club, condemning old man Osborne in *Vanity Fair* for using the power of money against his daughter-in-law.

"Tobias was a totally difficult man," Kearney said quietly. "But he was not all bad. If he'd gotten on with his father, or if Robyn had been a different kind of woman, things could have been different."

"Bill, I'm glad to hear the whole tale at last."

"Does it help you any?"

"We'll have to see," Frost said as he prepared to leave.

Once back home, Frost read though the chronology of Tobias' actions that was a part of his computer "index." With Kearney's revelations, it now all made sense. So did Tobias' shouting the night he was killed. In some eerie drunken clarity, hadn't he seen through Pace Padgett's disguise, hadn't he seen his demanding illegitimate son when he shouted, "What do you want this time?" Frost and the others had been wrong when the lurching figure of Tobias had appeared to be addressing Deybold; he was railing instead at the retreating figure of Pace Padgett. And now there was no doubt in Frost's mind who the "prick" was.

Frost did want to check one thing—the conclusion in the Chase & Ward memo that an adult could legally adopt another adult and that such an adoption would terminate any rights the adoptee had against a natural parent. He was sure the memo was correct, but he wanted to be absolutely certain.

With this in mind, he picked up his Chase & Ward directory and found Bob Millard's direct-dial number. I wonder if I'll get the baby on the phone again, he asked himself as he dialed. With a jolt, he slammed down the phone. The adoption question could wait; his own query to himself had given him a flash of insight that had to be pursued immediately. He must find Bautista at once.

Frost was trying feverishly to track Bautista down when the detective appeared at the front door.

"I've got them!" he said to Frost, as he came in. "Cynthia was right. Decker, the agent, had three different glossies of Rourke."

"Never mind that," Frost said, deflating Bautista's enthusiasm. "What kind of records does the telephone company keep of local telephone calls?"

"Hell, they keep everything. Every call is recorded on the computer and then they keep a microfiche of the computer records."

"How long do they keep them?"

"I don't know. Years, I think."

Frost then asked another question about the telephone records that Bautista said he couldn't answer without contacting the phone company. He also passed along to Bautista the conclusion he had come to minutes earlier.

"I like it," the detective said.

"And I hope you like it enough to get on it right away."

"I do. And I will. I'll call the phone company now and get them to work. I'll have to have a subpoena for the records, of course, but your friend Munson can get one tonight. But don't you want to see the pictures?"

"Yes, of course I do."

Bautista took the glossies from an envelope and showed the three pictures of a balding, middle-aged actor to Frost, who studied them carefully. "My visual imagination isn't the greatest," Frost said, "but I'd say that if you drew a mustache and some black hair on these, you'd have a pretty good likeness of Pace Padgett. Cynthia would be better at this than I am, though. I think she's upstairs.''

He called to his wife, who had been resting in their bedroom. Shown the pictures, she was even more positive than her husband. "I remember his high cheekbones," she said. "I noticed them at the time. They were like Igor Youskevitch's, my old colleague at NatBallet. And there they are—Igor's cheeks.''

"I have another surprise," Bautista said. "Decker gave me a biography of Rourke. His biggest success till now has been a one-man show for kids called—are you ready?—*A Man of a Thousand Faces*.''

"Great!" Frost exclaimed. "Now, will you pursue the phone business?''

Bautista made several calls and reported back to Reuben. "They're going to start digging tonight, and Munson's getting the subpoena. And, *amigo*, there's other good news. The phone company *does* have a record of calls that are forwarded from one number to another.''

Frost was jubilant, instinctively confident that the phone records would show that the calls Rourke claimed to have received at home that fatal Sunday had been automatically forwarded on to the Vandermeers, where "Pace Padgett" had answered them. Rourke may have triumphed as "The Man of a Thousand Faces," but his performance as Pace Padgett had almost certainly outdone that.

"Now, since there's no rest for the wicked," Frost told Bautista, "will you please double-check what your man Shillaber found out about Rourke's whereabouts Tuesday afternoon?''

"That was the next item on the agenda, Reuben.''

"Well, do it!''

"Okay, chief, you're the boss.''

"Don't tell your colleagues that. Besides, it isn't true.''

"Let's say it is," Bautista said. "That means you've got a decision to make. Should Springer and Mattocks be taken off what they're doing and help me put a full-court press on Rourke and his friends?''

Frost pondered for a moment. "That's a hard one," he finally said. "No, let's wait a bit. Let's wait to see if NYNEX comes through.''

"Aye, aye, sir."

"Cut it out, Luis, and get to work."

After Bautista had hurried out, Reuben asked Cynthia to dinner.

"We still have the problem of Robyn's murder, but how about a little celebration? I'm sure as anything we're at least halfway home."

Cynthia, who had been given a full explanation, agreed with him.

"The Sign of the Dove okay?" he asked. "It's such a pretty place, and I'm told they've done something about the food after all these years."

"I've heard that, too."

Reuben was happy and contented as he sat with Cynthia amid the flowers and plants and bare-brick walls at Sign of the Dove. The roast baby pheasant with lentils was very good, the Château Giscours '82 even better. But as the end of the meal approached, the celebratory edge wore off, and Reuben was beset anew with doubts. The case against Rourke looked promising, but the telephone company might prove to be a dead end. And there was the matter, still untangled, of his alibi for the afternoon when Robyn had been murdered.

"You know, Cynthia, if Rourke somehow had a double to cover for him at that rehearsal, that gives our friends a better chance to crack the case," Frost said. "There's no honor among thieves, and Rourke and his co-conspirator will be found out. I'm sure of it."

"Have you considered another angle, dear?"

"Like what?"

"We've been assuming that the same person killed both Tobias and Robyn. But is that necessarily so? Even if Rourke murdered his father, couldn't someone else have strangled Robyn?"

"I've been thinking the same thing. That's why I didn't want Bautista's sidekicks to stop what they're doing."

"Take Sherman Deybold, for example. We now know what a slippery character he is, but we've never figured out why he might have killed his best customer. But killing Robyn for the Jasper Johns is different. He may have thought he could sell it in one of his far-off parking lots, not for ten million, perhaps, but for a lucrative price. To a reclusive Brazilian who would never show it, for example. And I suspect people haven't called him and Michael Costas S & M just because of their first names. He might even have *enjoyed* killing Robyn.''

''That's disgusting.''

''So is everything else about this muddle. But do you see what I mean?''

''Yes, Cynthia, I do.''

''Or your new pal, Kearney. There certainly was no love lost between him and Robyn. Or Wayne Givens, who was so shocked to find that he'd have to bide his time until Robyn died for the Bloemendael to receive its windfall.''

''All true, my dear.''

''And, speaking of Givens, I'll bet you anything Robyn got around to announcing her plans for the Bloemendael to him.''

''My guess is you're right.''

''I'm sorry to dampen our celebration.''

''Not at all. Justice will triumph, I haven't a doubt. Except for street crime, murder's going to become obsolete. All the computer records these days—which we hope will trap Rourke—those DNA fingerprints I keep reading about, and so on and so on. Killing someone undetected has become very difficult.''

As Reuben made his pronouncement, the waiter brought the check. Reuben picked it up and examined it.

''Look at this, for example,'' he said to Cynthia. ''Not only does it tell what we ate and drank, but that there were two of us, sitting at table forty-seven, that we were served by Team One and that they made up our check at 21:13:44. Right down to the second.''

''I wonder if they have a system like this at the San Felice?'' Cynthia asked. ''It's a new place, they probably do.''

''My God, Cynthia, you may have something! Come on, get yourself organized. Let's go home and call Mattocks.''

CLOSER STILL

FROM SPENT MORE THAN AN HOUR TRYING TO REACH MAT-
tocks. When he did, the detective promised to find out about
the San Felice.

"How are things going otherwise?" Frost asked.

"No big news. I interrogated Givens this afternoon when
he got back from Washington. He tells the same story as
Baxter did. I'm going to prowl around that Foundation tomorrow morning. You'll be the first to know what I find
out."

Mattocks reported back sooner than expected, appearing
at the Frosts' shortly after eleven on Friday.

"Well?" Frost said expectantly. "Is the San Felice auto-
mated or not?"

"The answer is yes. The time the check is made up is
recorded. They were pretty cross about it, but when they
found out I wasn't about to leave until they dug out Givens'
check from Tuesday afternoon, they did it. Right there, Reuben, big as life, his American Express receipt stapled to it.
Sixty dollars' worth of chicken paillard and four glasses of
white wine."

"The hell with what they ate. When did the time record
show?" Frost asked. Mattocks' sally was innocent enough,
but Frost was in no mood for irrelevancies.

"It showed that Givens' check was made up at 14:46:22."

"So it's not very likely he was still there at three-thirty."

"No, the maître d' remembered they'd paid the check when it was presented."

"So he was wrong when he said earlier they left at three-thirty?"

"Yes, he admits that. His excuse is the place was busy Tuesday. Once he saw the time on the check, he backed off."

"What does Givens say now? And Baxter?"

"I haven't gone back to them yet. I just came from the restaurant. I wanted to tell you right away—and also what else I found out this morning."

"Fire away. I'm liking this," Frost said.

"Springer was right. There's some hanky-panky with Givens. I sweet-talked his secretary this morning, and she finally admitted that Givens and Baxter are getting it on. One of their tricks is to go off to lunch, almost always at the San Felice, on Tuesday or Wednesday, every week. The secretary—and Baxter's secretary too—has instructions to say they've gone off to lunch to celebrate Baxter's birthday. Except to Mrs. Givens, of course, but the secretary says she never calls."

"She's a wise woman. She knows better," Frost observed. "Why the birthday story?"

"They don't come back after lunch. The secretary thinks they go to Baxter's apartment, though she's not completely sure."

"So the birthday party, the celebration part, is to explain to anybody who asks why they're not back at the office?"

"That's it."

"I must say, some adulterers are smarter than others. It sounds pretty dumb to me."

"Yeah."

Frost got up from his chair and pulled down the first volume of *Who's Who* from the shelf. "Let's make sure Tuesday wasn't her birthday," he said. "I hope she's prominent enough to be in here."

She was, with more distinguished credentials than Frost had supposed, including membership in the National Academy of Sciences and several other learned societies. And a listed birth date of January 9, 1950.

"Maybe they were celebrating a little late," Mattocks said.

"And maybe not. Dr. Baxter told your partner Springer at least two lies—the nature of her lunch with Givens and the time they left the restaurant. I wonder what else?"

"I mean to find out," Mattocks said.

Frost thought for a moment. "I've got a better idea. Do you suppose Dr. Baxter would like to have lunch with a charming old man like me? Just lunch, I mean, no 'birthday' celebration?"

Mattocks shrugged his shoulders.

"It's a long shot this late in the morning. Let me try just the same," Frost said. He called Dr. Baxter and turned on the charm. Was there "any chance" she might join him for lunch? he asked. "I realize it's very short notice, but I have a matter of great importance to discuss with you." No, he preferred not to discuss it on the phone, Mattocks heard him say.

The bait worked. They would meet at Aurora at one.

"Come back around three and I'll give you a report," Frost instructed Mattocks.

Frost arrived at the restaurant first and was already seated when the long-legged Dr. Baxter, in a chic navy suit with a short skirt, appeared. She smiled and sat down, friendly enough, yet ever so nervous.

"Dr. Baxter, thank you for joining me. Especially with so little warning. Will you have a drink?"

"I'm sorry, Mr. Frost. Those of us in the foundation world usually don't drink at lunch."

"Not even white wine and soda? Or Campari, which I've even seen bishops drink during the day?"

"You're a smooth talker, Mr. Frost. Yes, a Campari and soda."

Frost ordered Dr. Baxter's drink and a martini for himself.

"Being retired, irresponsible and from another generation, I can have a martini," Reuben explained. "However,

I don't want you to get the idea that this is a frivolous old man's lunch. It isn't.''

"You hinted at that on the phone. I scarcely know you. We met at the Bloemendael meeting the other day, and I know your firm represents the Vandermeers. So I assume there's something about the Foundation you want to discuss.''

"I'm glad you were intrigued enough to find out.''

"Of course, I was intrigued. My whole life is the Foundation, and anything that affects it affects me—at least emotionally.'' She gave him a broad, bold lipstick-drenched smile that under happier circumstances would have turned him to jelly.

"I don't mean to prolong the mystery, Dr. Baxter, but perhaps we should order.'' The two decided against appetizers, with Reuben ordering lobster in a lime-and-sauterne sauce and his guest baked salmon in a horseradish crust.

"Dr. Baxter, the deaths of Tobias and Robyn Vandermeer have become a preoccupation with me,'' Reuben began, wasting no time. "By hook or by crook, I've been close to the police investigation of both of them.''

"I don't quite understand how that involves me.''

"A fair question. Let me try to explain, and I'll try not to be obtuse about it. I want very much for the killer—or killers—of Tobias and Robyn Vandermeer to be found. I want to get this whole thing behind us, to stop the cheap and sleazy speculation we've seen in the newspapers and on television. It's not doing your Foundation any good, and it's grossly unfair to the innocent parties who've gotten enmeshed in it.'' Frost did not tell her of his own exoneration; let her think he was attempting to prevent any more *New York* exposés and pictures.

"Having said all that, I want the investigation to proceed with as little harm as possible to those who've been swept up in it.''

"Mr. Frost, I'm afraid you're talking in riddles. I still don't know why I'm getting a free lunch. Or is this Dutch?''

"No, Doctor, it's my treat. Not a Dutch treat. Am I really talking in riddles? You have been questioned by the police?''

"True enough," she said nervously, shaking an excess of salt on her salmon. "They wanted to know where I was or, really, where Wayne was, the afternoon when Mrs. Vandermeer was killed."

"Yes. And you lied to them."

"I beg your pardon?"

Frost was grateful for the wide-spaced tables at Aurora as he bore in. The giggling Japanese drinking Johnny Walker Black at the next table were paying no attention, and were not close enough to hear, even if they had been.

"Dr. Baxter, you told the police that you were having lunch with Dr. Givens on Tuesday at San Felice—"

"And I was."

"But you also told them it was a lunch in honor of your birthday, when in fact you were born on January ninth."

"Oh, that! Pardon me if I laugh, this is too funny," she said, with great confidence. "You must understand that Dr. Givens and I are old friends. We have many little jokes between us. One is my birthday. Which Dr. Givens treats like the Queen's birthday. In other words, it can go on and on forever. Whenever things get difficult at the office, or whenever either of us has a tough problem, we go out to lunch and celebrate my birthday. It's an old joke and, believe me, quite innocuous."

"Then why did you tell the police you were having a birthday lunch?"

"It was a terrible mistake. The police officer was so serious. Springer, is that it? I couldn't resist. Besides, I figured that dumb secretary of Dr. Given's would say it had been a birthday lunch. She's in on the joke, and she always does."

Dr. Baxter, calmly eating away at her salmon and dismissing the birthday matter so lightly, almost threw Reuben off his pace. Nonetheless he persisted, even while thinking that Springer might have missed the joke.

"Dr. Baxter, I don't mean to seem offensive. Obviously I'm dealing in secondhand information, and I shouldn't even be confiding it to you, but there seems to be some indication that the Queen's birthday—yours—is celebrated by you and Dr. Givens on a regular basis at least once a week. On Tuesday or Wednesday, usually. After which neither one of you returns to the office.''

"Oh, that woman!" Baxter exclaimed, in great anger.

"Who?"

"Givens' secretary. Meddling, stupid woman! There's no privacy anywhere in this City."

"I can attest to that, Dr. Baxter."

"All right. So what can I tell you? That Wayne Givens and I have had a matinee or two? I don't think, Mr. Frost, that that makes us ax murderers."

"Or even poisoners, Dr. Baxter."

"Thank you."

"I do think it would be very helpful if you told me exactly what happened Tuesday afternoon, leaving out, if you like, the details of the last couple of hours at your apartment. My concern is that the police have a complete and accurate account of how you and Dr. Givens spent Tuesday afternoon. It will be best for all concerned if they do. I know the police. They are suspicious and dirty-minded. Without going into it, I know that better than most. And I can tell you, as sure as God made green apples, that if they don't have a straight account from you, they will triangulate their targets—you and Dr. Givens—in ways that will be unfortunate."

"I don't follow you."

"By 'triangulate,' I mean by asking questions in quarters that you may not like. By trying to zero in on you in ways that will make the privacy you seek disappear utterly."

"For example?"

"Like seeing what Barbara Givens knows about your 'birthday parties.' Or like finding out what the other members of the National Academy of Sciences think about your good moral character. Or the American Society for Pharmacology and Experimental Therapeutics, or, not to be confused with the foregoing, the American Society for Chemical Pharmacology and Therapeutics. Or your old colleagues at Rockefeller University. One might well ask all of them if they thought you had slept your way to your present eminence, after a series of Queen's birthday parties."

"Mr. Frost, that detective who questioned me has never

heard of the National Academy of Sciences or any of my other organizations, I can assure you.''

''But I have.''

''I believe, sir, there are libel laws that prevent what you have in mind.''

''Slander, Dr. Baxter. I would never put anything in writing. And I can assure you that any discreet inquiries I made would be well within the law. Which isn't to say that your colleagues, if they are like most other academics I've ever encountered, wouldn't draw nasty conclusions that will spread around like a brush fire.''

''I don't have to sit here and listen to this.''

''No, you don't. But if you don't, you'll miss out on Aurora's saffron ice cream, and either I or that plodding young detective you mentioned will be asking questions all over America, as I described. Isn't it simpler to tell me what happened last Tuesday? On the understanding, by the way—and I mean this—that I will reveal anything you say only as and when necessary to the proper authorities.''

''Wayne Givens is my friend,'' she said. ''I don't want to hurt him.''

''Yes, I understand that. If he's innocent, whatever you tell me will be irrelevant. If he's not, the truth will come out eventually, I have no question about that. And in ways that may hurt you and your eminent professional standing.''

''Could I have a glass of wine?'' she asked.

''I'm sorry. Of course. I assumed the Campari was all you wanted.''

''It was until now.''

Dr. Baxter did not speak until she had taken a deep sip from the white wine the waiter brought her.

''All right, Mr. Frost. Dr. Givens and I had lunch last Tuesday. We had many things to discuss, the food was enjoyable, or at least I thought so while I was eating it, so we lingered. We left about three-thirty. I know because I looked at my watch when we went out the door. Once we got out into the street, I began to feel a little queasy. I'd had mussels for lunch and they must have been bad. So I asked Dr. Givens to take me home, which he did. I still wasn't feeling well when I got home, so he stayed with me until—"

"Dr. Baxter, I don't think this conversation is getting us anywhere. You're repeating the same lies you told the police."

"You have a nerve, Mr. Frost," she answered, half-rising as if ready to stalk away.

"Sit down, Dr. Baxter. I'll concede you didn't repeat the lie about your birthday. But you didn't have mussels that upset your stomach. You had chicken paillard, as did Dr. Givens. And you left that restaurant just before three o'clock."

"How do you know that?"

"The triangulation process has begun, Dr. Baxter. Now, would you like to go back and clean up your account?"

Frost summoned up the same toughness and fierceness he had brought, if necessary, to the negotiating table when he had been in private practice. It was always a mistake to lose your temper for real; that always gave one's adversary a gratuitous advantage. But calculated anger was at times a shrewd and useful weapon. This was one of such times.

Dr. Baxter was, as Frost had hoped, intimidated by his display of wrath.

"You're quite right," she said quietly. "The truth would've come out anyway. We left the restaurant at three. I *did* look at my watch, by the way. Wayne said that he had an errand to do and that he'd meet me back at my apartment, to continue the 'birthday celebration.' He left me and I went home."

"And he returned?" Frost asked, now attempting to get a calm and soothing tone back into his voice.

"Yes."

"When?"

"About four-thirty."

"And then the party continued?"

"You said you wouldn't ask about that."

"You're right."

"But the answer is no. Wayne said he wasn't up to it, and I took him at his word."

"He stayed with you, though?"

"Yes, until about six. He opened a bottle of wine and we sat and drank it."

"He was nervous?"

"No, not really. He just begged off making love."

"Anything else you'd like to tell me?"

Dr. Baxter sighed and took another long sip of wine.

"What the hell?" she replied. "When he came to the apartment, he said he'd been shopping. He was carrying something that was rolled up and taped along the side. It looked like a canvas, or maybe a piece of paper. I didn't look at it very closely at the time. He left it in the back of my closet. He said it was a surprise—for me, I assumed—and that I shouldn't look at it."

"But curiosity got the better of you, and you did?"

"Yes. I took it out and opened it last night."

"And?"

"And it was a Jasper Johns painting."

"Like the one in the Vandermeers' dining room?"

"I don't know, Mr. Frost. Dr. Givens only went to the Vandermeers' with his wife."

"Did you tell Dr. Givens?"

"No, I've been trying to decide what to do. I guess, thanks to you, I've decided."

"You must have talked to him, to concoct your story."

"Yes. He begged me to tell the police we hadn't been separated Tuesday afternoon. And that we'd left the restaurant at three-thirty."

"Did he tell you why?"

"He said he'd had a meeting with Mrs. Vandermeer, at her request, early last week. They'd discussed her ideas for the future of the Bloemendael and ended up having a violent quarrel about her becoming Chairman of the Board. Dr. Givens didn't know who she might have told about their meeting, but was sure it would go badly for him if the police found out both about his confrontation with her and his movements on Tuesday at the time she was murdered."

"Didn't you put two and two together and realize he had killed her?"

"I was in love with him, Mr. Frost. Even after I opened

that painting and knew the truth for certain, I didn't want to believe it.''

"Weren't you afraid of him?''

"Not until now.''

Frost called for the check and attempted to organize the thoughts swirling around in his head. What should he do? The most important thing was to isolate Dr. Baxter from Givens. And to make sure the Jasper Johns was still in her closet.

"Does Dr. Givens have a key to your apartment?'' Frost asked.

"Yes.''

"You stay right here while I make a call.''

Frost could not reach Mattocks, but did find Springer.

"There's a detective coming here,'' he explained when he returned. "I want you to go with him to your apartment and show him that painting. It'll take a little time to sort things out. While that's happening, I don't think you should be alone. Stay with Detective Springer.''

"How long will this go on?''

"If my plan—which I improvised while we were talking— works, everything will be settled this evening.''

"Should I thank you?'' Dr. Baxter asked.

"Let's see if we can keep the birthday parties out of the papers first,'' Frost answered, though he doubted that it would be possible.

A LITTLE MEETING

Once he had left Dr. Baxter in the custody of Springer, Frost rushed home. A message from Bautista was on the machine. He called the detective and was greeted with shouted enthusiasm.

"Reuben, you're a genius! The phone thing checked out completely." Bautista went on to explain how the phone company had gone over Decker's and Gunther's records—and the records from the pay box near the movie theater where Terry Hartley had called Rourke on the afternoon Tobias was killed. All three showed calls to Rourke's number between four-thirty and seven on the fateful Sunday. And the records for Rourke's phone showed that all three had been forwarded to 288-7173—the Vandermeers' number.

"I'm going to pull him in," Bautista said.

"No. Not yet. Where is he?"

"We've got a tail on him. He went to his apartment about an hour ago."

"Let me explain my plan," Reuben said, outlining it to Bautista.

"So you're going to call him?" Bautista said.

"Yes. And you and Mattocks should be here around five-thirty."

Frost immediately got back on the phone and called both

240

Rourke and Wayne Givens. His voice was now authoritative yet soothing; the anger displayed toward Dr. Baxter was gone. Both conversations were similar. Frost was sorry to be calling so late on a Friday afternoon, but he was, as they knew, the senior lawyer for Tobias Vandermeer's estate and the Vandermeer Trust. Something had come up that he felt they should know immediately. Could they possibly come over for a drink at six o'clock? He was all apologies and all graciousness, and the Vandermeer bait worked. He even had the nerve to tell Rourke that he was looking forward to meeting him.

Shortly afterward, Springer called. The painting in Marguerite Baxter's apartment was still there, and, yes, it was the Jasper Johns. Frost instructed him to remain there or else to get another policeman to stay with Dr. Baxter.

"You may want to do that and come over here and join the fun," Frost said.

"Fun?"

"Never mind. If you're coming, just be here by five-thirty. You'll screw things up if you get here any later."

Bautista and Mattocks appeared promptly at five-thirty. Springer, disobeying Frost's warning, came ten minutes after they did. It was all right, though, since there was plenty of time before Frost's impromptu cocktail party, time that he used to bring the detectives up-to-date.

Frost said he would receive his company in the library.

"Where should we be?" Bautista said.

"There's a buzzer on the telephone in the library that connects to the one in the kitchen. You can wait there."

"What about me?" Cynthia asked, having returned from her afternoon errands to find the generals coordinating their battle plan.

"Since this is supposed to be a legal chat, I'm going to have to see the two of them by myself. We can't make it a social occasion. Do you mind staying in the kitchen with the boys?"

"Reuben, this is foolish," Cynthia said. "You shouldn't

be alone with these characters, with help way away in the kitchen."

"It's how I want to do it. But if I press that buzzer, Cynthia, you duck, and the rest of you come running as fast as you damn well can."

The detectives also had misgivings about Frost's strategy, but Bautista knew him well enough to back off from dissuading him, and he convinced his reluctant colleagues to go along.

Rourke arrived first. Ah, the cheekbones! Reuben thought. There was no doubt in his mind that he was shaking hands with Pace Padgett.

"I'm sorry we haven't met before," Frost said apologetically, meaning, of course, not having met him as Stephen Rourke. "I was away when your lawyer called on my partner, Mr. Millard. That was quite an interesting story he had to tell."

"Yeah, I suppose it was," Rourke said, grinning. "So what's this all about?"

"If you don't mind, Mr. Rourke, I'd like to defer that for a moment. I've invited Dr. Givens, the head of the Bloemendael Foundation, to join us. When he gets here I'll explain everything."

The mention of the Foundation seemed to make Rourke uneasy. Did he see his legacy being threatened? Frost wondered.

Frost was going to ask Rourke about the play he was rehearsing, but realized in time that his only knowledge of that had come from the detectives waiting in the kitchen. He was spared inventing more innocent small talk by Givens' arrival.

"Reuben, what the hell is this all about? Barbara and I were going to the country and now we won't get there until the middle of the night!"

"I'm *very* sorry, Wayne. But something has come up that really couldn't wait until Monday."

"Well, what on earth is it?"

Frost was in no hurry to get to the point. He introduced Rourke to Givens and offered them drinks. I should either make these very weak or very strong, he told himself as he mixed them. He made theirs weak, his own strong.

"Gentlemen, I know this all must seem very mysterious,"

he said, after they were seated in the library, Frost next to the telephone with the buzzer. "Perhaps I can lead into the subject by reviewing the state of the Vandermeer property after Tobias' and Robyn's tragic deaths. As both of you gentlemen know, I believe, the bulk of the Vandermeer fortune is in the Vandermeer Trust, created by Tobias' father."

Rourke nodded and Givens looked troubled. Who was this fellow who knew the terms of the Vandermeer Trust?

"On Tobias' death, Hendrik's will dictated that the Trust assets are to be distributed to the issue of Tobias, or failing issue, to the Bloemendael Foundation, subject to a life estate in the income that Tobias appointed in favor of Robyn. With her death, this means everything will go to you, Mr. Rourke, as Tobias' surviving son."

"Reuben! What are you saying?" Givens shouted. "Tobias had no son!"

"That's what we originally thought, Wayne. Until Mr. Rourke came forward."

"But he must be a bastard! Tobias never had any children by his wives. He didn't want any children."

"Wayne, the polite legal phrase these days is 'born out of wedlock.' And legitimate or illegitimate, a child can inherit. That's the law, at least in New York. And Mr. Rourke is Tobias' son."

"So my Foundation gets nothing?" Givens said, maddened enough by Reuben's calm and the complacent look on Rourke's face to refer to the Bloemendael as his very own.

"Normally you'd be right. Mr. Rourke is Tobias' son and would receive everything in the Trust. Unfortunately, that is not likely to be the case."

It was now Rourke's turn to explode. "Why not, for Christ's sake?"

"Because, Mr. Rourke, there's a rule in New York that says you can't inherit if you've committed murder in order to do so."

"Old man, you're crazy! Why are you talking about murder?"

"The police are now convinced, Mr. Rourke, that Tobias Vandermeer was poisoned by Pace Padgett, the waiter from

Bright Lights who was working at the Vandermeers' the night Tobias died. And they're also convinced that you are Pace Padgett.''

"But I was at home then!"

"If that's true, it's very odd that your phone records show that your calls were forwarded to the Vandermeers' that afternoon. And I don't think anyone there is going to have trouble identifying you, mustache or no mustache. Wig or no wig. Green contacts or no green contacts. You were there. Wayne, wouldn't you agree?''

Givens had now gotten control of himself and was positively giddy after the scare Frost had given him. ''Reuben, you're right. He's the waiter!''

"You made very elaborate preparations, Mr. Rourke, to make sure Pace Padgett disappeared and that you had an alibi. They weren't good enough. Though I'm confident they'll be sufficient to establish that your crime was pre-meditated.

"And if I were a betting man, Mr. Rourke, which I'm not, I would wager that your friend, Ms. Hartley, doctored up the Inderal capsules that killed your father."

Rourke, who had been sitting in an almost catatonic state while he listened to Frost, now shouted, "Leave her out of this!" and edged forward in his chair. Frost ignored him and coolly turned to Dr. Givens.

"I'm sorry I scared you that way, Wayne, but I wanted to take things in order. If Mr. Rourke is convicted, and I don't think there's much doubt about that, the Bloemendael Foundation will take everything from the Vandermeer Trust."

"I want my lawyer!" Rourke interrupted.

"Yes, of course you do. If you'll just be still for another minute or two, you can call him," Frost said, then turned back to Givens.

"Just to finish up fast, Wayne, I'm sure the Bloemendael Foundation will prevail. It's only a pity you won't be around to run it in its new golden age of prosperity."

"What does that mean?" Givens said, losing his aplomb anew.

"I don't think the Bloemendael directors will want to retain a murderer as their President. I don't think the likes of Eliza Russell would find it seemly.''

"What? What are you saying?" Givens almost came at Frost physically.

"Wayne, there seems to be pretty solid evidence that you strangled Robyn Vandermeer sometime between three and three forty-five last Tuesday afternoon.''

"That's unmitigated crap! I was with Marguerite Baxter the whole afternoon. At San Felice and then at her apartment. She was sick.''

"She's feeling better now. Relieved," Frost said, surreptitiously poking the buzzer by the telephone.

"But you're wrong! I can prove it. The headwaiter, Marguerite, everyone will support me.''

"Maybe so. But there's always the Jasper Johns in Dr. Baxter's closet to explain away. A nice attempt to implicate Sherman Deybold, but it didn't work. And if I do say so myself, Dr. Givens, murdering Robyn was certainly a very strong reaction to your deep-seated neurotic anxieties, whatever they may be.''

Givens went out of control as Frost mentioned the painting and his psychoanalysis of Becky Sharp, but the detectives broke into the room, guns drawn, and with Bautista in the lead, before he could do any harm.

"All right, gentlemen, let's just take it easy," Springer said, slipping handcuffs on Rourke, while Mattocks did the same to Givens. As the prisoners were piloted toward the door, both shouting obscenities to no avail, Frost stood up, as if out of politeness to his departing guests.

When they had disappeared, he gripped the desk. He was short of breath, perhaps even hyperventilating.

"You all right, Reuben? You're breathing hard," Bautista said.

"Who wouldn't?" Frost replied grumpily.

"Yeah, I guess that's right. I guess you're entitled to breathe hard after a home run.''

"No, no, Luis. You've got it wrong. Just a double play.''

ABOUT THE AUTHOR

The pseudonymous Haughton Murphy retired from a major Wall Street law firm after twenty years to devote more time to writing. He and his wife live in Manhattan. Haughton has written four other Ruben Frost novels, MURDER FOR LUNCH, MURDER TAKES A PARTNER, MURDERS AND ACQUISITIONS, and MURDER KEEPS A SECRET.

HOUGHTON MURPHY
and
MURDER

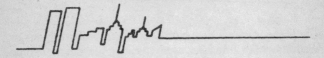

TAKE A PEEK...
IF YOU DARE